La Bouscarela

AMBER McCARROLL

Amber McCarroll

Bellew Publishing • London

First published in Great Britain in 1997
by Bellew Publishing Company Limited
8 Balham Hill, London SW12 9EA

Copyright © Janet Todd 1997

ISBN 1 85725 121 0

Typeset by Antony Gray
Printed and bound in Great Britain by
MPG Books Ltd, Bodmin, Cornwall

Contents

Acknowledgements

I would like to thank Château de Berne for all their help and support; also for the many glasses of their wonderful wine, sipped on their terrace at sunset, filling me with golden imaginings.

I am in debt to my friend Pat Mitchell for her film *New Voices from the Front Line*, a two-hour documentary on the role of women in areas of long-term conflict. I was inspired by its depths of observation.

A special thanks to Ian McCorquodale and to my publisher Ib Bellew.

To all my dear friends who encouraged me over long Provençal lunches, I send my love and thanks.

The jacket for this book was designed around the wine label of Château de Berne.

This is a work of fiction, a product of the author's imagination. Any resemblance to characters in real life is pure coincidence.

for Dino, Jasmine, Harry and Bill

I send my destiny for your approval,
As day gives way to the night.
I send you a fleeting moment of life's energy,
Ardently written with sweet joy.
The dove of peace sings in my breast
As I long for the time that freedom will beckon.
On swift wings will I fly to the sun of my future,
Knowing that I have been anointed with true friendship.

Georgina

Georgina Fox paused from what she was doing for a moment to look up at the sky. The cloudless blue that met her eyes caused her mind to wander and her thoughts to drift back to the lunch party in France. Just three days ago she had been sitting on the terrace of her friend Emma's home in the Alpes Maritimes, enjoying the good food and company always to be found around the long ash-wood table where Emma held court. Georgina had been the last to leave, lingering over a calvados and absorbing the peace of the afternoon. Emma read her tarot cards as they sat under the shade of the huge olive tree that dominated the terrace. Emma had read Georgina's cards many times, often guiding her to make sound decisions.

'A journey to meet your destiny,' she thought as she got back to packing the boot of the car. That's what Emma had said. For some reason, those words struck a chord. Emma was a very spiritual person and new-age in her thinking, but her tarot readings normally yielded practical advice. This was bordering on fortune-telling – not Emma's style at all.

Georgina had her own very strong spiritual beliefs, having had a psychic experience. Emma's statement had brought back to her that strange phenomenon which occurred all those years ago, the experience which had helped to heal the emotional lacerations in her heart and paved the way for everything that had happened since. She had never mentioned this to Emma because she didn't feel that she understood it well enough herself, but for Emma to make such a statement came as no surprise to her. It was more a confirmation of Georgina's own belief in fate.

The Chariot crossed by Death had startled her when Emma first laid down the cards but Emma had explained that the Death card did not actually mean physical death, more often it meant change beyond one's control. Death, the Grim Reaper, was understood in many mythologies as the carrier of destiny. Emma had told Georgina on several occasions that she felt a psychic presence around her. Georgina, for her part, found herself drawn to Emma. They had been schoolfriends but, for various reasons, had drifted apart. It was more then twenty years before they met again, at one of Emma's wonderful terrace lunches.

After squeezing in the last suitcase, Georgina called back into the house, 'Is that everything?' She wondered how her daughter Jasmin always managed to end up with so much luggage and how she fitted everything into her tiny room in their equally tiny mews house.

'Yes, mummy, I'll lock up. You wait in the car.'

Kensington was still quiet at 6 a.m. as they crossed the High Street and headed towards Shepherd's Bush.

'We should be in good time for lunch as long as the M6 doesn't get too blocked. I don't want Mac and Lallie fussing and worrying because we are half an hour late.'

'They're getting old, mummy, poor dears.'

Georgina couldn't think of Mac and Lallie as old. They ran Tarn House like a couple of sergeant-majors, but Mac was seventy-seven last February and Lallie would be seventy-five in November.

Mac was Georgina's mother. She and her sister Lallie lived in the family home, Tarn House. It was just outside Kendal in Cumbria, which they stubbornly still called Westmorland, refusing to change their headed notepaper, even though the printer advised them otherwise.

When Georgina's grandfather had been alive all the land around Tarn House belonged to him. Then, when he died, Uncle Harry, Mac and Lallie's elder brother, inherited the estate, but exorbitant death duties made it necessary for him to sell some of the land. The rest had been sold for the same reason when Georgina's son, Sebastian, inherited the house from Uncle Harry when he died two years ago.

Now only six acres remained with the house. Not that it made any difference to how everything looked: the sheep still grazed in the fields and the ha-ha kept them off the croquet lawn, as it always had.

Georgina hoped that Sebastian would choose to live at Tarn

House one day with his own family. The idea of not spending Christmas there was inconceivable.

'Do you think Sebastian will live at Tarn House one day?' Jasmin asked.

Georgina smiled. 'That's just what I was thinking, darling. I hope so. I know he loves the place. Still, while Mac and Lallie are there he doesn't have to make any decisions. He's a young man and young men have a need for city life.'

Sebastian Fox was the eldest of Georgina's children. He was twenty-four years old when he inherited Tarn House.

'Uncle Harry left the house to him because he thought that if any of us could hold on to it, Sebastian could.' She glanced across at Jasmin. 'Don't worry, darling, I have every intention of spending my Christmases at Tarn House when I'm as old as Mac. We won't let it go out of the family, we all love it too much. It's where I go to heal and it knows all my secrets.'

'Do you have secrets, mummy?'

'We all have a few, don't we?'

They both laughed, enjoying the warmth and intimacy of each other's company.

After a minute or two's silence, Jasmin spoke again.

'Have you heard from Giles lately?'

'No, have you?'

Jasmin gave one of her exasperated looks. 'He never gets in touch. If I don't phone him, I never hear from him. He's so lazy.'

Giles Fox was Georgina's younger son. He had recently dropped out of university and taken a job in a factory canning pet food. At this point, he was being decidedly non-communicative with his whole family.

'Don't be too hard on him, darling. He's just playing at being the angry young man. He'll grow out of it.'

'He's hardly a baby, mummy!' Jasmin sounded very much the child feigning the adult when she said this. 'It's time he grew up.'

Georgina laughed. 'You sounded as old as Mac when you said that. I know he is being a pain at the moment, but I think he really was the most affected of the three of you when your father and I divorced.' She glanced across at her daughter, trying to gauge her facial expression before continuing. 'I'm not making excuses for him and until he wants to help himself we can't do much but wait. Daddy was Giles's hero and I think he feels let down. A good reason not to make heroes out of ordinary people. It isn't fair on them.'

'Do you think Giles is doing things deliberately to upset daddy?'

'No, not deliberately, but subconsciously. I think we are probably all mirroring his feelings. Daddy feels angry with him, Sebastian feels rejected by him, you feel frustrated by him and I feel lost and helpless. These are all the things Giles feels in one big muddle.'

'Why do you think Giles was the most affected by you and daddy divorcing? Don't you think Sebastian and I were affected as well?'

'Oh, darling, I'm being insensitive. Of course you were both affected. Life is about being affected by things; learning from our experiences; growing from them, ideally in a positive way. What I really mean is that Giles has put his feelings on hold for the moment. They're sort of stuck in a groove like a scratch on a CD.'

'Do you think that's what happened to Mac?'

'Mac? In what way?'

'Well, how old was Mac when grandpa died?'

'Let me think, I was four, so Mac would have been thirty-five. Why?'

'Mac never remarried so perhaps she never got over grandpa's death.'

Georgina thought deeply before answering. When she did, she spoke slowly as if she were thinking things through with each sentence.

'I don't really remember much about my father as he was away a lot of the time. Now my memory is even more confused, and I find it very difficult to differentiate between what I truly remember and what I was told about him. I think Mac was used to being alone a lot of her married life; she was always independent. When your grandfather died I don't think Mac suffered that desperate loneliness that some people feel when they are accustomed always to being with a partner. It takes time to get used to living alone and most people are afraid of that. Mac went back to live at Tarn House after grandpa died and that's why I grew up there. Grandpa Williamson and Lallie were there to give Mac their support. Mac grew strong again but she didn't become hard and bitter, so to me that means she dealt with her feelings. I think the reason she didn't remarry was because she didn't meet the right man.'

Jasmin adjusted her seat-belt, which was rubbing against her shoulder, and kicked off her shoes.

'Didn't Mac have any boyfriends after grandpa died?'

'I'm sure she did. She was still very attractive. One of my favourite photos of her was taken with me on my fifth birthday. Women like Mac know exactly what they want and go and get it. She used to spend a lot of time with Uncle Harry in London. I suppose he would have been what we now call in fashionable circles her "walker". They were very close. They both enjoyed ballet and were great supporters of the Royal Opera House.' Georgina stopped talking for a moment. A minute's silence for the family favourite. Even Paul, Georgina's ex-husband, had loved Harry. In some ways Paul had been the son Harry never had.'

'Uncle Harry was the best,' said Jasmin, sensing the moment. 'It's still hard to believe I'm never going to see him again. I always felt he knew the whole world.'

'Yes, it did seem like that. No wonder Lallie nicknamed him William Hickey.' They both laughed.

Harry was the only member of the family who had called Lallie and Mac by their given names Alice and Maharla. When Mac was starting to talk, she couldn't say Alice and called her baby sister Lallie. The name had stuck. The same thing happened when Alice started to talk. She had called Maharla 'Macara', which was shortened to Mac.

Georgina noticed the sign for the next service station. It was five miles away and they had just passed through Birmingham.

'Let's stop for coffee. We're halfway there now, so it's a good time to fill up with petrol.'

'Good idea, mummy. I wish we were still in France, I could murder a *pain au chocolat* right now. Oh well, I'll have to make do with a greasy doughnut instead.' Georgina raised her eyebrows. 'Come on, Jasmin, it won't be that bad. Anyway, when we get to Scotland there's always Drumossie Dundee cake to look forward to.' Georgina knew Jasmin's weakness for sweet things.

'Oh, you're making me really hungry!'

They lapsed into a peaceful silence until they reached the service station.

The restaurant was crowded. It was 8 a.m. and it seemed as if everyone on the M6 had stopped for breakfast.

'You go and find a table, mummy.' Jasmin picked up a tray. 'What would you like?'

'Oh, a cup of coffee and a croissant, please, darling.'

Georgina found a seat by the window and looked out at the people passing by. All strange faces with their own thoughts. She wondered how it would feel to meet her old schoolfriend Jane Stevens after such a long time. At school they had been inseparable, both being day girls at a boarding school. Jane had been a bridesmaid at Georgina's wedding and Georgina was godmother to Jane's daughter Camilla. Jane and her husband, Marcus, were giving a party for Camilla's eighteenth birthday and this was the reason for the trip to Scotland. Life seemed to fly by these days. It was a shame that it took a birthday for her to find the time to visit Jane. She was looking forward to seeing a lot of old friends, many of whom had been invited to the shoot dinner arranged for the following evening to celebrate the opening of the grouse season. In Marcus's eyes, the 'Glorious Twelfth' was just as important as his daughter's eighteenth birthday. Between Jane's organisation and Marcus's passion for his sport, it seemed a little more than a coincidence that Camilla's birthday fell at that time.

'Penny for your thoughts.' It was Jasmin.

'I must have been day dreaming. I was just thinking about Jane. It's been years since we last saw each other. She's very grand now, of course, and holds court for the rich and famous.'

Jasmin laughed. 'What! People like daddy and Anthony Lawless, you mean?'

'Well, they're certainly both rich and Anthony Lawless does have an infamous reputation, especially where his willie is concerned! I've been told he doesn't wear underpants so he can get it out quicker!'

'Mother!' They both laughed.

'That's probably why he's trying to buy half the world's newspapers. He needs to give himself a good press, to counteract the other half who will give him bad headlines. I think it's his new sport since he became too old for rugby. There's an example of a fallen hero if ever there was one. He was daddy's for a long while, but now I think daddy sees him in a different light. The main problem with Anthony Lawless is he sees himself as a hero.'

'Do you think he'll be at the shoot?' Jasmin asked.

'I'm sure he will. The only reason your father won't be there is because he and Sebastian are in Atlanta on business this weekend.'

'Atlanta? Oh what a shame, I thought daddy would be there. I was looking forward to us all spending some time together.'

'Well, you know your father, business is his pleasure. At least he and Sebastian will be together and I'm sure their having a good time. Anyway, you'll see him in London when we get back. Come on, drink up, we need to get on the road.'

They got back into the car. The motorway was busier now and they had to wait to pull into the main stream of traffic.

'How long will it take to get to the Stevenses from Kendal?' Jasmin asked.

'About four hours. So don't worry, we won't have to leave too early in the morning. We're not expected until the afternoon. So we can stop for lunch somewhere on the way. I want to make the most of our time together.'

The motorway now needed Georgina's full attention. Jasmin put on her favourite tape of the moment, *Soulful Grooves*, then closed her eyes. Georgina glanced across at her. 'She'll be asleep in a few minutes,' she thought. 'Still such a baby really.' It was difficult to reflect upon the fact that at Jasmin's age Georgina was already engaged to Paul.

Georgina had met Paul in London while she was still at art college. He was six years her senior and already had his own business, a small but successful estate agency in Fulham. She remembered her friend Sally MacDonald had called that fateful morning and invited her to a party the same evening.

'We'll pick you up about eight. Brian's bringing a friend of his along. His name's Paul Fox. Do you know him?'

'No, Sally, I don't think so.'

'Well, watch out for him Georgie, he has a dreadful reputation as a womaniser.'

'Thanks, Sally! So he's my blind date is he?'

'Don't be silly, we're all going to the party together. I only told you to beware because he's too good looking for any woman's safety. What's wrong with you anyway, Georgie? Have you turned into a prude or something?'

'I'm sorry, Sally. I'm just a bit homesick, that's all. I should have gone north this weekend, but I have too much going on in London. I hate being in the city at weekends.'

'Well, we'll cheer you up. Why don't you wear that red dress you wore to the jazz club last Thursday, you look so stunning in that?'

'Yes, I might. Thanks, Sally, I'll see you later, then.'

Georgina put the phone down feeling slightly guilty, knowing she should have declined the invitation because she was already behind with her project for college.

Fortunately, the evening had been fun. They had all gone to a restaurant recommended by Paul and had such a good time there that they hadn't even bothered to go on the party. Instead, they went back to Paul's house for a drink. It was a large terraced house just off the Fulham Road. He lived in one room with a kitchen leading off. The kitchen had an *en suite* bathroom, an unusual and probably an illegal design feature. The rest of the house he had divided up and rented out as bedsits.

Paul went straight to the clock on the mantelpiece as they walked in and took a ten-pound note from under it. He smiled at Brian and put the money into his pocket.

'Thanks, Anthony,' he said to nobody in particular. 'Always leaves the rent for me.'

'Is he one of your tenants?' asked Georgina, innocently.

'No, he's a friend of mine who's having an affair with one of his cast of thousands. He always leaves me money under the clock when I let him use my bed.'

Brian laughed. 'Let's drink to Paul Fox, a true capitalist.'

Georgina wasn't sure how she felt about it – excited or disgusted? Paul was certainly interesting and she was fascinated by his easy manner. He was older than any of the other men she knew. Compared to them, he really seemed a man of the world.

Brian and Sally left together as Paul had offered to take Georgina home. She was quite expecting him to live up to his reputation and try to get her into the bed which she reflected was probably still warm from Anthony and his mistress.

Instead they talked for a long while. Paul was very interested in her interior-design course. She had taken a foundation course the year before and Uncle Harry had been the one to suggest she follow it up with the design course, as he had lots of contacts in that field and could help her to get established. Paul was interested in art and from the few paintings and antique pieces he had scattered around his room, she could see he had good taste. By the time he escorted her to his car, Georgina had decided she liked him very much. When they arrived at her flat, he walked her to the door.

'May I call you next week?' he asked.

'Yes,' she replied. He kissed her on the cheek and left.

He called her the following day and invited her to a dinner party. After that they were inseparable.

They were married within the year. Uncle Harry and Mac were a little uneasy about the speed of the whole thing but Lallie thought it truly romantic. She didn't believe in long engagements.

All three of them liked Paul immediately. He had made all the right noises to Uncle Harry, who had given them a generous cheque as a wedding present. Enough for a deposit on a flat.

Paul found what he described as a 'good deal' and Georgina spent her time painting and decorating. They sold it six months later for double what they paid for it and bought a bigger flat with the same idea in mind.

Paul had kept his Fulham Road house and let a friend stay in his room to keep an eye on things. Between them they had come to a business arrangement over the bed, a new one, which now dominated the room. They had bought some very large pieces of mirrored glass which they put all around the bed and on the ceiling. Apart from Anthony, they now had a bank manager, an insurance broker and an up-and-coming politician as clients. The ten-pound notes were split fifty-fifty. Paul didn't tell Georgina about this continuing and now expanding business.

The first eighteen months of their marriage passed happily. During this time they had moved twice, each time making a substantial gain on the property transaction. They now owned a large detached house in Parsons Green, living on the first two floors and letting out the top floor as bedsits. Georgina took over a small south-facing room, which she turned into a studio for herself, started to paint seriously and was enjoying the results. Paul had gone into partnership with Anthony Lawless, a man who seemed to have his fingers in numerous business pies. They had set up a property-development company, mainly residential refurbishments in central London.

By Christmas of 1968 Georgina realised she was pregnant. Even though it wasn't planned, she was delighted with the news, seeing a baby as being a happy addition to a successful marriage. It seemed that she was now moving more in Paul's world than her own and had left behind many old friends from her schooldays, girls who were still unmarried and enjoying being free. One of her closest schoolfriends, Emma, had married Ben, the son of Lord and Lady Davis. They were living hippie-style on Ibiza, getting themselves splattered all over the gossip columns as a result. Paul didn't approve of Emma, so Georgina had lost touch. Jane had been different: she had married Marcus Stevens, whom Paul liked. Jane was the only real friend of her own she still had contact with and she treasured that friendship.

Sebastian was born in June 1969, to a delighted mother and a father who wasn't sure he would take to fatherhood very well but told his wife he was over the moon. By the time Sebastian was three weeks old, Paul had employed a nanny and sent them all to stay at Tarn House for two months, the excuse being that he was too busy working and Georgina needed a rest.

Georgina had objected to being away from him for such a long period, but he had convinced her of the wisdom of his decision. He promised that he would spend his weekends with them. She could rest and the clean country air would be the best thing for the health of their son.

Male domination was a new experience for her. Not having had a father to rebel against, she felt resentful and confused, but Paul's masterful concern was also quite exciting.

That summer had been a very happy one for Georgina, with Mac and Lallie doting on Sebastian and Paul coming up at weekends. It was not quite every weekend but when he did arrive she felt he was getting used to his new role as father and, indeed, he did eventually warm to the idea.

They would take long romantic walks down by the river and discuss their future. Paul's business was going from strength to strength and he wanted Georgina to know his plans for them both.

'Everything has gone so well in London that Anthony and I have decided to open a commercial office in Amsterdam later in the year. Anthony has a lot of contacts over there.'

'Does that mean we will have to move to Amsterdam?' She hoped he wouldn't say yes. Sebastian had changed their life enough as it was for the moment.

'No, Georgie. There's more design work coming up with the London company and I want you to handle it. We are a good team and I hope you don't want to stop work now you have Sebastian. He will be perfectly fine with a nanny and I'm sure you'll find the time to share the job of looking after him.'

'But you'll be away in Amsterdam.'

'After the initial set up, I can commute easily from London. Most of my trips can be arranged as day trips. You won't notice any difference in our daily life.' He pulled her towards him and locked her in an embrace. The confidence of Paul's statement and the warmth of his body dispelled any doubts in her mind.

By the time their second son, Giles, was born in the September of 1971, they had moved twice more. This made four moves since they were married. As a result of their joint skills, they now owned a beautiful Georgian house in Edwardes Square, Kensington.

Anthony and Paul were floating their property company on the stock exchange at the height of the market and Paul was spending more and more time in Amsterdam. On the design side of the company the workload was just as hectic and Georgina found herself wishing there were at least sixty hours in every day.

She was twenty-three years old and life embraced her. Paul was her idol, his dreams and desires were her own. There was no one but Paul, and Georgina was his willing slave.

When the London property market crashed in 1973, business became very slow. Paul was still busy in Amsterdam and away from home just as much. For the first time in five years, she was able to think about herself, relishing the sudden realisation that she had needs and desires of her own. Now having more time to pursue her art, she began to enjoy spending her free moments in her studio.

This she had created for herself in the basement of the house. Although artificially lit, the atmosphere seemed to be conducive to her creativity. Her studio became the other world and she found there all the qualities she associated with Tarn House, feeling at peace in the cocooned environment and allowing it to replenish her tired soul. Edwardes Square had become a very important part of her life and she imagined her sons growing up there. She enjoyed the extra time she now had to be with them. Teatime became a ritual and she felt guilty if for any reason she had to miss it. Sebastian and Giles were adorable and being with them helped to fill the gap that Paul's frequent absence left. Mac and Lallie started to spend more time with them in London, taking Georgina to the Ballet which she loved. They helped to fill Paul's role as far as adult company went. When it came to Christmas it was spent, as always, at Tarn House.

Jasmin arrived two weeks early, in March 1975, whilst Paul was away on business; by the time he arrived at Queen Charlotte's Hospital, she was already two days old. He seemed thrilled with his daughter but slightly preoccupied.

When it was time for him to leave he said, 'I think we should sell Edwardes Square.'

Georgina's heart was in her mouth when she asked, 'Why?'

'Because I have been offered a lot of money for it and to sell on this market at the sort of price I've been offered is an amazing stroke of luck. Anyway, we don't need to decide anything now. Think about it, darling, and we can discuss it when you come home. I'll be here at ten o'clock in the morning to collect you both.'

He bent over the crib, dismissing what he had just said as if it were nothing of importance. 'Our daughter is beautiful.' He kissed Georgina on the cheek and was gone.

By the time a nurse came into her room, she was sobbing uncontrollably.

'Come on, lovey, cheer up. You've just given birth to a princess.' She put her arms around the weeping Georgina and gave her a hug. 'It's post-natal depression you're suffering from, I expect. Would you like me to make you a nice cup of tea?' The nurse hurried off to get the tea while Georgina tried to pull herself together.

'Thank you, you're very kind.' She sat up in bed sipping her tea, its calming effect working on her strained emotions. She would think about selling the house when she got home. The nurse was right, it was probably post-natal depression. She convinced herself that she would feel better in the morning, when Paul arrived to take them both home.

It was a week later before he brought up the issue of moving again. The household had been in a whirl of excitement with the boys fascinated by the new arrival and Paul taking a genuine and loving interest in both his wife and baby daughter. Georgina was feeding Jasmin when the subject was broached.

'I've found a beautiful Norman Shaw house in Bedford Park.' He cleared his throat. 'It needs to be completely refurbished as it's divided up into bedsits at the moment. We'll need to get vacant possession before we can start work on it, but I know you will be able turn it back into a lovely home, Georgie.'

'Paul, I really don't want to move at this point.' She looked at him with pleading eyes. 'We have moved so many times since we were first married and when Sebastian was a baby. I'm happy living in Kensington and I don't know Bedford Park. I want to enjoy the children, not spend the next six months, at least, on a building site.'

Paul sighed. 'Be practical, Georgina, the property market is dead at the moment. To be able to realise the price I have been offered on this house is a chance we just can't turn our back on. I can buy the Bedford Park house for a quarter of the price, then invest the gain very well. In fact, Anthony Lawless has offered me an opportunity to invest in a leisure business with him and I really think that's where the future is.'

'Always Anthony Lawless. You seem to look at him as if he were a god.' She felt her chest constricting. Hating arguments at the best of times, she definitely wasn't ready for a verbal fight at this moment, exhausted mentally and physically by the new baby. Something was going to happen between them that would be irreversible, she could sense it.

'Don't be so bloody childish, Georgina. I'm not going to let you stand in my way on this. You knew I had ambition when I met you. It's all the way with me.'

'How far is all the way, Paul?'

'To the top, Georgina. We're selling the house.' He got up and walked out, slamming the front door behind him.

Two months later the removal van arrived to pack up their home and put it into storage. Georgina took the children and their nanny to Tarn House.

Maria had been with them since Giles was born. As a Hungarian refugee, she sympathised with Georgina's plight of having to move with such a small baby. When she was only four years old, she had hidden beside her mother in a cabbage field for hours, waiting for the communist guard to pass by. Maria never fed cabbage to the children, which was probably one of the many reasons they loved her!

They all stayed with Mac and Lallie until they could move into the house in Bedford Park. Paul commuted as and when he could and the marriage went on hold. It took six months to relocate all the tenants and another three months to re-wire and re-plumb the house back into a single dwelling. They moved in at that point as Georgina decided she could get things done quicker if she was on site.

Jasmin spent her first birthday amongst the building rubble.

Not long after that things began to improve. The house was very spacious and elegant and Georgina had brought it back to life. The ceilings were high and beautifully stuccoed. There were original William Morris tiled fireplaces throughout and the stained-glass windows in the hall and dining-room, which were still in excellent condition, were attributed to him as well. The garden was walled and well established with a beautiful Victorian potting-shed, built in a west-facing sun spot, which she had turned into her studio.

By 1977 the London residential property market was booming again and Bedford Park became very expensive and fashionable. Paul had got it absolutely right as usual. The house in Bedford Park was worth more than they had sold Edwardes Square for, three years earlier.

With time their marriage seemed to have repaired itself but it was different, more of a business partnership now. Something in Georgina had died since she left Edwardes Square, but she put it down to lost youth and made her children her *raison d'être*.

Georgina spent most of her free time in her studio, hiding she thought. Her work progressed slowly and she had not been able to paint anything inspiring since their last move. She had somehow detached herself from her true feelings. When they all went up to Tarn House she would go for long walks on the fells, alone. There she could really lose herself in their wildness, feeling comforted by their changeless stability. She imagined herself as a character from a novel, a lost soul, wandering through the heather-scented hills, allowing the wind to wash over her confusion.

By 1981 both Sebastian and Giles were away at prep school and Jasmin was attending the local kindergarten. Georgina was working hard again for Paul's company and happy to be bridging the gap left by the boys' absence. That was the year she and Paul had met Tina Obstroullias at one of Uncle Harry's little soirées.

Betina Obstroullias was small, even birdlike, and could never be considered a beautiful woman. However, her couture clothes and ostentatious jewellery left no doubt in one's mind, when meeting her, that she was wealthy. Take away the props and she could be a chambermaid in a cheap Earl's Court Hotel. It was her eyes that told the world she was a woman used to getting what she wanted.

Paul had been impressed by her from the start. 'She's one of the richest women in the world,' he told Georgina, with the sort of admiration he usually reserved for Anthony Lawless. 'Shipping, you know, is the forte of the Greeks. Her family are very powerful. They make the rules in their world.'

Georgina didn't answer him. There wasn't anything to say, she didn't understand Paul these days.

When Tina's secretary called the following week and invited Paul and herself to a dinner party, she was surprised but Paul seemed delighted and personally took on the responsibility of calling back to accept the invitation.

They arrived, after more fuss and preparation on her part than Georgina was prepared to admit to herself. Grandma Williamson's sapphire-and-diamond earrings, which had been given to her by Mac for her twenty-first, had been taken out of the bank for the evening. After a lot of consideration, she decided to wear her black silk-chiffon Armani dress. High at the neck with long sleeves but completely backless, it emphasised her beautiful shoulders. She wore her hair in a chignon and pinned a black velvet bow to the nape of her neck. This and her earrings were her only accessories.

Tina was an extremely gracious hostess, paying Georgina a lot of attention and making sure the party flowed along with herself at the helm. When they sat down to dinner, Tina had Paul sit on her left and Georgina was placed at the other end of the table, next to a outrageously handsome Argentinian polo player. She remembered how he flattered her, helping to make the evening a great success.

On the way home Paul was buoyant. This was the world he wanted to spend more time in. A club he wanted to join. 'Tina has asked me to look over her property portfolio,' he enthused to Georgina. 'She seems to have a lot of negative-cash-flow property in California that she thinks she should sell. It would look very good for the company to be seen handling a private portfolio of that size.' He didn't tell her that Tina had invited him for dinner the following evening and that he had no intention of talking shop.

The next day he called Georgina from the office to say that he unfortunately had to go to Amsterdam. He would be staying overnight as he often did when he thought his meetings would end very late.

When Paul arrived at Tina's house in Grosvenor Square at eight o'clock that evening, his mind was totally geared for seduction. As he was shown into the drawing-room, she stood up. He walked across the room, noticing for the first time her slim shapely legs, emphasised by the perfectly cut lines of her black satin cocktail dress. The look in her eyes told him he had a willing victim.

During dinner Tina asked him about himself and he told her with great pride of his poor-boy-made-good background.

'My father is a bank manager in Kingston-upon-Thames and we get on well, I suppose. I'm an only child and I think I was quite hard to come by, so my mother dotes on me.' He laughed. 'I went to Kingston College and passed the Oxbridge exam but I convinced my parents that I should take a year off before going to university. I got myself a job working for a large estate agent and after the year was up I had no intention of going to university. After staying another year with the company to really establish my contacts I left. Using the money from an insurance policy my father had taken out for my further education, I opened my own agency in Fulham. Now I am a self-made millionaire.'

'Weren't your parents disappointed that you didn't go to university?'

'Yes, of course they were. My parents are kind but boring people. They live in a nice, boring, safe, detached house near the river. My mother thinks of me as a prince and treats me like one. But I see myself as a future king in the business world with my own empire.'

Tina was impressed by Paul. He was definitely made of the material business empires are built on. He was certainly ambitious but she wondered if he was ruthless enough to go the whole way. At this point she suspected not. She didn't see him as a killer shark, because his mother had shown him too much affection for that to be possible.

He escorted her back to the drawing-room, where the butler had left them coffee and warmed brandy glasses on a silver tray.

He looked down at her legs as he poured the Rémy Martin Cordon Bleu into the glasses and then up into her eyes, his own blue eyes smouldering behind his thick black lashes. As he passed her a glass, she stood up and took his hand. 'Let's take these to the bedroom with us,' she said seductively, raising her glass to him.

The bedroom was a place Paul knew he was already king. He walked with her to the bed, kissing her for the first time as they stood beside it. He began slowly and deftly to undress her, she felt the sensuous satin of her dress sliding over her body, then his strong arms lifted her up and in one movement laid her on the bed. He then undressed himself, looking at her all the time and telling her how wonderful she was as he did so. He believed sex to be an art form and every detail had to be thought through. He loved to create whatever illusion he felt appropriate, priding himself on perfect timing and total mastery of his theatre.

He lay down beside her, kissing her and caressing her hair and face before he ran his hands expertly over her body, feeling it in the way a couturier touches and kneads a piece of fabric to see how it moves and folds; every sigh was registered in his brain. He was determined to learn her love language from their first contact and just thinking about dominating this powerful woman was giving him an erection any stud in a pornographic film would be proud to call his own.

As he felt her body relaxing he slowly started to kiss it, beginning with her forehead, her eyes, then just behind her earlobes, making sure he gently blew into her ears as his lips passed over them. He cupped her breasts, passing his tongue over her erect nipples as lightly as a feather falling to earth on the softest breeze.

He continued down, slowly lingering wherever he got the most response, mentally thanking every woman he had ever slept with during his heyday in Amsterdam for teaching him how to please them.

Tina's sighs were turning into deep-throated groans as he confidently, without stopping the flow of pleasure for a moment, rubbed his hard penis against her clitoris. He played with her in this way as a fly fisherman plays with a salmon, letting her go then reeling her in. When he finally entered her he felt confidant he would be responsible for the best orgasm she had ever experienced.

He left Tina early the following morning, before she was awake, so he could shower and change at the office. Just before he turned into South Audley Street, he called her from his car.

'Good-morning. You looked beautiful lying there asleep when I left you.'

A voice heavy with sleep answered him. 'Why did you leave so early? I wanted to make you breakfast in bed.'

'There's only one thing I want in bed at the moment, my darling, and that's an encore of last night.'

'Oh, Paul,' she sighed.

'I'll give you my private number at the office. Call me when you can.' He gave her the number, blew a kiss into the phone and hung up. He knew she would call him before the day was out.

When his secretary arrived at the office, the first thing he arranged before he started his working day was to have flowers sent to both Tina and Georgina.

He always sent flowers to Georgina when he betrayed her. It made him feel better.

Georgina received a lot of flowers, which she always thought of as a sign of Paul's love and affection.

Paul didn't answer his private line all morning in case it was Georgina. At midday he called her to say he'd just arrived back from Amsterdam.

'I've booked the Waterside Inn for dinner this evening, Georgie. It's a long time since we've been out together alone.'

'That's sounds wonderful, Paul, you know that it's one of my favourites.'

'That's why I booked it; tonight I feel like spoiling my beautiful wife.' He turned the conversation to business.

After she put the phone down, Georgina went into the kitchen to make herself some coffee. She stood looking out of the window for a long time, over towards her studio, as if somehow it held a message for her. There had been a time when to lock herself away and paint would have cured all of her ills. Now she was so emotionally drained that it had become a frustration more than a joy.

'Sometimes I wonder if I'm going mad,' she thought. 'I don't know what's wrong with me. I have a loving, hard-working, successful husband and three adorable children, a job that fits in easily with my family life. Yet I have this sadness deep inside me, like a cold stone. I can't even paint any more – I feel as blank as the empty canvases in my studio. What gave me such pleasure now only makes me dwell on my confusion. Maybe I need to see a doctor? Now I come to think of it, I'm sure there was something wrong with Grandma Williamson. People used to say she was a bit strange. I wonder in what way? I must remember to ask Mac about it when I next speak to her.' The kettle reached the boil, clicked off and her chain of thought was broken.

During the afternoon red roses arrived but she still didn't feel any better.

Paul pushed his chair away from his desk and put his feet up, meticulously making sure the heels of his shoes rested on his ink blotter. He looked at his watch, it was 4 p.m. and as he glanced at his private phone, it rang. Marvelling at his perfect judgement, he picked it up. 'Paul Fox speaking.'

'Paul? This is Tina. Thank you for the flowers. Orchids are so exotic.'

'And so are you, my darling. When can I see you again?'

'I'm supposed to be going to the theatre this evening and then on to dinner but I could cancel it, if you're free.' He was pleased to hear the urgency in her voice. It had been easier than he had anticipated to win her.

'No, darling, not this evening, I'm a married man remember. I'll call you tomorrow and we'll see what we can arrange between us. It shouldn't be too difficult; don't forget, we do have a genuine business reason to be together some of the time.'

'All right, Paul, but you remember, I'm a woman who is used to having what she wants.'

'Tina, darling, I'm a man who always gets what he wants!' He paused. 'Don't worry I plan to send Georgina away for a few weeks. I'll call you tomorrow. In the meantime you can think up some bedroom fun for us both.' He put down the telephone, threw his head back in his chair, smiling to himself, and thought, 'Yes, Tina, power is a wonderful drug.'

When he arrived home, Georgina had already dressed for dinner. He found her in the study, looking over some drawings of a large house in Sussex Gardens that had just arrived from the architect. They were converting it back to a single dwelling; at the moment it was five flats.

She looked up and smiled as he came into the room. He looked across at her and thought what a beautiful woman she had grown into. Her shoulder-length blonde hair was tied back at the nape of her neck and she was wearing the gold, antique, oak-leaf earrings he had bought in the Burlington Arcade for her last birthday. Her simple black fitted dress showed off her tall elegant figure to perfection. She was one of those women who glided when she walked. Time was going to be kind to her, he was sure, and there was real admiration in his voice when he spoke.

'I think you grow more beautiful as you get older, Georgie. I'll have to keep my eye on you. I don't want anyone whisking you away from under my nose.'

She laughed as she walked around the desk to kiss him. 'I don't see enough of you these days to get fed up with you, darling, and anyway this Sussex Gardens project looks as if it will be taking up most of my spare time.' She kissed him before saying, 'Thank you for the roses, they're lovely, and it's such a good idea of yours to go out this evening. I've been feeling a bit down today.'

'Well,' he hesitated, controlling his feelings, 'your prince has arrived to escort you to that gourmet paradise in Bray-on-Thames. Come along, princess, we'd better hurry or we'll be late.'

Paul habitually drove too fast on the motorway. He was full of enthusiasm for Georgina's ideas on the Sussex Gardens project. She wanted to recreate the orangerie that had existed on the first floor of the house when it was originally built. It had been shattered in the blitz but still showed on the original drawings the architect had managed to track down. They talked about it all the way to the restaurant.

They were shown to Uncle Harry's favourite table, by the window, overlooking the river, and as they settled themselves into their surroundings the head-waiter came over. 'Good-evening, Mr and Mrs Fox. How are you both?'

'Very well, thank you, Mario,' Paul answered. It was important for him to be known in restaurants and, thanks to Uncle Harry, he was. The only other interruption to their privacy, apart from ordering the food, was when Paul discussed the Château Talbot 1966 which had just been decanted for them by the *sommelier*.

Uncle Harry had taught Paul a lot about wine and he was always keen to display his knowledge.

The food was delicious and the waiters were completely unobtrusive. Most of the conversation stayed on business but eventually they talked about their sons away at school and Paul's plans to take them sailing on their next exeat weekend. Paul's father had his boat moored on the Hamble and sailing was one of the few things he and Paul had in common. Paul's own sons loved spending time with their grandfather and learning under his patient tuition how to sail. The evening felt special as they had not been alone together for weeks but for Georgina it seemed a lot longer. Talking about the family and not business, for once, gave her the courage to speak about her own feelings. As the coffee was served, she searched for the words to try and make him understand.

'I was feeling so sorry for myself today, Paul. I do miss the boys when they are away at school, and now you have to be away such a lot of the time yourself, it all gets too much for me.'

'You still have Jasmin at home, darling, and she's a three-act play all by herself.'

She smiled at that remark. 'You're right, Paul, she is amazingly good company for such a little imp.'

Paul saw the opportunity to exercise his plan. 'I think you need a break, Georgie. Why don't you go up and stay with Mac for a few weeks. You could take a set of drawings with you to work on up there because we won't be starting any work on site for at least a month and I'm going to have to be away a lot during the next two weeks, so I'd feel much better if I knew you were taking advantage of the time to see Mac and Lallie. You and Jasmin would have them to yourselves and you know how you love sleeping in your old bedroom with all your dolls and teddy bears! It gets me quite excited thinking about it.'

'Paul Fox, if you weren't my husband, I'd be disgusted by that remark.'

He laughed. 'No, seriously, Georgie, I think it would do you good to get away from London for a while.'

Paul's easy manner comforted her. 'You could be right, Paul, especially if you're not going to be there. Anyway I have a few things I want to talk to Mac about.'

'What sort of things.'

'Oh, just northern gossip, darling. Nothing that would interest you.'

Two days later Paul drove Georgina and Jasmin to Euston Station to catch the nine-fifteen to Oxenholme, where Mac would be meeting them. This was a real treat for Jasmin who had never made the journey north by train before. In her excitement a quick kiss and hug replaced the usual sulks when her father could not join them.

The three-and-a-half-hour journey passed by quickly for both of them. Jasmin was easily entertained and was pleased to be spending this unexpected extra time with her mother. Georgina had thought seriously about taking her out of school for two weeks but had decided it wouldn't hurt at this age. Anyway, she would have Lallie's full attention while they were at Tarn House and Lallie was a very good teacher. Georgina could personally vouch for that.

Mac was on the platform when they arrived at Oxenholme station. She was carrying something in her arms and Jasmin was delighted to find that it was a black labrador puppy. Mac passed him to Jasmin to hold while she helped Georgina with the luggage.

'His name is Blue,' she said, as she stroked the puppy's head to help him settle in Jasmin's arms. 'Now hold him tightly or he'll start whinging – puppies need to feel secure.'

Georgina turned to Mac. 'He's absolutely adorable. You never mentioned him on the phone.'

'Well, you sounded like you needed a little cheering up and I thought Blue would be the perfect surprise.' She squeezed her daughter's arm.

They walked to the car with Jasmin in front snuggling the puppy up to her face. They put the luggage in the boot then helped Jasmin and Blue into the back seat.

Taking the back road to Tarn House, avoiding Kendal, they passed through the beautiful countryside of South Lakeland. Jasmin was happy with the puppy in the back of the car, showing him the pheasants perching on the walls and pointing out the old oak tree where Mac had once told her about the big white owl with eyes that shone in the dark that lived there.

As they turned into the drive, Mrs Taylor, the housekeeper, was standing at the window of the lodge. She waved as they drove by.

'She'll be up at the house after lunch. You can say hello to her then,' said Mac.

She drove on slowly, allowing Georgina time to enjoy the carpet of daffodils that spread all the way up the drive under the lime trees. At the gate Mac stopped the car for her to admire the view she so loved. The moss-and-heather-covered hills that guarded the valley as it swept into the River Lune never failed to inspire Georgina.

She parked the car at the back of the house and they went through the back door which led past Grandfather Williamson's old farm office, now a junk-room, past the laundry-room and into the kitchen, where Lallie was waiting for them.

Jasmin pushed open the door and ran into her arms. Mac put Blue in his basket next to the Aga and after a lot of excited chatter, they all sat around the kitchen table to have lunch.

The kitchen was one of Georgina's favourite rooms in the house. It was a large room, always warm from the Aga which was never allowed to go out. The pine dresser which dominated one wall was covered with blue-and-white china. A huge old, almost square, scrubbed pine table filled the middle of the room, and it was here they were all now seated. Two easy chairs stood in front of the French windows which opened on to a sheltered terrace where Grandpa Williamson had put a little table for Georgina to feed the birds on when she was a little girl. It was still there.

After lunch, Lallie and Jasmin took Blue with them as they went on their walk while Mac and Georgina settled into the easy chairs with their coffee. Somewhere during the conversation, Grandma Williamson's name was mentioned and Georgina seized upon the opportunity to ask about her.

'What was wrong with grandma? I mean, did she have something wrong with her mind. The locals always said she was a bit odd?'

Mac laughed. 'Well, for the locals, she was a bit odd, I suppose. She was an "off comer" for one thing and French to boot. It's bad enough up here now, but you can imagine what it was like at the turn of the century when your grandfather brought his French bride home. She spoke English with a very heavy accent and told stories that led the locals to think of her as fay.'

'In what way? What sort of stories?' asked Georgina, wondering why she hadn't heard about the stories before.

'Well, when she first came here she saw a ghost! She described a woman dressed in Elizabethan clothes, whom she saw walk through the wall upstairs at the back of the house, were Lallie's flat now is. That's the old Tudor part of the house which was the original farmhouse, before the Georgian addition turned it into your great-grandfather's country mansion. She wouldn't have known about the Tudor part, of course, because it isn't immediately obvious and the back of the house in those days would have been the servants' quarters, so naturally wouldn't have appeared as grand. A few years later, when work had to be done in that part of the house, the plaster was taken off the walls right back to the stone and your grandfather was amazed to see an old wooden door-lintel exactly in the spot where grandma had seen her ghost.'

'Tell me more, Mac.' She pushed herself farther down in her chair, hugging her coffee cup with both hands.

'When Harry, Lallie and I were children, she told grandpa that she would never see her grandchild and when your grandfather asked what she meant by grandchild, in the singular, she replied that they would only have one. Well, can you imagine, that was a very strange thing to say in the days of large families and sketchy birth control – how could she have known then that Uncle Harry would remain a bachelor or that Lallie would be jilted and never marry and that I would be widowed after having you quite late in life?'

'How do you feel about it all, Mac? Do you believe in ghosts?'

'Not in the old-fashioned sense of haunting and things that go bump in the night. Your father, as you know, was a pioneer in the computer industry and some of his theories have become fact. Look at the hologram, for instance, it's only a play of light and shadow; perhaps time is like that, sometimes revealing its eternity in form. Like a star we see in the sky that has been dead for thousands of years and we are still receiving the light from it. Your father had a time-line theory, far too complicated for me to explain, but sometimes time-lines cross, and perhaps that's what happened when grandma saw her ghost. As far as ESP – extra-sensory perception – is concerned, I suppose that's the category grandma's premonitions would come under. Russia and the USA are both backing scientific research into the paranormal and have been doing so since the Second World War. Police have been known to use mediums in their detective work, so there must be something in it all. Anyway this is too deep a discussion to get into with a daughter who hasn't been home for far too long.

'I know, Mac. It's just that I've been feeling very down and there's no apparent reason for it. I thought perhaps grandma suffered from some melancholic illness and I had inherited it.'

'You've certainly inherited her gift for painting and also her good dress sense. Whether you have inherited her sixth sense, I wouldn't know.' She smiled at Georgina. 'You should spend more time here. You know Uncle Harry got planning permission to convert the barn so why don't you and Paul turn it into a second home for yourselves. It looks over the kitchen garden, beyond to the river, and in my opinion it has even better views than the house. I'm sure Paul would agree with the idea of having a place for yourselves here as the children get older.'

They sat and discussed this idea, until Lallie and Jasmin came back from their walk. After that, Jasmin and Blue became the centre of their attention.

A knock on her door woke Georgina the following morning. 'I have a breakfast tray for you, Mrs Fox.' It was Mrs Taylor.

Georgina asked her to come in. She put the breakfast tray on a chair by the bed. 'Shall I open the curtains for you.'

'Yes, please,' Georgina replied, drowsily.

Mrs Taylor walked over to the window. 'Your mother thought you would like your breakfast in bed, seeing as you're not going to the market with them this morning. Jasmin's in the kitchen having breakfast with your aunt.'

'Thank you, Mrs Taylor. Please would you ask Jasmin to come up here when she's finished so I can supervise her wardrobe. She has some strange ideas if left to her own devices,'

'Bright as a button that one. She's been here before,' Mrs Taylor said around the door as she closed it.

Georgina rearranged her pillows into a back rest against the brass bed head. She always slept well in this room and was beginning to feel better already. As she lay back remembering her happy childhood in this house she marvelled at the comfort it still gave her in times of stress.

After everyone had left for the market Georgina put on her thick Arran sweater and went into the kitchen garden with her sketch pad. She went through the gate, double checking that it was shut tight, a habit left over from childhood. The kitchen garden was surrounded by dry stone walls on three sides, and the fourth side was the back of the barn. The ground was divided up by low box hedges which separated the vegetables and soft fruits. Around the periphery were planted different varieties of fruit trees. She sat down on the grass under an apple tree, noticing that its buds were almost ready to burst into blossom. In two months' time the grass she now sat on would be covered in oriental poppies. The white lilac would also be out by then and it would hang over the wall from the other side, almost reaching the ground. It was all so vivid in her mind.

She started to sketch the barn, adding windows and doors in places she thought would enhance the view yet not detract from the aesthetics of the building. As she worked a drowsiness overtook her and she allowed herself to fall back on to the grass. Looking up at the sky she watched the clouds racing past, drawing her mind upwards as she drifted into a daydream. At first she was relaxed and comfortable lying in this half sleep. Then, as if from nowhere, for no real thoughts entered her mind, the deep sadness returned. It slowly crept through her like a germ laying her low. She became hot then cold and began to shiver. She sat up, suddenly knowing that she would never live at Tarn House with Paul.

Gathering up her things, she went back into the house, deciding to take Lallie's car to Kirkby Lonsdale and meet the others at the market, hoping that she could persuade them to go to the Whoop Hall pub for lunch.

The following morning red roses arrived from Paul.

As soon as she saw them, any fears she may have had the previous day vanished; during the afternoon, he telephoned. Mac answered the phone and had a long chat with him before putting him on to Jasmin while she then went off to search for Georgina, who was in another part of the house.

As Georgina walked into the sitting-room she could hear Jasmin chattering and laughing with her father. She finally handed her mother the telephone.

'Daddy want's to speak to you.' Smiling all over her face, she ran out of the room to find Mac.

'Hello, Paul.'

'Georgina darling, did you get the flowers?'

'Yes, thank you. They were just what I needed to make my day. The weather here has been glorious and Jasmin is over the moon with Mac's new puppy.'

'Yes, she told me, his name is Blue.' Paul tried to keep the impatience out of his voice. 'Listen, Georgie, I have to go to America tomorrow.' He swallowed. 'This portfolio of Tina's, I need to have a look at some of the residential stuff. I'll be in Florida first and then I have to go to California, which means that I'll be away about a week.'

'Oh, Paul, I wish you didn't have to travel so much, I do miss you.' Determined to overcome her disappointment, she pushed her feelings down into the dark hole she had created for them.

'I know, darling, and I miss you too. I'll come straight up there when I get back and we can spend a few days together with Mac before we come home. Why don't I take you all to the Sharrow Bay for dinner? I'm sure Mrs Taylor will babysit.'

All the pleasure was now gone from the phone call for Georgina. As usual their conversation turned to business. She didn't mention to him about Mac's idea for them to convert the barn. When she put the phone down she knew she was going to ask Mac not to mention it either.

The rest of the time passed pleasantly enough and Georgina's work progressed. She went for long walks with the family and visited old friends. She sketched Blue in his basket and gave the result to Mac to go with her kitchen paintings. These were a collection of Georgina's artwork from the age of six, which Mac had framed and hung in the kitchen. She was relieved to see that her work had improved over the years, after seeing some of her early attempts! She just wished she could find some inspiration for a painting, something she could throw herself into with true feeling. Something she could be proud of.

Paul arrived from California with a suntan and gifts for every-body. Aunt Lallie, who loved to flatter and fuss over him, told him that he got more handsome with every visit. Georgina noticed, for the first time, the grey streaks that were beginning to appear at his temples. She had to agree with Lallie, the contrast in his thick black hair was very attractive and his eyes looked even bluer than usual in his suntanned face.

'Well, ladies, what have you all been up to while I've been working.'

Mac laughed. 'Working on your suntan by the looks of you.'

'I'll admit to you Mac, that I did find time to play tennis most days but I did a lot of business as well and put in some very unsocial hours. As you probably know America is the land of the breakfast meeting. Most Californians seem to be up at six in the morning jogging. The beach seemed full of them, all healthy looking and body beautiful. I don't know what happens to the overweight or lazy. I think they must have banished anyone fat and ugly to Arizona. Just thinking about all that exercise is enough to make me tired and hungry – which reminds me did anyone book the Sharrow Bay for tonight?'

'Yes, I did,' said Georgina. 'Mrs Taylor is coming up to the house about seven and I booked the table for eight. That gives us plenty of time to drive slowly, not at your usual breakneck speed, Paul. Remember we'll have Lallie in the back seat and every time you go over eighty-five, she'll be tapping you on the shoulder with her umbrella.'

'That's the only reason I carry it.' Lallie tried to sound gruff when she said this. Paul went over and hugged her and told her she was becoming an eccentric old bat. Mac suggested that they all eat lunch, after which Paul and Georgina took Jasmin and Blue for a walk.

They went down to the river. The good weather still held, which was unusual at any time of the year in the north-west. They walked along in silence, seemingly comfortable in each other's company and enjoying the peace whilst contentedly watching their daughter running and playing with the puppy.

'It's good for a child to have a pet,' Georgina said. 'Perhaps, now that we won't have to move house any more, we could have a puppy for the children.' She squeezed Paul's hand. It was so nice to have him back.

When he spoke it brought her up with a start. 'Georgie, I want to talk to you about moving to California.' He hesitated. 'I – I have incorporated a company in California.' He rushed on. 'Some of Tina's negative-cash-flow residential properties are on excellent lots of land. I have the opportunity to buy them at a very discounted price. I can buy them as a package, then sell them on individually. Tina is changing her tax structure in the States, so the properties won't work for her any more. They need a lot of work to upgrade them. It would therefore be a golden opportunity for you, Georgie. You would need to go to real-estate school and get your licence, but apart from that everything would be straightforward.'

'Straightforward!' She looked at him in shock. 'What about the children.'

'Jasmin can go to school in California. The boys are already at boarding school; they could come out every holiday or we could come back to England depending on the business situation at the time. I think it would work very well; it would be a great adventure for all of them.'

'But I've never been to California, Paul, I may hate it. The only time I've ever travelled is when we've been on holiday to France and Spain, or when Lallie used to take me to Italy when I was child – oh yes! and one weekend you took me to New York.'

'Well, a good reason for you to start experiencing some more, Georgie. You've lived a far too sheltered life so a challenge like California is exactly what you need.'

'Whether I need it or not, it looks as if you've made up your mind for both of us.' She wanted to say more but could feel the tears welling up. She thought to herself. 'Why do you always make me feel as if I'm running one step behind, living in your shadow. We never really talk about what I would like, only we – and that, as far as your concerned, means you. Her head was down now and she was fighting back the tears.

'Georgina you always have to be a spoilt brat. I only do what's best for us as a family. I live in the modern world and in that world the only language is money. It's all right for your Uncle Harry to go around acting out his Noël Coward look-a-like, giving his elegant soirées, but it's people like me who will save your precious Tarn House at the end of the day. Let's face it, Georgina, you have no idea. Sometimes, I don't think you will ever grow up.'

Georgina didn't answer him and they walked on in silence for a minute or two. Paul stopped and turning her towards him by putting his hands on her shoulders, he looked down into her sad, upturned face. 'Come on, Georgie, you're not going to sulk are you? Let's go and have a look at California together and at least give it a fair chance. You can't say no before you've even seen the place.'

He pulled her towards him. Her head nestled into his chest and she could feel the tears spilling over on to her cheeks. She wanted to say. 'You've already decided, so I have no choice. Why is it that every time I start to feel safe and happy, accepting how things are, you go and change the rules. But she knew she would say none of those things.

'All right, Paul,' was all she finally said.

'Mummy, daddy what's wrong?' Jasmin came and stood beside them with the puppy in her arms.

'Nothing, darling. Mummy and I were just talking about a trip we are going to take. How would you like to go to Disneyland and see Mickey Mouse.'

'Yes, please, and please may we take Blue with us – he would like that.'

'When he gets bigger, perhaps,' said Paul. He picked her up and she passed the puppy to Georgina.

'Hold Blue, please, mummy, because he's very tired. Daddy, will you give me a piggy-back?' He bent down for her to climb up and they set off for home.

'Let's just tell Mac and Lallie we're going to California on holiday for now. I don't think I'm ready to discuss more than that just yet,' Georgina spoke very quietly, almost to herself.

She began to wonder if the feelings that she had experienced in the kitchen garden the other day were a premonition of what she was now hearing. 'If Paul and I enjoy America, we may never come back to England to live,' she thought. 'I wonder if I have inherited my grandmother's sixth sense?'

Paul glanced at Georgina's face as they walked back to the house. He could almost see the cogs of her mind turning to try and reason with herself. He knew that by the time they reached the house, he would have won the argument and going to California would be a good idea. She was positive and desperately loyal, just like his mother, he thought. He was glad he had his emotions under control, otherwise Georgina would be his downfall.

When they got back to London life became action-packed as usual. Georgina had the Sussex Gardens project to work on with the architect. Paul said he had to go to Amsterdam, but would be back for the boys' exeat weekend. The week after that they would take Jasmin with them to California.

Giles had been very put out that weekend when he heard of his sister's trip. 'Why does she have all the luck? I've always wanted to go to Disneyland. All the boys at school have been.' He continued to sulk for most of the weekend but finally his good nature reasserted itself. Both boys had gone back to school contented with dreams of a summer adventure and promised gifts from America.

'I'll send lots of postcards,' Georgina had called as she waved goodbye to them both.

They flew to LA the following Wednesday. The flight was full when they finally boarded the plane. Paul whispered in her ear as they looked down the cabin. 'Aren't you glad you don't have to travel sardine class?!'

The thought of a long-haul flight under those conditions gave her a feeling of claustrophobia. She was sure Jasmin would be too excited to sleep. Without Maria with them, she expected to work hard keeping everybody happy for those long hours in the air. To her surprise and relief Jasmin fell fast asleep during the film.

As she sat comfortably next to Paul, drinking champagne and chatting about the trip, she realised she was enjoying herself. It occurred to her that it was rather a romantic thing to be doing, being up in the sky with her husband and daughter heading for the New World.

'Do you think I'll find it difficult working in America, Paul?'

'America is a very efficient place in terms of business. Darling, between us we are going to conquer the place! I think you will like La Jolla, it's small and exclusive. The lots of land are in one of the best locations on the coast. One block back from the sea. At the moment they all have old, badly built beach shacks on them. They were probably built as holiday homes in the forties. La Jolla was just a beach town then. Now it's becoming very smart. The properties are nearly all let to students on six-month leases but one of them is on a month-to-month lease. As the leases expire, we will renew them all on month-to-month terms. That way we will have more control and still keep the rental income while we develop the lots.'

Georgina was feeling drowsy; there was a lull in their conversation and her eyelids were becoming heavy. She was bored with talking business and wished they could talk about each other. She drifted into a half sleep. She saw a little girl picking flowers at the side of a railway track. The child was totally engrossed in what she was doing and hadn't realised she had wandered on to the track. A train came up behind her and she started to run. Faster and faster through a tunnel. The train was gaining on her, then all of a sudden she was out of the tunnel and running up the railway bank. The child had turned into Georgina.

She woke up with a start. She had been dreaming. She looked over at Paul. He had his briefcase open and was busy with some paperwork. She decided not to bother him with her dream. She felt it was a good omen, even if she couldn't analyse why.

They finally touched down. Going through customs was not a welcoming experience after such a long journey. 'They make you feel like a criminal,' said Georgina after they had been filtered along the 'Aliens' passage, questioned and finally allowed to pass through.

'It's always a shock the first time. The first impression of America is that the natives are rude and unfriendly. A deprived childhood is probably one of the requirements for a job in customs.' Jasmin jumped on the trolley with the bags as Paul pushed it and guided them towards the Avis desk in search of a car.

It was early evening by the time they booked into the Beverley Hills hotel. Even though the sun had set, the air was still warm. The hotel looked majestic, bathed in the red glow that was splashed through the sky. Its beauty was emphasised by the exotic palm trees which looked like tropical monuments as they lined the approach to the entrance. Georgina could not help but feel excited. It certainly looked the place that dreams were made of.

They were shown to their suite. Paul tipped the bell-boy and turned round in answer to Jasmin who was pulling at his trouser leg in a desperate attempt to get his attention. She was very bouncy for a child who had just made a thirteen-hour plane journey.

'Do you realise that this is the first time Jasmin has stayed in a hotel.' Georgina could see Paul was getting a little agitated with Jasmin's excitement and she wanted to justify it before Paul became cross. 'We've always rented villas for our holidays. She reminds me of myself when I used to go to Italy with Lallie.'

'I thought you stayed in Tuscany with that old schoolfriend of hers, who had a daughter your age.'

'Yes, that's my friend Marina, she came to our wedding. You remember her, she lives in Switzerland now.'

'Yes, I remember her. Wild black curly hair and long wild curvy legs.' He winked at Georgina. She picked up a cushion from the sofa where she was sitting and threw it at him.

'Anyway, when Lallie and I made our journey to Tuscany every summer we flew to Nice and stayed at the Negresco overnight before taking the train to Florence. The Negresco is where Lallie was supposed to stay for her honeymoon. I think she stayed there every year to prove to herself that she had recovered from the shock of being jilted for a wealthy widow. Can you imagine the scandal in those days, Paul?'

He didn't have to answer her as another cushion came hurtling across the room followed by Jasmin's high-pitched childish laughter.

'Right, young lady.' He got to his feet and scooped Jasmin up into his arms. 'I am going to have some supper sent up here for you and you can watch television while you eat it. Then straight to bed; we must get on to West-Coast time as soon as possible. I don't want you falling asleep in Disneyland the day after tomorrow.' He sat her down in front of the television and switched it on. He started searching through the cable channels until he found a cartoon for her to watch.

'What's West-Coast time, daddy.'

'I thought that question would come up,' laughed Georgina. 'I'm going to start unpacking and then take a shower. I'll leave you two to discuss time zones.' She went into the bedroom, thinking how lucky Jasmin was to have a father to ask questions. Grandpa Williamson had been the only father figure around when she was Jasmin's age. By then he had become a garden fanatic. Time for anything else was very limited. She remembered helping her grandfather to prick out seedlings in the greenhouse, or standing beside him while he discussed with the gardener the planting of a new variety of onion sets in the kitchen garden. But most of the time she would be with either Mac or Lallie.

After taking out and hanging up the things they would be needing in the next few days, she took a long shower. As she let the water relax her, she stood thinking of all the things that would have to be arranged if they were going to live in America. Paul was so sure that this was the right thing for them to do and, now she had resigned herself to the challenge, she already saw it being a success. Paul had always been much more adventurous then she was. To keep their marriage alive it was important for her to help him fulfil his dreams. That seemed to mean following his lead for as long as it took to make him happy. He was so much older and wiser then her and quite right when he said she was a spoilt brat. Now she had the chance to make him proud of her. From now on she'd learn more about business in general and be a true partner to him in every way.

In this positive frame of mind she began to discover California – Rodeo Drive and its shops, the amazing mixed-up architecture of the houses in Beverley Hills and the pace of life which she would have to get used to.

Disneyland was a pleasant surprise for her; she had imagined it would be an ordeal, but losing herself in the fantasy of the place, she enjoyed herself as much as Jasmin. The holograms in the Haunted House reminded her of Mac's explanation of ghosts. They looked so real that she wanted to reach out and touch them. Mac had chosen a very good example when she had explained her ghost theory. Helping Georgina to see things with more clarity had always been one of Mac's gifts.

Her spirits were high as they drove down Interstate 5 towards San Diego. When they reached Del Mar they turned off the motorway and drove along the coast, taking the Torrey Pines road into La Jolla. Paul had told her that the name meant 'jewel' in Spanish. As she look down at the coastline of the chic overgrown village which nestled like a multi-faceted diamond between the sea and the mountains behind, she could see why it had got its name. It would be very easy to fall in love with the place. The vegetation was lush and beautifully manicured. Gardenias which had been trained into hedges fenced in many of the gardens. The architecture of the houses varied considerably. Some were built of wood in the colonial style of New England, others were futuristic nightmares. The style which she found the most pleasing was that of the old Spanish homes scattered throughout the village. Bougainvillaea was to be seen everywhere and huge eucalyptus trees lined the sidewalks, making it hard to believe that this was naturally a desert. Automatic sprinkling systems made sure everything remained green. A heady scent from this lush and exotic landscape filled the air and heightened its charm.

Paul parked the car outside a Spanish-style pink-stucco building which was the La Valencia Hotel. Everything about the place was quaint, pretty and understated and the view of the sea was breathtaking.

They settled themselves in and started to devise plans to make the best use of their time. Paul had to be back in LA the following day for two days of business, so it was up to Georgina to explore for herself and to keep Jasmin amused while he was away.

The first thing they did was to go and see the lots of land that Paul had purchased. He also took her to meet the real-estate agent he had instructed to find a property for them to live in.

The agent had some news for them about an apartment that had come up for rent on Coast Boulevard, which she wanted to show them immediately as she felt it would be snapped up very quickly. So within the first four hours of arriving in what appeared to be a laid-back sleepy town, they were sitting in the bar of the La Valencia signing a two-year lease on an apartment on the beach with a three-hundred-degree view taking in the sea and the coast.

Their Californian lifestyle was about to begin and there was no turning back.

She found no difficulty in occupying her time and keeping Jasmin happy while Paul was away on business. Sea World was at the top of the list. Jasmin fell in love with the dolphins and they both screeched when they were soaked by the killer whale.

They went to see the school Jasmin would be going to and she met her teacher. The school was run by nuns and her teacher was Irish. There was an old-world feel to the place that pleased Georgina. It would take a while to acclimatise completely to this new life and she needed all the crutches she could find to support her in the beginning.

Jasmin on the other hand took to everything like a duck to water. She was enjoying herself immensely and loved all the attention staying in a hotel with mummy and daddy entitled her to. She wished life could always be like this, and if they lived here forever maybe daddy would buy her a pet dolphin of her very own to play with. This was the best thing that had ever happened to her so far in her young life, and if it was a dream she didn't want ever to wake up.

About an hour before Paul was due back at the hotel, red roses arrived for Georgina. Again she counted her blessings.

He was back on time and they went out for an early dinner with Jasmin to let her give Paul an update on all that had been going on while he had been away.

'I like my new school, daddy, and the teacher is very nice and the nuns all wear black dresses and cover up their hair because they are married to God.'

'I'm not sure if that's quite right, Jasmin, but I know they will teach you some new ways of looking at things, just remember it's only one way and not *the* way. There is no such thing as *the* way,' Paul said, in a suddenly didactic tone.

'Paul!' Georgina frowned at him, thinking his statement unnecessary. 'I think that went right over Jasmin's head.'

He gave her a sheepish grin and changed the subject. 'Mummy told me you both got soaked at Sea World.'

'Yes, because we were sitting at the front next to the water, so when the whale jumped up and crashed back down again the water from the pool went everywhere and all the people in the front got wet and screamed which made the people at the back laugh.' She screwed up her face as she remembered the shock of the water hitting them – but then that was all part of living in a dream, the unexpected could happen at any minute. What daddy had said about the nuns was strange, grown-up talk that she had forgotten already. She knew the nuns were married to God because one of the girls who had shown her around the school had told her so. The nuns wore wedding rings for God too. Even daddies didn't know everything, Jasmin was beginning to think.

The rest of their stay was taken up with arrangements for the move they would be making. School uniform had to be bought, although this didn't take long – unlike the performance in England when the boys first went away to school. Essential furniture for moving into the apartment had to be bought and delivery dates arranged.

It seemed as if they had only just arrived when it was time to leave, with a very reluctant Jasmin in tow, who feared that if she left her dream, it would never come back.

She looked out of the window all the way to the airport without saying a word to either of her parents. She wanted to have everything very clear in her mind so she could bring it all back if she needed to, like playing with Blue at Tarn House. Sometimes if she couldn't get to sleep she thought about Blue and the way he smelt, all doggy and warm. She would pretend that he was at the bottom of her bed, keeping her safe, and then she would fall asleep and sometimes dream that they were down by the river together with Lallie. That's what she intended to do with this place when she missed it, as she knew she would.

They arrived back to a typical London day, grey and drizzly. It was such a contrast to the sunny beach town they had left behind.

'I'll call Mac as soon as we get home and tell her our news,'

Georgina said excitedly. 'I'm so looking forward to living in La Jolla, Paul. I can't believe I ever doubted that it would be a good idea.'

The taxi sped towards London and for once the M4 was clear.

'There will be so much to organise in the next month, I hope I'll be able to fit it all in.'

'Of course you will, darling. That's one area where I know you have no rivals. When it comes to organisational skills, you would have made a good logistics officer in the army.

The taxi dropped them at the house and after helping with the luggage, Paul left them to go to the office. Maria made some coffee while Jasmin told her about their trip. Georgina took her coffee into the study, as she needed to call Mac right away. She saw this as the most important decision in her life so far, and she hoped Mac's reaction would be positive.

The telephone rang for what seemed an age and she was just about to put it down when she heard, 'Tarn House.'

'Mac, I was just about to put the phone down.' The desperation eased from her voice as she spoke.

'Georgina, you're back! How was your holiday?'

'Oh, Mac! We had a marvellous time, in fact, we've decided to move to California for a while. Paul has a lot of business out there, for both of us.'

She paused, her heart beating fast, for she realised how important Mac's reply would be to her well-being.

'Georgina, how exciting! I hope you've made sure there's room for Lallie and me to come and stay. It's about time we did some serious travelling.'

'Mac, I love you.' She felt herself relax.

They spent a long while chatting, with Georgina answering Mac's questions. Then they discussed the arrangements for the boys exeats. These were to be split between Tarn House and Paul's parents.

When Georgina finally put the phone down and tasted her coffee, it was cold. Feeling contented she sat back in her chair, knowing she was a very fortunate woman to have a mother like Mac and hoping she would always be as close a friend to Jasmin.

From that moment until the day they left England, there was no time to reflect upon the decision to move to America. Paul was away on business at least two nights of every week and Georgina had the Sussex Gardens project to finish before they left. She was looking forward to working on less traditional lines, as a Californian property would allow her far more creative scope than a refurbished Georgian house in London.

A few days before they left, Uncle Harry invited them both to dinner. He seemed to think it was a good idea that they were making the move. He directed his conversation towards Paul. 'I hope you will be spending most of your time with Georgina and Jasmin in California, they will need all of your support in undertaking such a change of lifestyle.' His face held a look of concern.

'Naturally, Harry, though in the beginning I will have to commute, as I still have a lot of business here and in Holland; but Georgina will be able to handle her side of things, I have great faith in her.' He smiled across at her and gave her an encouraging nod, then directed his gaze back at Harry. 'You must make a point of being our first visitor.'

'It's a long time since I was in California. I don't seem to want to travel as much as I used to. I remember staying at the Hotel del Coranado in the sixties. I enjoyed it then. Now I've heard San Diego has grown and the whole area has become very built up.'

'Well, you'll be able to see for yourself when you visit us.' Georgina said this with tongue in cheek. Uncle Harry's failing health was something never discussed and she knew he was too ill to travel even though he would not admit it.

Paul left a week before Georgina to organise the apartment; he was travelling via New York as he was now handling Tina's commercial portfolio there. He would arrive in La Jolla two days before Georgina to arrange the services and delivery of essential furniture they had bought on their last trip.

Georgina was having very few personal things shipped to America as they intended to keep on the Bedford Park house for the time being. Maria would stay on as housekeeper and Georgina would look for a nanny in America; at the moment a visa for Maria would be too difficult to acquire.

So many things to attend to at the last minute didn't allow for any regrets. It wasn't until Georgina was on the plane that she had time to reconsider what she was doing.

'Living in two places will be good fun,' she said to Jasmin as she helped her fasten her seat-belt ready for take-off. This was said for her own benefit, Jasmin didn't need any convincing.

Paul was there to meet them at San Diego airport and after the size and aggression of LA, where she had cleared customs and changed planes, she felt immediately at home. Paul had a surprise waiting in the car park for her: a 450SL Mercedes sports car, in her favourite colour blue with grey leather upholstery. On the passenger seat was a bunch of red roses.

'Welcome to California, darling,' Paul beamed, like a small boy with a new toy.

'Oh, Paul, it's beautiful but it's a very grown-up car for me. I never thought about owning anything as smart in England.'

'Ah, but in America, Georgie, a car is as important as having the right address or going to the right school in England. People are always asking each other what car they drive, you'll see. In California they choose small European cars as a mark of their status. Anyway, jump in, girls, and your chauffeur will drive you both to your hotel. I'm staying at La Valencia and I thought we would leave going to the apartment till tomorrow when we feel more ready to face it. There is still a lot to be done there.'

She felt proud sitting next to her husband who looked so confident and comfortable in the driving seat. He would be able to teach her all she would need to know for their new life in this land of opportunity.

They had dinner in their suite and Georgina was happily exhausted when she finally admitted she could stay awake no longer.

'Well, you go to bed then, darling. I'm going out for a while. I'm wide awake and I would only disturb you, staying here restless. I'll go to the bar and have a drink.'

Paul went down to the bar, ordered himself a Scotch and sat drinking it until just before midnight. After which he left and drove to the apartment.

He fumbled for his keys, tottering slightly, and finally opened the door. He went straight out on to the terrace, picking up the portable telephone as he passed through the kitchen. He lay down on the chaise-lounge and kicked off his shoes. He lit a cigarette and looked up at the clear star-filled sky. The sound of the Pacific pounding on the rocks beneath registered in his ears as he dialled Tina's number in London.

'Hello.' The drowsiness in her voice excited him.

'Tina, good-morning, darling. This is your wake-up call from California.'

'Paul, I haven't heard from you in three days, you bastard, what's going on? I'm very annoyed with you and I won't be ignored – you know I need attention.'

'Tina, darling, but that's why I'm here on other end of the phone. I've called to make erotic love to you. The gift I left – you haven't opened it yet, have you?'

'No, you told me to wait. Why the mystery?'

'Because it's a gift that needs my participation; it's a long distance love charm.'

'How thrilling! It's here beside the bed. I admit there have been times when I was tempted to open it.'

'I want you to open it now.' He stubbed out his cigarette.

She unwrapped the paper to find a black satin box with the word 'Pandora' embroidered in gold on the lid.

'This looks like a very dangerous gift, Paul. I don't know if I should open the box,' she teased.

'Open it, darling, the only danger is addiction.'

Inside the box was a life-like rubber penis lying on a black velvet cushion, surrounded by silk orchids which looked so alive she had to touch them to see if they were real.

'How outrageous!' was Tina's response to the gift.

'Magnificently sculpted, don't you think, darling. Now lift him from his bed and I will bring him to life for you. Listen and do exactly as I tell you and I promise you won't be disappointed in our love-making. It will be theatre at it's best.'

After he put the telephone down he lay back on the chaise-lounge and lit another cigarette. 'I should have been an actor,' he thought.

In a way, Paul was the director of his own life. Georgina had to remain the emotionally innocent virgin or she would not be his child bride. Tina was his sexual fantasy. He allowed her to discover the dark animal in her soul and it bound them to each other like sorcerer and apprentice.

It had been easy for Tina to become addicted to his world of sexual fantasies. Having blocked her own feelings as a neglected child of a mega-wealthy, spoilt mother and a busy ambitious father who hardly knew of her existence, she had learned to live in a psychotic vacuum. She filled the void by mirroring other people's strong sensations. A sad human aerial for emotion.

Paul casually stubbed out his cigarette, gloating over the success of his self-centred world. He got up from the chair, now ready to go back to the hotel and climb into bed next to his sleeping wife.

The moment she walked into the apartment the following morning what she saw reconfirmed that she had made the right decision in moving to California. The cream calico module sofas she had chosen the last trip looked perfect on the limed-oak parquet floor. The apartment was dominated by the ocean and two walls out of the four in the living-room were glass. The terrace wrapped around the whole apartment and gave a very spacious feel to the accommodation. The one-hundred-and-eighty-degree view was breathtaking. She stood on the terrace holding Jasmin's hand, watching the surfers coming in on the waves; the sun sparkling on the water created a light-hearted atmosphere.

Jasmin looked up at Georgina, her face reflecting the magic below. 'Mummy, please may we go down to the beach and swim?' To her child's eyes the water looked as if it was playing with the sun. 'It looks so pretty down there. Are we really going to live here for ever?' She gave a contented sigh. 'I hope I'll make some friends soon.'

'Of course you'll make friends, darling. Once you start school you'll meet lots of children. The beach is the meeting place for everyone under thirty. Today I feel decidedly under thirty, so let's go down and play. Even your decidedly-over-thirty daddy won't be able to resist the invitation if you ask him. You go and find him, while I organise everything we need to take down with us.' The apartment could wait. It was the first home Georgina had lived in since Tarn House that wasn't a business investment. The thought only occurred to her as she was descending in the elevator towards the beach. At last, home and business were divorced. It was a completely unexpected feeling of freedom, which she hadn't thought of as an issue until that moment.

Georgina lay on a towel, the soft sand making a comfortable mattress beneath it, drowsily soaking up the sun, which felt wonderful after the grey of London, when the shock of a cold drip hit her warm, naked stomach; she opened her eyes and found herself looking up into Paul's own twinkling blue ones. The colour of borage flowers was her first thought, a cross between periwinkle and aquamarine – the times she had tried to mix their colour on her pallet without success!

'Life is a beach, Georgie. Come into the water with us. Jasmin wants me to buy her a buggy board this afternoon – she'll be surfing before the end of the month. I'm surprised how well she swims. Even so, Georgie, keep a close eye on her. When I'm not here, you must both be very careful and make sure that you and Jasmin aren't alone on the beach while swimming. The undercurrents here can be treacherous.'

'I promise, Paul.' She tried to put on a serious face. 'I'll find myself a nice surfer to take care of the two of us while you're away, then perhaps even I will be surfing before the year is out.'

'Behave, Georgie!' he wagged his finger at her. 'Come and have a swim before lunch. Tonight I'll make you forget any ideas of beautiful young surfing gods you may be nurturing.'

He pulled her up and they ran into the water. Jasmin, who had been waiting at the water's edge on her father's instructions, joined them with squeals of delight.

It was hard for Georgina to get into a work mood at first but once she did she began to enjoy it. Jasmin settled into her new school and within a week she noticed a slight American twang appearing, especially when other children were around. 'Jasmin's definitely assimilating,' she thought, using an American expression herself without even realising it.

She had started her real-estate course and was interested to learn about the other side of her business. Real-estate law was basically the same as in England, but it was all new to Georgina. The principles of property she knew thanks to Paul, in fact she was surprised at her knowledge on the subject. She saw all of this as an even closer bond between herself and her husband. 'Soon, I'll be able to run a whole project alone. Paul will be so pleased with me. If only he didn't have to travel so much, life would be perfect.'

Friends were made and new places were being discovered. All without the participation of Paul. Georgina found herself courting single women because this fitted in better with her grass-widow status. Some were divorced women of her own age and others single women with business ambitions that didn't allow for relationships.

She joined a gymnasium and spent at least one hour a day working out. Yoga came next, then health-food fads and by the end of the first six months Georgina had assimilated perhaps a little to well.

The boys arrived for their summer holidays. Mac and Lallie decided to visit at the same time, which definitely meant a full house, but it was all good fun. The move seemed to be suiting everybody; the only pang of sadness was the absence of Uncle Harry. After the summer, Paul was there less and less frequently, which became the norm as time passed.

Georgina was becoming very independent and was now making quite major business decisions alone. She was working with a very creative architect; they complemented each other's style and between them were coming up with some very imaginative designs.

Jasmin had made friends with a surfer named Frog. He was in his mid-twenties and appeared to spend most of his time on the beach; he always seemed to be there whenever Georgina or the new nanny, Dolores, took Jasmin down.

Frog had got into the habit of coming over and sitting with them, teaching Jasmin how to read the waves and retelling, over and over again for her pleasure, stories of dolphins riding the waves with the surfers. He made up wonderful adventures of the world under the sea, which seemed to be full of mermaids and seal princesses, of wicked crab stepmothers and handsome dolphin princes. The sound language the dolphins used to communicate had to be imitated by Frog then mimicked by Jasmin before she would allow the story to end.

Dolores and Jasmin got on very well. Dolores was kind without being weak. She worked hard at her job, paying attention to Jasmin's needs without spoiling her. The only problem with Dolores was she couldn't swim, so Frog was a gift from the gods as far as

Georgina was concerned and she had to admit she enjoyed his company and his stories as much as Jasmin.

On the occasions when Paul did arrive he seemed somehow out of place in this new world. He didn't appear to be making any moves to change the status quo. Georgina found it hard to communicate with him. The subject of his spending more time in La Jolla caused them to argue. Or was it that she was answering back for the first time?

Everything about this new life was confusing. Georgina had always thought that her problems with Paul were because of her ignorance. Now here she was going forward in leaps and bounds, only to find new barriers waiting for her. It seemed sad that Paul was missing precious parts of Jasmin's growing up. At Halloween, Jasmin and Dolores had made a clown outfit for the parade at school and Frog had helped her carve a pumpkin on the beach. When she spoke to her father on the phone, he seem to lack any understanding of Trick or Treating. Then Paul had not come home for Thanksgiving, saying that it was an American holiday and did not mean anything to him. Jasmin had been very disappointed when she and her mother had shared the family dinner with some of her mother's single women friends instead. Such a lot of moments when he should have been there were lost. Jasmin was growing up in a world Paul refused to understand.

It was almost time to go back to England for Christmas. Perhaps that would bring them back together.

'I'm finding it hard to believe that it only two weeks before Christmas and here we are sitting on the beach.' Georgina lay back on her towel. Frog was sitting next to her, his wet-suit still dripping water.

'This is when we get some of our best weather. The Santa Ana wind feels good on your body, does it, Georgie?' Frog's deep voice drifted into her ears. Warm like the wind.

'Thank you for looking after Jasmin when she's in the water and the patience you show when she asks for one of your stories, O great teller of tales. I'll miss them myself.'

'How long will you be going for?' He flicked his wet hair back from his face.

'Just two weeks. Unfortunately the school holidays here aren't as long as they are in England, or we would stay longer. I'm looking forward to seeing my sons. We're all going to stay with my mother in the north of England. It will be cold and damp there, but if we're lucky it will snow. A white Christmas would be wonderful.'

'I'll think of you both while your away, although it will be hard for me to imagine what living in England would be like. I've only ever lived in La Jolla.'

'Don't you ever travel, Frog?'

'Yes, I go down to Mexico sometimes. I go if the surf report is good, and I ski every year. I go to Mammoth or Big Bear, sometimes Squaw Valley. I have friends with condos there. One day I'll go and check out the world, but for now I'm just fine here, lovely lady.'

Georgina wanted to ask him if he worked or whether he was at university. The beach seemed to be the only place he spent his time. This was the first time she had been alone with Frog, or spoken to him for any length of time. Normally Jasmin was with her and Frog was busy answering her questions. She noticed him for the first time as a man and not the young boy on the beach entertaining her daughter. She decided he was probably a bit older than the twenty-five years she had originally put on his shoulders.

'What do you do when you're not on the beach?' She hoped this didn't sound like a leading question. She was becoming quite confused by her feelings towards him.

'Not much. I collect my rents, talk to my accountant, those sort of things. My grandmother died a very rich old lady. She left me with a lot of responsibilities.' He sounded bored with the question.

Georgina looked at him. Yes, he meant what he said. She could understand how it would be an inconvenience for him to be wealthy. It was also very refreshing for her to hear; since she had moved to California everybody there seemed totally obsessed with money. Frog, in her estimation, handled his very well.

'I would like to take you and Jasmin out for Christmas dinner before you leave.'

'What a nice idea, Frog. I know Jasmin would be delighted.'

'How about you, Georgie?'

'Me too,' she replied honestly.

He arrived at seven o'clock wearing faded blue jeans and a thick white cotton sweater. His sun-bleached blond hair was combed out of his eyes for once but he still smelled of the sea as he bent down to kiss Georgina on the cheek.

They all climbed into his Toyota jeep. 'I thought we would go to the Fish Market. Do you know it?'

'No, but I like the sound of it.'

'It's in Del Mar. The fish is barbecued over mesquite wood and it tastes as good as the fish I catch and cook myself when I go down to Mexico to surf.'

'Then it must be truly delicious. My grandfather used to fish, so I know how much difference there is between caught and bought.'

The Fish Market had a friendly bustling atmosphere. It was very busy and they had to put their name on the waiting list for a table. They went into the bar; it reminded Georgina of an English pub, one of those pubs on the Hamble, where Paul's father kept his boat. The good thing about this restaurant was the absence of the cigarette smoke one always associated with pubs in England. It was the perfect place to bring Jasmin, with plenty of things apart from the food going on to keep her interest.

'What would you both like to drink.' He caught the attention of a waitress.

'Coca Cola, please,' said Jasmin, without a minute's hesitation.

'OK, and you, Georgie.'

'Some white wine would be nice.'

The waitress came over to the table. 'A Coke and a bottle of Minnelli 'seventy-eight Chardonnay, please.' He turned to Georgina, 'I think you'll like that.'

The wine was delicious. Georgina watched contentedly as her daughter and her friend from the beach entertained each other. He was so gentle and yet so much a man, why had it taken her so long to stop seeing him as a boy? There was something special about Frog; somewhere from the back of her mind came the phrase 'a free spirit'. Yes that's exactly what he was, she decided; she envied him for that.

Their name was called and they were shown to a table close to the where the fish was being cooked. All around the walls of the restaurant there were sepia photographs of fishermen standing next to record-size fish that had been caught at the turn of the century.

Georgina was really enjoying herself. She could feel the emptiness deep inside her lifting. It had become almost an accepted part of her, she had lived with it for so long. It was being replaced by a feeling of youthfulness and happiness; she wanted to rush home and paint. She imagined painting Frog surfing on a big wave, a dolphin riding next to him with Jasmin on its back; the afternoon sun, low in the sky, would be blazing behind them, its rays spilling on to the beach, washing the sandpipers with their glory and giving to the whole scene a spiritually uplifting effect. 'I feel like a teenager,' she said to Frog. 'I'm having such a good time. I've been so locked away in the world of business and friends connected to business that I'd forgotten it doesn't have to dominate most of an evening's conversation. Thank you for that.' Their eyes met but she looked away.

'I used to paint, when I lived in England, but somehow along the way I lost my inspiration. Tonight I feel inspired again.'

'I'm glad I've made you happy, Georgie. You're far too pretty to be lost and sad. When you come back from your trip, I'll take you both down to Mexico; you can paint and Jasmin and I can go fishing.'

Hearing her name being mentioned in connection with what sounded like an adventure with Frog, Jasmin became interested in the conversation and automatically said, 'Yes, please let's, mummy.' To what she wasn't quite sure but if it included Frog she knew it must be a good idea.

'We'll see,' was Georgina's reply to Jasmin. She looked across at Frog. 'Thank you for the invitation, we'll talk about it when I get back.'

After saying good-night to Frog and putting Jasmin to bed, she made herself a big mug of herb tea, took it on to the balcony and lay back in her chair, listening to the waves. Relaxed and content she started going over the evening in her mind. Frog had inspired her to paint again. She was looking forward to the New Year when she would take some art classes at UCSD. Even if Paul decided to spend more time here next year, she would work them into her schedule. The warm mug was comforting in her hands. That's how she felt with Frog, comforted. She thought she should feel disloyal to Paul and realised she didn't. Frog was a friend who just happened to be a man that was all.

She had to admit to herself though that she wouldn't mention to Paul about the invitation to Mexico, or this evening's dinner, unless Jasmin did.

During the rest of the time before they left for England, Georgina was too busy to go to the beach, having some last-minute Christmas shopping and business to attend to. She bought Frog a beautiful bronze dolphin she had found in a gallery on Prospect Street. They found a photograph of the cove and Jasmin wrote a Christmas message from both of them on it.

They met him on the beach the day they were leaving. Jasmin gave him strict instructions. 'Happy Christmas, Frog. Don't open it before Christmas, otherwise Santa Claus will be very cross.' She passed the gift to him in a clumsy way as it was a little heavy for her.

'Well, thank you, Jasmin.' He rescued the parcel with athletic grace. 'I hope you have a good time over there in old England. I'll think up some more stories while you're gone and save them for when you get back.' He turned to Georgina. 'Have a good time, Georgie, and be happy.'

'Thank you, Frog, and you have a happy Christmas.'

It wasn't until she was on the plane that she realised she didn't even know his real name.

The boys had both grown since she had seen them in September, when they left California to go back to school. It was far too long to be separated from their mother, she decided. Next year she would come home for half term.

Jasmin was pleased to be reunited with Maria, who asked her a lot of questions about her new life. School was neat, her friends were neat.

Paul was not amused by Jasmin's American accent, or her colloquialisms. He told Georgina he wanted her to go to boarding school as soon as possible. They argued about it as they did over most of things lately.

'I hope things improve between us.' Georgina was lying in bed looking at Paul's back, as he took a suit out of his wardrobe.

'They will, Georgie. It's just that we've both been working too hard and haven't had the time for each other these past few months.

You'll see, once we get up to Mac's and get into the Christmas spirit, everything will be back to normal.'

'Perhaps you're right. I'm going to put Maria and the children on the one-thirty train. Mac's meeting them at Oxenholme. I have some last-minute shopping to do but I should have everything packed and ready to put in the car by about three o'clock.'

'Good.' He came over to the bed. 'I won't be late, Georgie; it will be nice for us to be alone, driving to the north. We'll stop for a drink somewhere before we join them at Tarn House.' He pushed her hair behind her ear and bent to kiss her neck.

His hands were soft and he smelled of expensive aftershave. Her body didn't respond to his touch as it always had done in the past. A new emotion crept through her for the first time – fear. The fear of losing the only lover she had ever known.

He was her husband, father, brother, lover. Life without Paul was unthinkable, yet here she was putting a question mark on her feelings. She was changing and it scared her to death.

The car journey was long and exhausting with roadworks and traffic jams all the way. They were both glad they had sent the children by train. The atmosphere between them wasn't as relaxed and comfortable as it used to be. Georgina noticed Paul was becoming competitive as far as the business was concerned. She had been about to remind him they were both on the same side at one point. He saw she was beginning to form her own opinions about life and their children that didn't always agree with his. He felt he was losing control and resented this new woman who seemed to be moving into his Georgie. His Georgie, she belonged to him. What had happened in such a short time to change everything? She would be better once they got to Tarn House, she would be her old self again. He realised that he would have to spend more time with her next year, whatever Tina said. He didn't want to lose Georgie.

Everyone was in the hall dressing the tree when they arrived. Giles was at the top of the stairs reaching over the gallery, the concentration showing on his face as he put the fairy in her place of honour. Jasmin watched her brother's effort with sparkling eyes, lost in images of Christmas and Santa Claus.

Blue was lying next to the big cast-iron radiator, which the open-galleried hall needed to heat it, no longer the tiny puppy Georgina had carried in her arms last March. He had grown into a handsome dog. He got to his feet as they came in and nuzzled up to them both, wagging his tail. She bent down to pat and hug him. 'Oh! Blue, it's so good to be home.'

The next few minutes were taken up with everybody hugging or kissing somebody as the family reunion got underway, the joy of the moment capturing all of them.

Mac had prepared the traditional family Christmas Eve supper of fresh oysters followed by baked salmon in dill sauce. Lallie always made the *crème brulée* that finished the meal – cakes and puddings were her speciality.

The centrepiece for the table had also been made by Lallie. She had waited for Jasmin to arrive so she could help to collect the holly and other greenery from the shrubbery. The pine-cones in the decoration she had collected throughout the year while on walks with Blue.

In the dining-room the fire was burning and the candles had already been lit. A beautiful Victorian oil-lamp on the Sheraton sideboard contributed the only other light to the soft subdued glow.

As they sat down at the table it was painfully obvious to the adults that Uncle Harry's health was deteriorating. Mac discreetly helped him to his chair; a slight distortion of the features was evidence of the pain in his weak lungs but he managed to maintain his dignified bearing.

The meal was interrupted by sleigh bells outside the dining-room window and all of the children ran out into the kitchen to look through the French windows as Santa Claus with a heavy sack over his shoulder made his way around the shrubbery. Nobody was allowed to leave the house for being seen by Santa would jeopardise their chances of his leaving them gifts. This was a tradition started by Georgina's grandfather when she was a little girl. In those days it was one of the gardeners who would have dressed up. This year it was Mr Taylor from the lodge.

By eleven-thirty dinner was over and the whole family was assembled in the vestibule with hats and coats on, ready to go to midnight mass in Kirkby Lonsdale.

It was good to see so many familiar faces in church after more than half a year in a new land. The smiles and nods of recognition warmed

Georgina's heart as they walked slowly to their pew at the front of the church, keeping in step with Uncle Harry's laboured breathing.

The Christmas mass had it's usual deep cleansing and calming effect on her. The thought of the birth of a God of love and forgiveness filled her with hope for the rebirth of her love for Paul. She prayed for that and Uncle Harry, whose suffering seemed so unnecessary in her uncomplicated world.

Paul and Georgina slept in her old bedroom as the house was full.

Their love-making had been a disaster for her, the responses she showed him were automatic and without feeling. This left her guilty and full of self-doubt. Eventually she fell asleep only to find herself dreaming of Frog.

They were lying on the beach; he was rubbing sun cream into her back. She could feel her body responding to his hands gently massaging her skin. He put his lips to her ear and whispered for her to look up to see who was above them. She looked up to see Paul standing on the rocks dressed for dinner in tails. Next to him was a table with a top hat on it. Beside the hat stood a group of miniature people, Lilliputians to his Gulliver.

He picked them up and started to juggle with them. She recognised Mac, Lallie, Jasmin, Sebastian, Giles, Uncle Harry, herself and last of all Tina. He smiled down at her on the beach as he threw them all into the top hat. She got up and went over to him. He pointed into the hat. She looked in and saw the face of her father smiling back at her; it was the face in the photograph Mac kept on the piano in the morning-room.

She jumped into the hat to look for him. In trying to find her father, she was subconsciously searching for her own character and destiny. Her present confusion was expressed perfectly in the dream.

She woke up on Christmas morning to the sound of Jasmin dragging her sack of presents across the bedroom floor to show her still sleepy parents all the gifts they had packed into it only a few hours before.

As usual they managed to sound surprised and delighted with her gifts from Santa.

'You know, Paul, however sad life gets, there's always something to show us how beautiful it really is.'

'Is that your thought for Christmas morning, Georgie? Thinking about poor Harry? I understand.' He kissed her cheek.

'Yes . . . ' and us, she thought.

Paul reached under the bed, feeling for the two artistically wrapped parcels he had hidden there. 'Happy Christmas, Georgie, I hope it's your best yet.'

'Paul, they are so pretty – I don't want to spoil the effect by opening them.' Taking care, she gently eased the tape that held the paper together. The silk roses that decorated the top of the parcels were in faded pinks and creams and the parcels themselves were wrapped in thick old-gold paper. She managed to extract the contents without damaging the flower arrangement.

'They're absolutely stunning.' She looked down at her gifts. Gold earrings in the shape of an artist's pallet and a necklace to match. The pallets were set with precious stones to act as blobs of paint and white-gold brushes were threaded through the thumb grip. The larger pallet which made up the necklace was set on to a heavy gold tight-linked chain.

'For my lovely artist.' Paul hugged her and Jasmin, who had managed to sneak in between them during the opening ceremony.

'I'll wear them at lunch. They'll look just right with my burgundy silk dress. You have such good taste, Paul.'

'I know, that's why I chose you.' They kissed again, then turned their attention back to Jasmin who had one of the books from her sack for them to read.

Lunch was a family menu which hadn't changed since her grandmother's day. Smoked salmon followed by roast goose with potato stuffing and *boudin noir*. Mac had diversified in recent years and now used black pudding as a substitute. The whole family agreed that it was an improvement, being courser in texture than its French brother but lacking nothing in flavour. When stuffed into the neck of the goose the *mélange* of tastes was truly delicious. Stilton cheese, followed by Lallie's Christmas pudding, mince pies with home-made mincemeat and the wine from Uncle Harry's famous cellar. This was the only thing he supervised at Tarn House these days but his love for his hobby was undiminished, even with his failing health.

Georgina noticed herself observing the feast. Everything was as usual. Happy smiling faces around the table; Jasmin looking up at Giles as he spoke to Sebastian, glad to be reunited with her big brothers, her heroes; Paul teasing Lallie; Uncle Harry and Mac so close they didn't need words to communicate. She felt a slight outsider from her family for the first time in her life. She felt detached, her mind was somewhere else on her favourite day of the year. She began to understand how some people could hate Christmas with it's great expectations of *bonhomie*. She was missing La Jolla, the simplicity of her new life. She missed Frog. He would probably be in Mexico now barbecuing his freshly caught fish, watching the waves, free and alive in every sense of the word. He was only a few years her junior but she felt old and tired in comparison, and in spite of his youth there was a wisdom in Frog she wished she could achieve. He, a man who had never travelled, seemed to know about unspoken things. She suddenly needed to ask him a million urgent questions,

After lunch the men stayed in the dining-room with their cigars and port while the rest of the family moved into the morning-room. When Lallie went off to make the coffee, the children spread out around the house to play with their new toys and games, each lost in his or her own world.

Georgina found herself alone with her mother in front of the fire. 'Mac, I need to talk to you.' She fiddled with her earring. 'I'm feeling very confused about my new life. I don't know if it's making me happy or sad, a bit of both I suppose. I'm finding it hard to navigate in the right direction.'

'What do you mean by the right direction.'

'Well, being loyal to Paul and my business projects. Accepting the idea of Jasmin in boarding school here while I'm there. Being alone.'

'You've met somebody whose making you ask yourself questions, Georgina. Who is he?' She gave her daughter a knowing smile.

'Oh, Mac! You know me better than I do myself. Well, yes, I have made friends with somebody. He's very different from me but I like the way he sees life. He's a surfer. At first I saw him as a friend of Jasmin's, a young man on the beach who watched out for us while we swam.' She justified her statement. 'The undercurrent can be very dangerous in the part of the sea where we swim. Gradually, I got to know him as a person and I found that I liked him very much.'

'What's his name?'

'I don't even know. He has a nickname like most surfers. They give each other names like Rocky, Squiff, etc. His is Frog. I forgot to ask him his given name.'

'What's so special about Frog that you're questioning all your values?'

'I think it's his free spirit that attracts me. He seems to have a secret knowledge of life that I can't touch but I want to try. He doesn't seem to feel that ambition and money make much sense.'

'He sounds like a young man who's found his bliss. I'm sure he has ambition, to surf a certain type of wave perhaps? He plays with a dangerous friend. The sea knows no mercy. I'm sure he has faced death more than once and so he doesn't fear it. That's probably the secret knowledge you feel he has. I had a *petit ami*, as the French say, when you were a girl. He was a racing driver, with a lot of the qualities you find in Frog. He fascinated me for a long time and for a while I thought I was in love with him.'

'Mac, you've never mentioned him to me before.' She felt a little put out.

'Georgina, I didn't meet anyone I wanted for a husband after your father. That doesn't mean I stopped living. I'm only telling you now because I feel it's worth knowing that all men don't make good husbands, any more than all women should be wives.'

'Sometimes I feel so naïve when I speak to you, Mac.'

'But you are naïve, darling. Look at you – married at eighteen, never had to go out into the world and find yourself a job, protected until now by Paul. I think you're just finding your own feet for the first time and you're having a little rebellion with yourself and anyone else who cares to join in.'

Georgina got up and went over to Mac, throwing her arms around her neck and kissing her on the cheek. 'Mac, I love you and I hope one day to be as wise as you.'

'Coffee, coffee, everybody!' Lallie arrived, her timing, as ever, so perfect as to be uncanny.

During this time the men in the dining-room had been having their own heart to heart. Harry had started the ball rolling with his concern for Georgina.

'Paul, I don't wish to pry into your affairs but I find there's not a month goes by lately when you're not in the gossip columns, escorting Tina Obstroullias. I'm pleased that Georgina is in America and away from it all. Be careful – the press can make or break, they are quite heartless.'

'Don't worry, Harry, I intend to spend a lot more of my time with Georgina next year. I've made up my mind on that already. She's becoming far too independent for my liking. I must admit she's doing a fine job in California and if I leave her alone any longer she will stop asking for my advice at all. As far as I'm concerned that would not be a good thing. I know two heads are always supposed to be better than one but I don't want my wife to turn into a women's libber. A macho Georgina would be unthinkable.' He laughed at the thought.

Harry smiled as he said, 'I don't think you need to worry about that. Look at Mac, an independent woman through and through and totally feminine. For a young man you have some very old-fashioned ideas.'

'Now don't lecture me, Harry. Let's change the subject. That Château Jourdan we had at lunch was excellent.' Paul, as usual, managed to defuse what could have turned out for him to be a tricky discussion. They continued to talk about Harry's favourite subject until Lallie called into the dining-room that the coffee was ready.

When the coffee was cleared away the adults decided to play cards. They were all more relaxed after their intimate conversations; a family reunited.

Georgina now saw her mother in a new light, not just as a mother, but as a woman. One to take an example from. A woman quietly in control of her life, with no regrets and nothing to prove.

The Christmas holidays came to a finale with a New Year's Eve party, given by their neighbours, the Walkers. Their parties were famous for their extravagant side-shows. The house was a restored Elizabethan manor and one hundred or so guests were entertained by a discotheque in the garden-room, a jazz quartet in the library and a juggler and puppet show for the children in the breakfast-room. A buffet was set out in the dining-hall. There were plenty of rooms and an abundance of food, drink and old friends to make the evening a stunning success. Judy Walker was a very good hostess as she had been weaned on entertaining. Her father was a well-known Tory MP, now in the House of Lords, and he had made sure that all the women in his life were there for his own glorification.

Georgina was pleased to spend some time with her old school-friend Jane Stevens and to see her goddaughter Camilla again after over a year. She and Jasmin were about the same age and got on well together. Jane was always up with the local gossip and happy to have a new ear to fill. She was careful not to mention Paul's business relationship with Tina to her friend, just in case she overstepped the mark. She had come to her own conclusion on that subject. Jane was an avid reader of the gossip columns.

By the end of the evening when she kissed Paul to wish him a happy new year and told him she loved him, Georgina really meant it and La Jolla seemed a long way away.

They arrived back to Bedford Park relaxed and cheerful. Paul had decided on the way down that they should sell the house and buy a flat. He had seen a penthouse in Kensington that had caught his eye. With four bedrooms and an enormous terrace it would suit his family perfectly. Also the price was right, but how to tell Georgina. She saved him the bother by bringing up the subject herself that evening.

'I've never really thought of here as home even though it turned into a beautiful house. I never miss it in the way I do Tarn House.' Or, she thought to herself, Edwardes Square.

'Perhaps we don't need it any more with our new lifestyle. I saw a penthouse flat in Kensington the other day that would suit us perfectly. A lock-up-and-leave sort of place. What do you think, Georgie?'

'I love Kensington. If the flat is big enough I think it would be a good idea, especially as you'll be in America with me this year.'

'I'll make an appointment to look at the flat tomorrow. If you like it we'll buy it and I'll arrange everything before you leave. It will be fun to see how quickly I can exchange contracts.'

'Oh, Paul! You turn everything into a game.'

'Life is a game, Georgie.'

The next day they went to see the flat. It was light and airy with good views. She liked it as soon as she walked through the door. The terrace was very wide and she planned to make a roof garden there when she had time. This was going to be a move to wash away the past. This was part of a joint decision to spend more time together.

When she and Jasmin left for America the house was on the

market and the flat had been bought. The boys were pleased to be told that all their holidays that year would be in California.

She set off on her journey back to California with revived spirits and great hope for her relationship with Paul.

The scent of jasmine and eucalyptus was overwhelming after the winter air of England. They arrived during a Santa Ana which suited their balmy mood. Jasmin was pleased to be back with her new friends, the American twang dropping back into her voice almost upon arrival. Georgina settled back into work and waited for Paul to join her. She purposely avoided the beach for fear of what her reaction to seeing Frog would be. She knew this was a cowardly act and promised herself to do something about in the next few weeks. But she wasn't allowed to hide for very long because Frog telephoned and invited her and Jasmin for Sunday brunch. She heard herself saying yes automatically and when she put the receiver down her heart was beating faster than she wanted to admit. His phone call had jogged her memory of the promise she had made to herself last year and she went to an art shop and bought pastels, charcoal and a sketching pad. Then she booked herself on to an art course.

He arrived the following Sunday wearing shorts, docksiders and a faded blue T-shirt.

'I bet you've been missing Mexican food while you were over there!' His Californian drawl washed over her, and his warm smile reflected in her eyes. 'I thought we could go down to Old Town and have some.'

'You're right, Frog, and I'd love a marguerita. I haven't had one since I came back.' She kissed him on the cheek in a sisterly way – and that was the mood she wanted to maintain.

They all jumped into his jeep and headed towards San Diego. 'I missed you, Frog,' said Jasmin. 'I had the best Christmas but I missed you.'

'I've missed you too and your mother. I made up a few beach stories for you while you were away. I met a dolphin while I was in Mexico and he told them to me.'

'Oh, Frog, I can't wait. Let's go to the beach after lunch so you can tell them.'

'Well, that's up to your mom, Jasmin; you'll have to ask her.'

'Mummy, please, please may we go?!'

'We'll see how we feel after lunch,' Georgina said, hesitating but not wanting to disappoint her daughter.

The margueritas were like nectar to her parched spirits. Mac was right, she had been protected. Growing up in one's thirties was a painful experience. She relaxed and started to enjoy what the day had to offer. Jasmin had already persuaded her that the beach was on the agenda for the afternoon.

'Have you thought any more about coming to Mexico with me? I had a bitchen time there while you were away.' When Frog used the word Georgina always had to remind herself that it meant something good.

'I'm expecting Paul to arrive next week.' She look into Frog's eyes. 'He will be spending more time here this year.'

'Well after he leaves then, it would ease the pain of being alone.' He grinned like a cheeky schoolboy who had just given the teacher an apple.

Georgina found herself smiling even though he had hit a nerve. 'How could we resist such an invitation. Yes, Frog, and that's a promise.'

'I wish you would tell the dolphin story now,' said Jasmin, trying to gain Frog's attention.

'Jasmin, dolphin stories are for the beach. I have to hear the ocean to catch my mood and let the dolphins speak through me. This afternoon isn't so far away.'

'You should write a book of children's stories, Frog.' She stroked Jasmin's hair as she spoke.

'I will one day and you can illustrate them for me. We can live in Mexico on the beach.'

'You always make life sound so easy.'

'But it is, Georgie, it is.'

The food arrived. They had all ordered the same thing. Cheese enchiladas, chilli riano, refried beans and rice. Frog said he would eat anything Jasmin couldn't manage on her plate. She managed almost everything.

'I hope I won't sink, I'm so full up,' she said as she tried to imitate her mother and wipe her mouth delicately with her napkin rather than the back of her hand. She usually tried to get away with this when nobody was looking. She had seen her brothers do it and thought it rather daring but today she wanted to act just like mummy because she noticed Frog liked the way mummy acted.

They left the restaurant contented and overfed. The jeep seemed a lot further away on the way back to the car park, but the walk did them good. Georgina was thinking of a sleep in the sun and Jasmin excitedly anticipated the story Frog had promised her. He was silently practising his tale as he ambled to the jeep in his laid-back fashion, life resting easily on his broad shoulders.

They drove back to La Jolla, collected their things from the apartment and went down to the beach. Settling themselves in their usual spot they prepared for a peaceful afternoon, feeling a little less full than an hour before.

The beach was crowded due to the weekend and the warm weather. Georgina lay back on her towel while Frog took Jasmin for a swim. Within minutes she was asleep, safe in the knowledge that Jasmin was being looked after. She slipped in and out of her dreams. They were pleasant nonsense, probably brought on by the margueritas.

Somewhere from her sleep she heard them chattering next to her. It seemed only minutes since they had left.

'Come on, Frog, you promised, it's time.'

'All right; sit quietly and don't wake up your mother and I'll begin.' His warm, deep voice brought her out of her sleep but she lay there with her eyes closed, rested and lazily waiting for the story to begin.

'Well, Jasmin, when I was in Mexico I met a very famous dolphin who surfed with me for a while. His name is Sidney Dolfus but he told me I could call him Sido. Sido is famous because he found Sofie Mermaid's lost pearl earrings. He told me his account of the story and how King Neptune made him one of his special agents. This all happened off Cabo San Lucas. Sido had been helping his sister with her dancing lessons that morning and was . . . shit . . . ' He got up and ran towards the water calling to Georgina to take Jasmin up to the apartment. She looked up to see a small plane which spent its days flying up and down the beach pulling an advertising banner, falling out of the sky and heading towards the beach. It veered slightly and finally crashed into the rocks at the other end of the beach.

She saw Frog dive into the water and swim out to the rocks. Some of the other surfers joined him; people were getting up from the beach and running towards the crashed plane. Georgina started to gather up their things. 'Come along, Jasmin, Frog told us to wait in the apartment. I'm sure he will be able to save the man.' She said this with more conviction than she felt.

They went up to the apartment. Jasmin was shivering and before going out on to the terrace to see what was happening Georgina rubbed her vigorously with a towel and found one of her own sweaters for her because she felt it would be warmer.

When they got on to the terrace, the rescue helicopter was hovering over the plane, lowering a stretcher towards the waiting surfers. They had pulled the pilot out of his wrecked aircraft and were holding him above the water. One of them grabbed at the stretcher when it was low enough and they all helped to lift the man on to it and secure him tightly. As the helicopter gained height it pulled the stretcher up and sped off towards the hospital in Mission Bay.

Georgina sat down and waited for Frog to appear; she hoped the man was still alive and that he could be saved. She thought about his family, and how what started as a normal day could turn into a nightmare within moments. Most of all she tried to keep calm for Jasmin's sake. She looked so small and pale sitting on the terrace in her mother's sweater which came over her knees, sucking her thumb and hugging her teddy bear.

Frog arrived about fifteen minutes later looking very shaken up. Georgina instinctively fell into his arms to comfort them both. 'I'll make some tea,' she said. 'Do you think the pilot will be all right.'

'I don't know, Georgie, we did our best; the doctors will do theirs. After that it's in the lap of the gods.'

Jasmin came in and stood beside them and put her small hand inside Frog's. He looked down at her. 'Sorry about the story – we'll have to finish it another time.'

'That's all right, Frog. I thought you were very brave today to save the man. I'm sure King Neptune will make you one of his agents.' She sounded very grown up. Frog knew he must take her statement seriously.

'Tea everyone, on the terrace.' Georgina had tears in her eyes as she put the tray down.

They sat down and drank the tea in silence, letting the emotional exhaustion wash over them. Georgina was the first to speak.

'Would you like to have supper here with us this evening, Frog. I'm just making omelette and salad.'

'Yes, thanks, Georgie. I'd like that.'

She looked over at Jasmin. 'And you, young lady, must get yourself ready for bed before supper as you have school tomorrow. Then you can stay up a little longer to watch your cartoon.' She spoke softly, giving a treat that wasn't usually allowed, knowing Jasmin would need something to take her mind off the afternoon's drama before being able to sleep.

An evening alone with Frog was the last thing she had meant to happen, but there it was. After Jasmin had gone to bed, hugging her teddy and her furry rabbit, named Pink Nose, for good measure, they took the rest of the Minnelli Chardonnay, a favourite wine of hers since the Fish Market, on to the terrace. There, as two adults brought closer together by a crisis, they sat and sipped their wine and talked, the easy conversation of intimates. Her relationship with Frog had reached a different stage.

She felt she should mention Paul to remind herself as much as Frog that she was a married woman. 'Paul arrives next week.

He will be spending more time in America this year. That was the plan we made over the Christmas holiday and I hope he sticks to it.'

'I do enjoy being with you and I would be a liar to say otherwise.' A huskiness had crept into his voice.

'I enjoy your company too, Frog, that's a problem for me. I feel that my loyalty to Paul is being tested; somehow I think I should miss him more than I do. I'm sure it's normal for survival to get on with life the best one can but I must admit spending a lot of time with Paul frightens me a little. I don't know what we'll discover about our relationship.'

'Did you spend all of your time together before you came to California?'

'No, not as much as we should have. We lived and worked together, both wanting the same things, trying for the same goals. At least that's what I thought, now I'm not so sure what my goals are any more. I think Paul still knows what he wants – more and more money!'

'I don't think anyone searches for just money. Money is a means to an end. Power can be attained through money. The wise seek freedom through it.'

'Well you certainly chose the latter.'

'I hope so.' He put his arm around her and drew her towards him, her head resting naturally on his shoulder.

'I think Paul wants money to have more fun, to play more games and to escape reality. He has a friend, at least a man he calls a friend, a man named Anthony Lawless. Now I think he has a very different reason to want money, of which he has plenty. I think he likes to control people to make them feel small and himself more like a god. He seems to have a much more sinister reason than Paul does for being rich. I don't know why I say that, I don't know anything about him really, it's just a feeling I have when I'm around him. I've only met him with Paul and he hardly ever speaks to me. I am of no use to him whatsoever, so he doesn't bother with me. I feel that Paul plays with life whereas Anthony is evil in his actions – although I have no proof of that. I think Paul loves life and he sees us all as part of a whole, whereas Anthony is perhaps incapable of love. Perhaps the power of money just stops him hating so much.' She sighed. 'But what do I know? I think I'm in love with Paul and here I am sitting on the terrace, comfortable in your arms, and questioning and testing that love.'

'Georgie, I want to say something to you and I want you to remember it. Love's gift cannot be given, it waits to be accepted. I love you, but you must never see it as a threat to your life with Paul and I will never push you into something you are not ready for, but I'll always be there for you. Don't live a lie that's all. It isn't fair on anyone, least of all you.' He kissed her on the top of the head. 'Now I'm going home because I'm beginning to sound like a preacher.'

They got up, somehow managing to stay in each other's arms. 'Thank you, Frog. I promise you I will sort my life out this year. It's about time I addressed reality. I'm so lucky to have you as a friend.' She hoped he wouldn't kiss her because she knew she would respond, but her safe soft cheek was all he kissed. Then he left, almost abruptly.

She went back to the terrace knowing she wouldn't sleep. She sat down going over what had passed between them in her mind. Her thoughts of Frog as the young man on the beach bore no resemblance to the emotionally mature person she now felt she knew quite well. The fact that they weren't lovers was irrelevant. They were intimates and as such a threat to her relationship with Paul, which was beginning to show so many holes. Not being lovers was from choice not from lack of desire on both sides; like an open wound, it was hard to know exactly if it would heal, or whether it would fester from lack of attention and remain damaged tissue from the wrong treatment.

'Life, how bitter sweet you have become,' Georgina murmured, with only the sea to hear.

By the time Paul arrived the following weekend her art course was well underway. On the second week of having to fit in with her schedule he voiced his resentment.

'I seem to be making appointments to see my own wife these days,' he said as she passed him a cup of coffee at the breakfast table.

'Oh, Paul, I know I've made a busy life for myself here, but last year would have been impossible without it. You were hardly ever around and it was all so strange and lonely for me. It will take you a little while to fill your time that's all. Why don't you join the tennis club?'

'There's a three-year waiting list. That dumb architect of yours is a member and he tried to get me in. He doesn't know the right people, that's pretty obvious.' Anger had crept into his tone.

'Paul! He isn't dumb.' Her voice rose to meet his anger. 'Why are you behaving like a spoiled child? When I came here last year, at your suggestion I may add, it was hard for me at first with only Jasmin for company. It took me a while to find my feet but I didn't go whimpering to you about it.'

'For God's sake, Georgina, you're beginning to sound like my mother.'

'Perhaps I'm beginning to feel like your mother. I will not let you try and make me feel guilty over something I have made a success of. I worked very hard and took total responsibility for my life here. I hoped you would be proud of me for it but I can see you resent all of my hard work.'

'Well, I don't know why you have to surround yourself with a crowd of women's libbers.'

'They are not women's libbers. They are women who live alone for one reason or another. Like me last year. I was hardly a couple so I tended to make friends with single women. That's normal. Paul, I survived, I've changed a bit, become more independent. That's normal too. It's just that you need time to get used to it. Please be fair.'

'Fair? But it isn't fair. I feel a stranger in my own home.' He spat the words across the table.

'Paul, now I know you're exaggerating.' She paused, calming her voice slightly. 'I'm not going to cancel my art classes. It's the first thing I've really done that's just for me and I will not be put off.'

'Georgina, you've become hard living here. I'm not sure if I like it,' he said coldly.

'I can't change the way I am now, nobody can go backwards. I don't want to spend our time together arguing but I am standing my ground, Paul. Please give it some thought and see if we can't meet halfway. Time is what we haven't spent together for a long while. We need to get used to each other again.' She put down the napkin she had been folding as she spoke and got up from the table. 'Now I have to go or I will be late for my class.'

Paul stayed on for two more weeks but things didn't improve between them. He saw her as a traitor and she saw him as her jailer. Each one was fixed in their resentment of the other. She began to wear her independence like a badge. He became more patriarchal by the day. Locked in their own agendas and not listening to each other, theirs was an impossible situation. They were both relieved when he finally got on the plane.

After he left she reflected on the failure of the visit and the consequences of their estrangement. She had to make it work between them – they had three children after all, three young lives depending on them both. She made a pact with herself to try harder the next time Paul came.

She avoided Frog. She didn't want to turn her life into a melodrama, running from one to the other. She kept herself busy sketching on other beaches or experimenting with paint at home. She sent Jasmin downstairs to the beach with her nanny, excusing herself because of work.

Eventually Frog called to remind her of her promised trip to Mexico. Even as the phone rang, she new it was him.

'Georgie, I know you're avoiding me. Stop making excuses and remember your promise. Come down to Mexico and have some fun. Jasmin tells me you've had a sad face lately. Out of the mouths of babes and all that!'

'Frog, you're impossible. I'm trying to do the right thing and work on my marriage, which at this moment seems to be in a real mess.'

'And going to Mexico with me is going to make it rockier? I don't think so, Georgie. Remember the truth will always come out even if you try and sweep it under the bed. You won't sort yourself out hiding away, you know.'

He arrived at the apartment at six o'clock in the morning on the following Sunday, as they had arranged.

The jeep was packed with fishing gear and a huge cold box. He loaded her easel and bags into the back and by six-fifteen they were on Interstate 5 heading for the border, with Jasmin still asleep, wrapped in a blanket on the back seat.

Her first impression of Tijuana was shocking. It was the first time she had ever been in a third-world country and the contrast to the affluence of San Diego made it even more depressing. The dirt streets teaming with people, the children begging, the shanty towns built out of cardboard and corrugated iron – all set a scene of suffering she had never imagined to exist so close to the richest country in the world.

'This is horrible, Frog. Look at those poor children over there, the smallest can only be about three years old.'

'I know it looks bad the first time you see it, Georgie, but look closer through the dirt. Those children don't look starved, they have happy faces and there is hope in their eyes, they see the border as a challenge. They dream of one day crossing over to America and starting a new life there. Tijuana is a wealthy town teaming with American dollars that come over the border every day. It's the people in the interior you should be feeling sorry for. The poor farmers who starve to death if their crop fails. They wait for their lives to be over. These kids are waiting for theirs to begin.'

She felt he must be right and tried to see things through his eyes. Tijuana didn't look wealthy to her, nothing she saw in front of her was making any sense. None the less she was glad she had seen it; her life needed more of these jolts into reality.

They arrived at the beach Frog had decided upon just south of Ensenada around seven-thirty. It was completely deserted except for a few seagulls and sandpipers; by now Jasmin was wide awake and was soon scampering on the sand. They set up camp and sat down to plan their day. Frog and Jasmin were going up the beach to fish and Georgina was to stay with the things and paint. Lunch was to be provided by 'the fishermen'.

It was one of those days we all keep in our memory; everything was right about it. The weather, the big opal-eye fish they ate for lunch, the wine, the dolphin story, the results Georgina achieved with her painting, the enjoyment they all found in each other's company. Jasmin fell asleep after lunch and they lay either side of her, talking. Their conversation was easy and relaxed as they talked in depth about life in general and their spiritual beliefs in particular. How each perceived God and the world. Frog had definite opinions but he wasn't dogmatic and he was genuinely interested in how she saw things. She noticed he spoke *to* her and not *at* her as Paul often did. Frog cheered her up and helped her to see that she was taking life far too seriously.

She arrived home feeling as if she had been on a week's holiday, not just a day trip to a different world. She thanked Frog from the bottom of her heart. He had shown her love comes in many different guises and each one is worthy. She had stopped feeling so guilty and was ready to face the challenge of her messy marriage.

When the Easter holiday arrived she was in a better frame of mind as she set about planning Jasmin's seventh birthday party. Paul and the boys were there and it felt like old times. They took the children to Disneyland at Jasmin's request for her birthday treat. Another day they went to the Boriego Desert and ate apple pie in Julian on the way home. They visited Sea World and Jasmin told the boys she knew how to talk to the dolphins, then proceeded to entertain them with her stories and sound effects. The boys were delighted with everything. Paul took them sailing and horse-riding. Georgina found time to paint without treading on anyone's toes. She felt rewarded by her new attitude since her trip to Mexico and her renewed determination to make her marriage work.

The holiday ended with everybody regretting it was over and genuinely sad to be separating again. The boys wanted to stay and go to school in America; they were secretly glad that Jasmin had passed her entrance exam for the boarding school she would be going to in England. They were jealous of her privileged position as a day girl in this magical land of beaches and sunshine. Georgina promised them that their summer would be even more fun. They had a sailing holiday to look forward to with Grandpa Fox in Brittany, as well as their long stay in California. She realised now that the more love was given the more it grew and kissed Paul with true affection when they said goodbye at the airport.

It was in June that her life started to fall apart. It began with a knock on her door and ended with a scream in her soul. On 24 June, Midsummer Day, she was sketching on the terrace. She had been restless all morning and couldn't really concentrate on what she was doing.

The buzzer went at the door. She picked up the intercom. It was Frog's friend, another surfer called Rocky.

'Georgie, it's Rocky. I need to speak to you. May I come up?' She pressed the button to let him in, her heart beating in her throat. She knew something had happened to Frog.

Rocky stood at the door looking grey. 'Come in, Rocky. What's happened, you look dreadful.'

'Sit down, Georgie. I have some bad news.' He led her to a chair. 'Frog has been killed in a surfing accident.' He swallowed hard. 'We went down to Mexico this morning to our usual place. There were big waves coming in, it was the best surf we've had in months. He was knocked out by his board.' His hands went to his face. 'He drow. . .' He had to stop talking he was crying so much.

She couldn't speak; she sat there cold and shocked looking at Rocky. All she could think of was how she was going to tell Jasmin.

'I'll make us some tea.' She got up and went into the kitchen. Everything she did seemed to be in slow motion. She saw herself putting the kettle under the tap, plugging it into the electricity, reaching into the cupboard for the cups, going over the fridge for the milk. Nothing seemed real. She took the tea into the sitting-room. Rocky had composed himself a little and was taking deep breaths to eliminate his sobs.

'I came to tell you straightaway before you saw it on the news or read it in the newspaper.' As he sipped his tea a bit of colour returned to his face.

'Thank you, Rocky, that was a very hard thing for you to have to do. I appreciate it.'

'I hope Jasmin doesn't hear before you can tell her yourself.'

'I hope not, Rocky.' She patted his hand, feeling suddenly very old.

After he left she sat down on the terrace, staring out to sea. It took half an hour for the tears to come. The tears for the treasure she realised she had lost. When they did they came with body wrenching sobs.

By teatime she had composed herself and waited to tell Jasmin.

The news that night was full of the tragic accident of Craig McKenzie French, son and heir to Frenchies fast foods. Heir to his grandmother Marion McKenzie's real-estate portfolio. She went into the bedroom to try and comfort Jasmin who had taken the news very badly, pleased for her sake that she was leaving to go to school in England. Only time could heal such a deep wound for both of them. For the moment she must concentrate on helping her daughter get through the rest of her summer.

'Come, darling, sit up and dry your eyes for a moment. Look at Pink Nose, his poor face is wetter then yours where you've cried all over him.' She handed Jasmin a handkerchief. 'I want to talk to you about Frog because I know he wouldn't want us to be sad for him because he died. Frog was taken away by the sea doing what he loved most in the world. He probably lives in King Neptune's palace now and is a very important member of the court. When you start your new school in England you will learn to write stories and then one day when you're older you can write down all the stories that Frog told so well and I will paint pictures, so the children who read those stories can see what King Neptune's palace looks like. I know Frog would love us to do that for him. Now, try and go to sleep and you can dream of Frog and his dolphins and they will be surfing together always.'

Tucking the bedcovers around Jasmin's small body, she could feel the pain in the roof of her mouth, as she willed herself not to cry. 'Sleep tight, darling.' She pushed the damp hair away from Jasmin's forehead and kissed her there. She left the door open as she went out of the room.

'Mummy,' Jasmin called after her. 'I love you. You won't leave me and go to live in the sea with Frog, will you?'

'No, darling,' she called, the long-held-back tears streaming down her face. 'I promise you.'

She and Jasmin now shared something together that would bond them in another way than just mother and daughter, for they now shared the memory of a man whom they had both loved in a special way.

July brought with it death of another kind. Death of trust. It was in the second week after the boys had arrived in La Jolla for the start of their summer holidays, as it seemed a better plan for everyone if they went sailing with their grandfather at the end of the holiday. This would give Georgina more time to organise Jasmin's leaving America to start school in England.

Tina telephoned asking if Paul was there.

'No, Tina, is he supposed to be?'

'Yes, he said he was with you; the bastard is two-timing us, darling.'

'What are you talking about, Tina?'

'Georgina, I've been having an affair with your husband for the past two years. You must have known, you couldn't be that stupid, darling, surely.' She laughed.

'No, Tina, I didn't know.' She felt her heart jump and her throat tighten as Tina's words pierced into her. 'My husband didn't change towards me, so why should I suspect anything was wrong – and anyway why should I believe you?'

'Because you're not a fool. The reason you didn't notice anything different in his behaviour – and by that remark, I suppose you mean in the bedroom – is because he has always been unfaithful to you.'

'Tina, that's a horrible thing to say. I refuse to continue this conversation.' She slammed the telephone down.

She felt sick. What an idiot she had been, it had never occurred to her that Paul was unfaithful. Before their recent problems, their sex life had been fine. Paul was always attentive and loving, so why should she suspect? Tina wasn't lying though, she knew that too.

Her female intuition told her Tina knew a lot more about her husband than she did.

It made a joke out of her and Frog. How they had wanted each other and denied themselves out of respect for her marriage. What marriage? she thought now – a farce, nothing more. Her shock turned to anger, she wanted to hurt Paul for all his lies. How long had this deception been going on – or was Tina the first? Perhaps she had lied to her about the other women out of her own frustration. She suspected not. She was beginning to see Paul as a charming playboy, always taking what he needed without any respect for other people's feelings.

That's how he had treated her all of their married life and until recently she had been a willing victim. All that would change now, she was ready to retaliate. She could feel herself going numb, first Frog and now this. She had to stop thinking, it was killing her.

Paul telephoned the following morning. 'Hello, Georgie, I'm in New York. How's everything.'

'Everything's fine, Paul. Tina rang – she was looking for you.'

'Oh really? It's probably about the business here.'

'No, Paul, she thinks you're being unfaithful to her; she told me about your affair.' Her voice was ice cold.

'You believed what she said.' He sounded hurt.

'Yes. Of all the things I may accuse Tina of, lying isn't one of them.'

'I don't believe I'm hearing this! You would believe Tina before me?'

'Paul, I don't wish to speak to you at the moment. I'm far too angry to be fair on you – in fact, at this point, I almost hate you.' Her voice was strained with fury. 'Don't come down here thinking you can smooth things over. It's to late for that. Far to much has happened to me in the past two years for me to be good old Georgie any more. So stop playing games. I will call when I have something to say to you. I am taking the children to Santa Barbara for a few weeks, I need a change of scenery. You may call this evening and talk to them, I will make sure Sebastian answers the phone. Tell them you have to work and that's why you won't be joining us. Your good at lying and I don't see why our children's summer should be spoiled by our mess.' She put the phone down, not waiting for his reply. She felt somewhat cleansed by her action and hoped her hard line would hold.

She put the answering machine on so that she could vet her calls. She had no intention of speaking to Paul for the next few days. She needed to think; she wanted to call Mac, but saw that as a weakness. This was something she had to work out for herself.

She wished Frog could be there for her and tried to imagine what advice he would give her. Good wise Frog, that would always be his name to her. She was pleased that it was only after his death that she found out who he really was. It made him even more special to her. She owed it to him to work on her art, that was something she would definitely see through. He believed in her but didn't want anything from her, unlike Paul who she now felt had used her for his own ends without any respect for her feelings.

Hard and difficult times. Paul sent roses, she sent them back. He tried calling, he always got the answering machine. He sent telegrams, she ripped them up.

She carried her anger with her through the summer, enjoying her children and keeping her time exclusively for them. Out of guilt or need, she wasn't sure, she devoted herself to them and they gave her the only happiness she could find at that point.

By the time she and the children left for England she had reached the point of emotional exhaustion. Her mental war with Paul was at crisis point, but she still wasn't ready to talk to him. The challenge of his glib tongue was too much for her parched wits. They flew to Amsterdam and changed planes there. She sent the boys to Heathrow to meet their father and she and Jasmin flew to Manchester where Mac was waiting for them.

As always she took solace in Tarn House. Just walking through the door made her feel safe and a bit calmer. Mac would help her put things into perspective; a few days was all she needed to get back on the right track.

That evening after Jasmin had gone to bed, she sat down with Mac to a pot of coffee and some serious talking.

'I don't know what to do Mac. Paul and I are not together at the moment.'

'Well, I guessed as much. Is it another woman?'

'Yes and no. I wish it were that simple. He has been having an affair with Tina – she's the woman we met at Uncle Harry's, the one with the property interests in America. I would like to leave the fault for our mess on her doorstep but that isn't really the truth. Something has happened to our relationship, slowly, over the years. I have been unhappy for a long while and I didn't know why. Now I feel a part of me has died and I don't know if it can be brought back to life.' Her voice sounded flat and defeated

'That's nonsense, Georgina, you've just had too many traumas, one after the other. First your poor friend being killed and then finding out about your husband's infidelity. Let's put the emotions to one side for the moment and be practical. You need to talk to Paul and decide what you are both going to do about your marriage. Are you going to stay married and have a working relationship or will you divorce? I think you both need time to come to that decision, but you must talk to each other.You may find that you're good friends after all, if so the sooner you start acting as such the better it will be for everybody. You're angry with yourself as much as you are with Paul. The sooner you can start forgiving yourself, the sooner you will start to heal. Also, never think children don't know what's going on. They realise more than we give them credit for. The sooner you tell them the truth the better, but you have to find out what the truth is yourself first.'

'Hard but wise advice, Mac. I don't know why I feel so sad about Jasmin going away to school. It seems worse than when the boys went somehow.'

'That's because another stage of your life has been reached. Try and make this the best yet – it should be. A beautiful woman in the prime of life with the best years still to come. I was about your age when your father died; it takes time, that's all; you will survive, Georgina. Now come here and let me give you a hug – a girl is never too old for that and a mother is always a mother.'

Over the few weeks left before school started her mood didn't improve, in fact it deteriorated into a deep depression. Mac became worried about her; it was if her spiritual energy were dying. Normally Mac would find the right words to help her daughter but this time there was nothing she could do to help. She just had to watch Georgina fading into the mist of her own misery. Mac telephoned Paul to say he must be patient a little longer as his wife seemed seriously depressed and not ready to talk or deal with anything more than their daughter's going away to school. She wished he would change his mind about Jasmin going to boarding school and tried to suggest this to him. He would not hear of it, believing it was the right thing to do. He called daily to speak to Jasmin and gave the excuse of work for his absence, promising they would spend her first exeat weekend together. Mac advised Georgina to see a doctor but she wouldn't hear of it. The negative shadow that shrouded her was becoming the only real thing in her life.

It was even harder than she thought it would be, leaving Jasmin at her new school. They both put on a brave face as they said their goodbyes but by the time she reached the bottom of the drive and turned out of the school gates, the tears were pouring down her face. She didn't bother to wipe them away, she just blinked to see the road more clearly. She was choking on a surfeit of pent-up emotion; her breathing was laboured and painful; she knew she should pull off the road and compose herself but she couldn't stop driving.

Too fast and almost out of control, she turned off the main road to take the back lane to the house. Her loneliness was closing in on her and she was speeding as if to escape from it. She was in total despair as she rounded the corner and met a tractor crossing the road. She saw her death and welcomed it; her whole life flashed in front of her mind's eye in those few seconds. Then darkness.

She woke up in the hospital. As the room came into focus, she saw Mac sitting on a chair by the bed.

'What happened?' she whispered.

'It's all right, darling, I'm here now.' She leant over and clasped Georgina's hand. 'You had an accident but you escaped without even a scratch. I'm going to take you home as soon as they've looked at your X-rays. You seem to be absolutely fine, thank heavens. It's lucky you were in the Volvo and wearing your seat-belt. What a shock. I should have insisted on going to the school with you; it was too much for you to take Jasmin on your own.'

The doctor arrived to give the all-clear. 'If you start vomiting during the night you must call us immediately. I don't think there is any concussion though. The X-rays show no signs of breaks or cracks. You were very lucky by all accounts.'

'Thank you, doctor. I feel perfectly OK. I'm sorry to have caused so much trouble.' She gave him a shaky but confident look of reassurance.

'Well, I expect the police will need to talk to you. I don't know though. Nobody was hurt fortunately.'

As they walked towards the car, Mac held her arm. 'You can't go to America tomorrow as planned, Georgina. You must stay at Tarn House and rest for a few days. I'm sure you will feel the shock of this accident later.'

'No, Mac, I'll be fine. I'm travelling first class so I will be able to sleep on the plane. If I don't go now I may lose my courage completely. It's very important to me at this point that I finish up everything in America personally; perhaps I'm trying to make a statement, I don't know.' The exhaustion in her voice was painful.

As much as Mac tried she could not dissuade her and the following morning she reluctantly drove her daughter to Manchester Airport to take the shuttle to Heathrow for her connecting flight to Los Angeles. After she had checked in her luggage, they went to the restaurant for breakfast.

'Are you quite sure you are going to be all right, Georgina. I feel I should be going with you. I had a shock myself when I saw the car. I still can't believe you got away without being injured.'

'I know, Mac, I saw my death too. It's funny. I've read in books how people see their lives flash before them when they die and that's exactly what happened to me. My biggest shock was waking up in the hospital and seeing your face.' She smiled at her mother.

'You look tired, darling, are you sure this is a good idea.'

'Mac, it's a long-haul flight and I'm looking forward to sleeping all the way. I'm trying not to think about how I'm feeling. I don't seem to have even as much as an ache at this point and I'm sure as you say there will be some repercussions, but it could be days before reaction sets in. I promise you that I will call you straight away if I feel I can't cope and I know you will be on the next plane.'

The waiter arrived with their breakfast and they ate it with relish; the trauma of the past twenty-four hours had made them both ravenous.

'Thank you for the pep talk when I arrived, Mac, it was exactly what I needed. That's another reason for me to go to La Jolla. I will be alone and I will have time to think about Paul and me. You were right about my being angry with myself. I feel a fool, I suppose.'

'Feeling a fool is better than being one. To feel a fool is to learn something about oneself – that's what we're here for, I think.'

'You could be right, but for most of us wisdom comes slowly, if at all.'

'I think that we are all given what we need in that area, it's just that we don't always see it – but I don't worry about you. You're one of those who will recognise the signs and won't be afraid.'

Mac's remark stayed in her mind as she boarded the shuttle for Heathrow. She liked the way her mother looked at life. She hoped she would always be there for Jasmin in the way that Mac had been there for her. Mac had let her find her own way in life, waiting until she was asked for advice rather then telling Georgina what to do. As a result she had made a lot of mistakes but at least they were her own. The more she learned about her mother the more she respected her. 'It takes a long while to really know even the people we love the most.' She thought as she fastened her seat-belt for take-off.

The LA flight was packed. She settled herself into her seat and took the glass of champagne the hostess offered her. She expected to sleep all the way across the Atlantic. Exhausted in body and mind, she was running on overdrive and hoped that the champagne would relax her and induce that sleep. She buried her face in a magazine and tried to centre her thoughts on an article about nail-care.

'Excuse me, but is this yours.' She looked up to see an extremely handsome man in his mid-forties smiling down at her, holding her raincoat.

'Oh! I'm sorry I was waiting for the hostess to hang it up.' She took the raincoat from him as he sat down.

The hostess came over and took the raincoat, offering champagne to them both. 'What a civilised way to start a journey.' He turned towards Georgina. He had a charming smile and captivating green eyes. 'Cheers,' he said raising his glass. 'My name is Samir Hariri.' He extended his hand.

She shook it, 'Georgina Fox.'

'Is this your first trip to Los Angeles?' He had a slight accent and a clear baritone voice and she was attracted to its warmth.

'No, I make this journey quite a lot. I've been working in San Diego for over a year.'

'I know San Diego very well, I lecture there sometimes. Where in San Diego do you live?'

'La Jolla, just up the coast.'

'Ah yes! A very pretty town. I spend time there myself. I head the literature department at UCLA but I also do freelance lectures. Several women's groups in San Diego ask me to speak and that sometimes takes me to La Jolla.'

'Do you only lecture to women?'

'No,' he laughed and she noticed he laughed with his eyes. 'I think I find women's groups some of the most interesting, that's all. It's always a pleasure debating with them. I enjoy the woman's viewpoint because I find that hers is usually the voice of reason in the end. Whatever their race or creed, women's priorities are generally the same. Freedom from hunger, healthcare, education and hope for their children. Women will always opt for those ends. They have much more awareness of life and death. Every month, they experience one or the other. Men in general have rather different things on their more complex agendas. Power is the first item that comes to mind.'

'I hadn't thought about it before, but I suspect I've lost my husband through lack of understanding of the male mind. I don't know if I ever will understand.'

She suddenly found herself telling this complete stranger her life story. Sharing her thoughts in a way she had never been brave enough to do with anyone before, including herself. The more she talked the more she needed to, it was as if the flood-gates had opened and nothing would stop the flow until her mind was empty.

The twelve-hour flight passed quickly and pleasantly with all idea of sleep banished by this new freedom. It felt so right up there in the sky to unload her troubles on this man who didn't seem to want to judge her or mould her thoughts for his own ends. His questions were sensitive without being prying. He opened doors in her mind and the more she talked the clearer things became.

He finally asked her what she intended to do next. Surprised to find that she had a definite answer, without hesitation she replied, 'I want to paint. I want to move to the South of France and paint. Paul I and spent our summer holidays there when our sons were small. I always thought I would have liked more time to myself then but the boys

87

were very demanding at that age. I was inspired by the light the impressionists were all so enthusiastic about. I felt very much a part of the atmosphere of the place. I always imagined myself there one day as a working artist, experiencing the different seasons. Those wonderful soft warm colours coming alive on my canvas.' She was completely carried away with the idea that had come from nowhere.

'Then that's what you must do. I know the South of France well. I spent a lot of my childhood there. It does have a special feeling and smell. Something that always stays with you. I used to get back there frequently but over the last few years I have been too busy. I can imagine you there, Georgina – becoming more and more bohemian over the years, wearing a big straw hat decorated with herbs and dried flowers.' He smiled at her. 'No, seriously I think you should do it. Move to the South of France. Your children would love it there and it isn't so far away from the people you love as California is. I support that idea one hundred per cent. Perhaps I may even be able to help you.' He gave her his card. 'Call me while your in La Jolla – ask for Sam. I would like to invite you to one of my lectures. I'll be in San Diego in the next week or so and I'll have to check with my secretary but I'm sure I'm scheduled to speak there.'

'Thank you, Sam, I would enjoy that very much.' She searched in her bag for her own card to give him.

The seat-belt sign went on at this point and she could tell by the pressure in her ears that they had started their decent.

She arrived at the apartment hot and tired, having missed sleeping on the flight from Heathrow. Without Sam's company, the rest of the journey to La Jolla had seemed tedious and frustrating. She took a long hot shower then she lay on the bed exhausted. So much had happened over the last forty-eight hours, her body had been pushed to the limit. She felt she would sleep for a week.

The sound of the Pacific Ocean rhythmically breaking against the rocks below helped to calm her mind. She could feel her body becoming heavy on the bed. A sudden wave of sensation rippled through her; then, before she could draw her breath, another, even stronger then the first. The experience was very pleasant, like an orgasm, but her whole body was feeling the ripples with the same intensity. The waves continued like caresses of energy, spiritually lifting her away from her torso, relaxing every muscle, every bit of tension she was physically holding deep within her. Cleansing, calming and lulling her body. Each ripple unfolding like a bud, exposing for the first time the full beauty of its petals. Spasm after spasm flowed through her for what seemed an age.

At the same moment her mind was levitating, rising above her body and hovering in harmony with the physical music of it. A bright light seemed to be drawing her away towards it. She wanted to go, it felt so safe there, so peaceful, a joy she had never known existed came from that light and she felt part of it. The energy sandwiched between the two parts of her, the physical and the spiritual, was playing the most beautiful game as if to create a new whole. Suddenly she knew that if she let this continue she would die of ecstasy and vanish into the mist of this beautiful experience before she was ready. Mentally she pushed herself back down into her body. The sensation slowly stopped. She sat up; her mind was clear, she felt wonderful. A great sense of physical well-being and a deep spiritual feeling of peace had replaced the dreadful lump of pain that had unremittingly constricted her heart of late. She felt truly happy. She lay down again, luxuriating in this new feeling.

Was that an out-of-body experience, she wondered. Perhaps the energy she had felt was the collective subconscious she had read about somewhere. She wondered why she hadn't been afraid of such a strange experience. Instinctively she had felt safe at all times with whatever the energy was.

She floated in her new state of awareness for some time. A vision of a house came into her mind. A farmhouse painted white with a slate roof. She felt its warmth and welcome with exactly the same feeling she always had for Tarn House. She didn't know this house, but she wondered if it could be the original Tarn House Mac had mentioned. She almost expected to see a woman in Elizabethan dress walk through the door. Nothing of the sort happened. The vision faded and as it did so it was replaced with the need for sleep.

She woke late the following morning, her body feeling purged and alive, her mind clear and ready to take on Paul with a firm decision as to what she wanted.

As soon as the time difference would allow, she telephoned him at their new penthouse home, a home she had never shared with him. She had no regrets about selling the Bedford Park house; Paul would be much better off in the penthouse if he was going to be alone.

She heard the distinctive sound of the English ringing tone. In the past that sound had always engendered a feeling of homesickness in her. Today no such feeling came, even when Paul's voice, husky with sleep, answered.

'Paul, its Georgina.' She waited a few seconds before going on, to give Paul time to register the fact that it was her. 'First of all, I would like to apologise for avoiding you these past months. I have been acting childishly. I didn't know how I was feeling and I was afraid you would manipulate me into something I didn't want.' She paused, when he didn't speak she went on. She could sense a new confidence in her own voice. The old Georgina seemed to be an observer of this new person handling her life. 'I want a divorce Paul, but only if it's the right thing to do businesswise.' She drew a deep breath and continued. 'I realise now our marriage became a business partnership over the years and I don't want to spoil the part of it that worked by confusing it with my personal feelings.'

'Georgie, don't.' Paul's voice sounded frail at the other end of the line. 'It's all over with Tina.' Tina's interest in Paul had waned the moment he was totally available to her.

'Tina isn't an issue, Paul. I would be lying to you if I said she was. I want to pursue my painting and I have decided to move to the South of France. I blocked my creative impulse over the years as I blocked my emotions. Now that my urge to paint has returned I can't jeopardise it by living in a false marriage.' She was speaking with a new passion, the reunion with her lost art giving her the strength she needed. 'Anyway, Paul, I wouldn't suit you now, I've grown up. You want somebody you can control and you've lost that with me.'

'You've become hard, Georgie.' His defeated tone was painful and she felt sorry for him.

'No, Paul, that isn't true. I've become confident in myself. It has taken a lot of pain to reach this point. I am clear-sighted enough to know that I am responsible for my problems with our marriage. I was just as much at fault. Putting you in the category of a hero, stopped me having to make decisions. I can't hold you responsible for my past weaknesses.'

'We need to talk about this, Georgie; we have children together. You can't just up and leave. This isn't something we can discuss over the telephone.'

'Paul what is the difference between my living in France and my living here? As far as the children are concerned they will cope in the same way they did with America. I am going to France with or without your support. There is nothing to discuss on that point. I want to be your friend, Paul. I think we have been friends and it would be sad to lose that, but it's up to you. Try to accept that I have changed. I'm not angry or hurt and I don't want to hurt you. If you want to hurt yourself, I can do nothing about that. As friends we can be of better use to our children. I think they deserve that.'

'Is there somebody else, Georgie?'

'No, Paul, and don't look for an easy way out. I want to do something for me, to see where it leads me, and I have total confidence that I am doing the right thing. It's too complicated to explain but I know something important has happened to me which is nothing to do with us. I need to find out what that something is.'

'Let me digest what you've said because it's a lot to take in. I feel I'm talking to a stranger rather than to my own wife. Please, when you come back, let's talk. I promise not to try and dominate you.'

'My mind is made up, Paul, but yes, we should talk. I would like you to help me form a plan that would suit everybody. I know we can work together as we have in the past. It's just that this time you will be helping me to do something that I want. Handle it with grace and we will all benefit from it.'

'Georgie, I'm not sure how I feel about anything at this moment but I do love you, I always have and I always will, whatever course that love takes. I'll be there for you. I need time that's all.'

'I think you could become the brother I never had and I hope things work out that way. Anyway, I'll call you when I get back to England. I will stay at Tarn House until we sort everything out. I'm glad we are saying goodbye on a civilised note. I hope it can continue like this.'

'I'll do my best not to become a male chauvinist but I am only human.'

'No, Paul, you're the magician. You always pull the right thing out of the hat.' As she put the phone down she was reminded of her dream. Paul the juggler. Now he had to juggle with his own feelings she wondered how he would manage.

She slumped into a chair. It was warm and muggy in the apartment. The call had gone better than she had expected but she felt drained all the same. She closed her eyes, allowing her mind to drift. The sensation of well-being returned as she saw the vision of the house she had experienced the previous evening. It brought with it a cooling soft breeze which enveloped her body. The slates of its roof were glistening after the rain and she noticed around the porch an arch of yellow roses and jasmine which over the years had entwined themselves into a marriage of colour and scent. She could smell their rich fragrance and feel the damp air in her nostrils. On the heavy oak door a brass knocker which had just been polished shone to welcome her. A great desire to enter overcame her, and the affection and warmth the house was exuding encouraged her to do so. Just as she thought she would, the vision faded, leaving behind the positive feeling of support she would learn to associate with it.

She didn't understand what was happening but yet again she wasn't afraid or disturbed by it. It was something she had to yield to, because when she had thought the journey into the vision was up to her and was about to take control, it left her. Time would explain all, she hoped, but for the moment she felt she was just meant to accept it without question. This wasn't something she wanted to share with anyone yet.

At the thought of sharing feelings, Sam came to mind. The man she had met on the plane had impressed her. He was a very handsome man and his green eyes held a compassion that made one feel safe. She had never been the sort of person to open up about herself easily. Yet in those few hours up in the sky this man had won her complete confidence. She decided to call him. She got up and went to the bedroom to get his number as his card was still in her handbag. She fished around her cluttered bag and finally located it; as she took it out the telephone rang.

'Georgina, it's Sam. I was just calling to find out how you are feeling today.'

'Sam, what a coincidence I was about to call you. I feel much better thank you. In fact, I have already spoken to Paul. It was much easier than I had expected it to be, and I think he will be reasonable about my decision.'

'That's one of the reasons I called. I've been thinking about France – but first of all I would like to invite you to one of my lectures. I am coming to San Diego next Friday and I will be speaking to a group of women called Christian Women United. Would you be free that evening?'

'Yes, Sam, I would love to come.' It was as if she had known him for years; she felt completely relaxed as she spoke.

'Good, I'll get my secretary to call you with all the details and arrange for one of the committee to meet you there. Perhaps we could have dinner afterwards.' Before she had the chance to reply he went on. 'About France, Georgina. I mentioned on the plane that I may be able to help you there. My family owns a house in the hills above St Tropez. It's a little overgrown but very comfortable. It faces southwest so the light is very good all year. I'm sure you could turn one of the rooms into a studio for yourself. There is a caretaker's house in the grounds. Rosie and Henri who live there have looked after our family for years. I'm sure they would be delighted to see the house opened up again and lived in. We are hardly ever there these days and have been talking about letting it. My sister has been opposed to the idea, as she didn't want strangers living in it. I told her about you and she agreed with me that you would be the right person to ask. So go and have a look at the house while you're in France and see what you think. It has been waiting for something to happen in it and I can imagine an artist working there.'

'That's an interesting statement, Sam. I believe houses have energy too. I'm sure I will love your house. Thank you, it really is a very generous offer.'

'Not generous, Georgina, it will please me to know the house is being used. I meet people all the time but very few have impressed me in the way you have. You are going to go a long way and I would like to think I helped a little to put you on your path. I think we will become very good friends.'

'I hope so, Sam. I want you to know that I don't normally go around telling perfect strangers my life history.'

'Fate can never be dismissed, Georgina.' He laughed. Then a

more serious note came back into his voice. 'You're special, Georgina. I mean that.' He went on again before she could answer – not that she had an answer – 'So I can look forward to seeing you on Friday?'

'Yes, Sam. I'll be there and thank you again.'

She put the phone down for the second time that morning with a feeling of this being the first day of her new life. Fate or coincidence, it didn't matter. Samir Hariri was the man who was helping to shape that life. There was a solid depth to him that she liked and she felt herself in safe hands. Only good could come from their new friendship. He was for her growth as much as Paul had been for her stagnation.

Their friendship blossomed from the first time Georgina discovered Sam as the brilliant public speaker he was. He opened new avenues of interest for her. She had never been politically aware, always seeing the world and its problems as very remote from her own daily life. Of women's groups and issues, she had no real knowledge. She associated them mostly with the burning of bras and equality in the workplace. Thoughts left over from her college days.

The women she met through Sam weren't looking for equality; they already saw themselves as equal. They were much more interested in defining and perfecting their roles, whatever they should turn out to be.

For the first time she thought about her generation and the pill. How it had changed and liberated them. Pre-pill women lived from month to month, not really being in control of their lives. Makeshift birth-control methods meant there was virtually no such thing as planned motherhood. The pill left them with definite choices as to career and size of family and time to find out who they were. With it came the chance to explore sex for itself in the relaxed knowledge that it wouldn't end up in pregnancy. Along with that came more expectation as to what they wanted from their partners in terms of enjoyment and fulfilment. Their need for equality had spread a lot further than the workplace.

The pill was something Georgina had always taken for granted, not something that had revolutionised her life. She became interested in women as a subject to explore through her painting. How much more importance had been put on the virginity of women even in modern cultures than on that of men. The nun and the prostitute at the extremes of good and evil. Only the spiritual superiority of Jesus Christ could blend them, making Mary Magdalen the most talked-about women in the New Testament. A subject for many works of art, she washed the feet of Christ with her loose gold hair, a symbol of her sinful past. The theme of delicate virginal beauties looking chastely into the eyes of Herculean heroes had been a favourite of the Victorian era. Now women had more physical control over their bodies; post-pill women were no longer invariably portrayed as soft and curvaceous but often as hard, muscular sex machines. The power shoulders of the eighties.

Through the various women's groups she was introduced to as a result of her friendship with Sam, she saw women searching for an identity. An identity purely feminine but not weak, an identity of choice. They didn't want to be second-class men. The role they saw for themselves was to honour themselves as women and it would follow that men would honour them. The doctrine of original sin wouldn't wash with them any more. They weren't here to suffer or be victims. They were here to stand equally beside their men as women, their values held by choice, not need or doubt. These were the women who had evolved because of the pill – a discovery made by a man. She thanked him for that gift, accepting all of the problems and questions that came along with it.

As she had sat across the table in the restaurant that first night with Sam, she had been a little in awe of him. In those two hours on the podium he had caused her to question and understand more about herself and the world in which she lived than had occurred to her in the course of all of her life until then. She felt his sensitivity towards women and his respect for them. He explained his theory that for many reasons women have a damaged persona, a distorted image of themselves brought about by cultural or economic need. That damaged persona had allowed her to lose her way in her marriage to Paul. Like the princess in the Bluebeard fairy tale, as long as she didn't open the door to his other life, she was safe in her ignorance. Once Tina had told her what subconsciously she already knew there was no turning back. She had been obliged to accept responsibility for her own life and not hide behind Paul's domination of her. She saw Sam as her teacher, in the father-figure role she had always until that point reserved for Uncle Harry.

They never became lovers. Now, more than ten years on from that night, as she drove north with her daughter asleep beside her, she could ask herself why. She was now a well-known personality in her own right, a successful artist still living and working in the beautiful old house she rented from him in the hills of Provence. That was home now to her and her children. The scent of Provence was always easily recalled to her nostrils, wherever she was. The heat of the summer nights, the sound of the *cigales* cooling themselves in the trees during those long summer days, the fireflies that arrived at the beginning of June and had gone by the end of it, lavender everywhere by the middle of July as if the hills had been painted purple overnight, the village market stalls laden with wild mushrooms every October – yes, her heart was there now. She had never fallen in love again, not with any man at least, but she was in love with Provence.

That wasn't to say she hadn't had her love affairs. They had come and gone over the years, some leaving sweet memories, but nothing had lasted. She was changing and developing too fast for that. Her success was something else she had had to learn to accept. Yes, she had become a woman alone but not a lonely woman.

It was through a documentary she had seen on one of her trips to America that she had got her idea for her one-man show. The documentary was called 'Women and War'. She had named her show after it. The best loved painting in the show she had called 'Homework by Candlelight'. It was of a woman standing over her son while he attempted to do his homework by the light of a candle. They were in an air-raid shelter. The mother's eyes were full of encouragement, helping him to make the most of their frightening situation.

As she turned off the motorway on the last leg of the journey to Tarn House she looked down at her still sleeping daughter. How differently her own life had turned out from the way she would have expected when she was Jasmin's age. How fortunate she was. What was it Mac had once said about Frog? – he had found his bliss. Well, she was also one of the lucky ones because she had defiantly found hers.

She still had her vision from time to time; it had become so much a part of her now she would be lost without it. She had long since given up wondering what it all meant. At first she thought it was the original Tarn House. Then, before she came to France, she dwelt on the romantic idea that it may have been Sam's house in Provence. Her experience of architecture should have taught her that an old farmhouse in Provence usually had terracotta roof tiles. Sam's house had turned out to be a soft warm pink that mellowed into its surroundings. The terrace was given extra shade during the hot summer months by an ancient, knotted grapevine. There was plenty of jasmine, but unlike her vision, it grew up a stone wall at the back of the house. There were yellow roses too but they had been planted under the olive trees that covered most of the land, to protect them from the heat of the midsummer sun. They pushed their way to the light through the branches, enjoying the companionship of such majestic bedfellows. Some of those knarled and twisted olive trees were estimated to be over three hundred years old. She had changed very little inside the house over the years, although she had been given *carte blanche*. She had bought two cream canvas-covered sofas which she had put either side of the fireplace; they were made warmer by two paisley-patterned cashmere throws. The colours of the garden were captured in them and when the fire was alight on a winter's evening they were the perfect thing to snuggle into. Jasmin called them her lounge-lizard sofas.

Along with Sam's house she had the Kensington mews house, Paul had bought it for her when they had finally divorced and it was a perfect London base. Now Jasmin was going to university, she would probably be using the house more than her mother. Sebastian and Giles had owned their own flats for some time. Paul had looked after them all very well and they had managed to stay friends, although they had their ups and downs. Giles and his father were having problems with each other at the moment, but she thought they probably would have had anyway, even without the divorce.

In about ten minutes' time she would be in the kitchen of Tarn House. She could almost smell the food and was already hungry – it must have been all that dwelling on the past. She saw Jasmin stir out of the corner of her eye. 'Wake up, darling, we're almost there.'

James

James Minnelli was late. He hated being late but the traffic on the M4 was moving at a snail's pace.

'Traffic's bloody diabolical this morning, guv,' the cockney taxi driver called through the glass window that separated them.

'Nothing like being late to put me in a bad mood.' James lay back in his seat as he spoke.

'You're an American?'

'Yes,' he replied lazily.

'Whereabouts?'

'California,'

'Really! Me bruvver lives in LA – he's in the movie business. I've been out there a few times to stay wiv 'im. Crazy sort of place. You from LA?'

'No, I live in the north.'

'I went up there once with the wife, a place called Calistoga. They specialise in mud-bath treatments up there, you know.'

'Yes, I know. Calistoga also has excellent mineral water.'

'Don't know about that, guv, but the mud-bath treatment was bloody fantastic once you got used to the idea – and then the massage afterwards. I felt like a million bloody dollars by the time they 'ad finished wiv me. My old lady said it made 'er feel like a movie star, 'aving some muscular young bloke give 'er a massage. Cheeky bitch.'

James smiled but didn't answer. He was glad he had taken a taxi; Anthony had offered to send a car for him but he always preferred to take taxis in London. London taxi drivers were a breed apart for an American visitor. He spent a lot of his time in London now, and had done for the past ten years or so, but he still saw himself as a visitor.

'Which terminal did you say again, guv?'

'Terminal one.'

'Going somewhere nice or is it just a business trip?'

'I'm going up to Scotland for a few days.'

'Oh, a bit of golf – or are you shooting or fishing?'

'Shooting,' he replied.

'It's been a bit bloody 'ot over the last few days. I 'ad some gents in me cab one year, just back from Scotland, complaining it 'ad been too 'ot for the bloody grouse to fly. Said it was a bloody disaster.'

'Well, let's hope that doesn't happen this year.' The cab pulled up outside departures.

James picked up his suit-carrier from the seat beside him and jumped out of the taxi. He paid the driver and rushed through the sliding doors and over to Counter 76 where the handling crew were waiting to take him out to Anthony's private jet.

Anthony Lawless had his head down looking at a document when James entered the cabin.

'I don't believe it! I'm later than you.' James smiled down at the top of his friend's head. Anthony was notorious for being late.

Anthony looked up, ignoring the remark and extending his hand to greet his friend. 'I knew you should have let me send a car for you.'

'It wouldn't have made any difference, Anthony. The traffic was almost at a standstill.'

'But at least you would have been more comfortable in the car.'

'I wouldn't have been able to chat as freely to one of your chauffeurs as I could to a London cabby.'

'Good god, man, what do you want to chat to a cabby for anyway.'

'Those guys are the salt of the earth, they see a lot of life. Trouble with you, Lawless, is you've lost touch with the common man.'

'Well, you know what salt does to the earth, James.' He raised his eyebrows. 'If by the common man, you mean the unwashed general public, your quite right.' He averted his eyes from James and looked towards the steward. 'Tell the captain we are ready to leave.'

'Yes, Mr Lawless.' He left them and went into the cockpit.

As the plane took off and began to gain height James could feel himself relaxing. The thought of a few days on his own seemed like a holiday in itself.

'I thought you would have brought Tina along,' Anthony said, glancing up from his paperwork.

'Give me a break, Anthony. I'm thinking of renaming her Velcro, she sticks so close to me lately.' He paused and after giving a frustrated sigh continued. 'I've been given an ultimatum which is why I'm allowed a few days to myself.'

'What sort of ultimatum?'

'Marry her! She wants a commitment. I've been with the woman for eight years, surely that's a commitment in itself. She doesn't need financial security, she has more money than the both of us put together.'

'That sounds like a good reason to marry her. Think of all the power a marriage like that would bring.'

James took a hard look at his friend and realised he was serious. 'But that would be like selling my soul.'

'If that's the price, maybe you should. I would, given the chance.'

Anthony Lawless had made a name for himself in the business world and was now enjoying the power that went with it. Recently his activities had been channelled into media and he now owned a network of newspapers in several countries, including his native Ireland. There he was a national hero, having been a rugby star in his youth. His charismatic personality had drawn both male and female under his spell. The seductive depth to his voice had moved women to comment publicly that it was his best physical attribute, and privately that it's tone seemed to touch erogenous zones they didn't know they had.

Anthony had met James whilst at university. James had gone to Trinity College and they had met on the rugby field, in opposing teams. James was a good rugby player and Anthony had been drawn to him; they became the best of friends and had remained so.

James's family background had fascinated Anthony. His father Joe Minnelli was born in New York, the son of a Sicilian immigrant, who had made his original money working for the Mafia operating a numbers racket. During Prohibition he had bought land in the Napa Valley, California, and set himself up as a grape farmer. He and his son had made a fortune supplying the Mafia with brandy made in illegal and well-hidden stills. Now Joe was as straight as a die and an upstanding member of the community, with friends in high places. His family nickname was Lucky and 'Lucky' Joe Minnelli certainly lived up to that name.

James's mother, Lana, was Irish, and had left Dublin at eighteen to live with a married cousin in New York where she had intended to seek her fame and fortune. She was beautiful, with a pale flawless skin and strawberry blonde hair that flowed down her back in Pre-Raphaelite waves. Her expressive green eyes were full of hope and innocence. She wanted to go on the stage but fortunately Joe met her before she could be discovered by some theatrical agent. She was so beautiful and naïve; he always liked to think that he had saved her from that business and the vultures who would surely have pecked at her kindness until they devoured her soft heart.

When they met it was love at first sight. They literally bumped into each other as they were both rushing to keep different appointments. Lana had been furious as she bent down to pick up the script she had dropped and when she looked across at the man who had bent down to help, her eyes were flashing fire. Joe could feel the heat of that anger across the pavement.

That was the first day of a relationship that was destined to last for more than fifty years. James was the youngest of their three children and the only son. Having two older sisters had made him at ease with female company. His parents became the toast of San Francisco, with their good looks and Joe's celebrated vineyard. They made many important friends and contacts and James grew up surrounded by these people. Life for him had been very easy and after university he had been happy to go into the family business, a business he had grown to love. It gave him the opportunity to travel and spend a lot of time in Europe.

Anthony had always taken the maximum advantage of his friend's contacts, having come from a very different background. He had been born into what on the surface seemed a normal lower-middle-class Dublin family, in one of Dublin's least prestigious residential areas. He was classic proof of the theory of mythomania. A single boychild with a hidden irregularity in the family will create his own myths about his family to give himself importance, and thus the myths become the child's driving force. Anthony had created for himself a world so different from most people's daily existence that it allowed him to forget his true past. His private jet, in which they were now travelling, was a symbol of that life.

'You must accept, James, that a relationship like your parents have, or the one you had with Annetta, come just once in a life, if at all. You can't bring that relationship back, so why not try power – it's an excellent painkiller.' Anthony issued this advice as a doctor would a prescription. Power was good for the health.

There was a comfortable lull in the conversation and Anthony seemed to be preoccupied with the papers in front of him. James lay back in his seat and closed his eyes. His thoughts drifted to Annetta, as they always did at such times. He missed her; it had been ten years since her death, yet she was there in his mind as if it had been yesterday.

In the beginning he had wished he had died with her and if it hadn't been for their son, Nikki, he thought he probably would have. The pain of her loss still caught him off guard and when it did it almost choked him.

He remembered her saying to him, during the last stages of her illness, when she was so weak, 'If there's a way back to you, I'll find it. If you think hard in the quiet, you will know my answer to any question you ask me. We are that close now and always will be.' It was true, he mentally shared every major decision he made with her. Annetta's existence had engulfed his whole being the moment they met and through all the years of their marriage.

She had been thirty-two when he first met her, four years older than him. She was already very successful, a well-known television journalist based in London. A war correspondent during the height of the Vietnam War, she went into areas of conflict daily and took great risks to get her stories.

He had come back from a meeting one evening to find her sitting in his parents' drawing-room talking to his mother. His father had told him many times, and anyone else who could still be bothered to listen, how he had bumped into his mother and it had been love at first sight. Well, it was obviously a family trait, because when he walked across the room that evening and his mother introduced him to Annetta, he immediately knew she was the woman he wanted to spend the rest of his life with.

'Ah! there you are, James. Let me introduce you to Annetta, the daughter of Mary Peterson, an old friend of mine in Dublin. Annetta, this is my son James.'

The palm of his hand felt sticky as he extended it. 'How do you do, Annetta?'

'James.' She nodded her head slightly as she looked him straight in the eye.

'Sit down, James,' his mother said, out of character. She had never been a bossy woman and he wondered if he looked as awkward as he felt. 'Annetta is staying with us for a few days' holiday and I hope you will be able to find the time to help me entertain her.'

'Yes, I'm sure I can. Welcome to Eagles' Ridge, Annetta. I'll start by getting us all a drink – what would you like?'

'The house white would be lovely, thank you.' She smiled. 'I'm not just being polite either. I always order a Minnelli Chardonnay if it's on the wine list.'

As he opened the wine and put the glasses on a tray, he studied her face across the room, where she sat talking to his mother. Pretty? No, not the word he felt suited it. Wise made it sound interesting but plain. Yet the word could not be dismissed when looking for a description. He felt her eyes oozed wisdom. He settled for dangerously beautiful. Dangerous for him, as he stood the chance of losing himself completely to the owner of it. She had even features, ashblonde hair and eyes the deep blue he imagined a Nordic fjord would be. He thought their colour would change dramatically with her moods, as he supposed a fjord does with the weather.

James liked women's company and was never uncomfortable around them. Young, good looking, rich, educated and well travelled, he was on the guest lists of all his parents' friends and acquaintances with daughters. Now he was faced with a new experience and the unease he felt around Annetta was not unpleasant. In fact, he was excited by it and there was an impatience in him to find out all he could about her. She seemed so cool and relaxed sitting there chatting to his mother about old family friends, he felt she must be picking up his disquiet, but she didn't appear to notice. Much later she told him just how in touch with that energy she had been. It was only her experience as a journalist that had allowed her to hide her feelings and keep herself centred throughout. For she had felt a sense of *déjà vu* when James first walked into the room that evening; it was like two old souls meeting across the ether.

It took three months and many telephone calls before they could finally meet somewhere. It was the beginning of May and Annetta chose Corsica. She knew the island well and loved to escape there whenever it was possible. A friend of hers owned a refurbished *bergerie*, on a hill overlooking the sea just south of Bastia. He lived in Paris most of the year and allowed Annetta the use of it whenever she could find the time.

James had never been to Corsica and was pleasantly surprised at how unspoilt the island was. Annetta had met him at Bastia airport, having arrived the day before to open up the house.

'Welcome to this erotic island,' she said as he bent to kiss her cheek. They drove silently down the coast road taking in the scenery and their closeness to each other.

The *bergerie* stood alone surrounded by cork trees. Part of it had been left as a ruin and a beautiful garden had been planted within its walls, with purple wistaria cascading like bunches of grapes. The scent of honeysuckle was heavy in the air, heightening their senses. The whole scene was bewitching, a secret garden steeped in mystery.

As they stood in the garden sipping their champagne and looking out to sea, they were at one with the magic of the place. After such a long wait to be alone together, just standing next to each other was madly sexual. The telephone had been an instrument of torture over the past three months, bringing them so near, yet keeping them so far away from each other. Now that they were together at last, they were savouring every second of the experience.

Neither of them was ready to surrender to their passion quite yet, the scent of each other's nearness being exquisite foreplay in itself. Finally, James put one hand on Annetta's bent elbow and with the other he removed the glass she was holding and put it down. The spell was broken. Just the touch of her flesh had sent fire coursing through his veins. His breathing became short and his heart pounded in his throat as he took her in his arms and hungrily kissed her. Her own passion rose to meet his and there was no power left in them now to resist another minute. They wildly tore at each other's clothes, one trying to assist the other into nakedness. They fell on the grass entwined, hands moving over skin as they discovered each other for the first time. Their love-making became trance-like, their lust for each other seemed insatiable. They drank of each other as if their thirst would never be quenched. She lost count of her orgasms, each one a little death, each one binding her to him. When he ultimately exploded into her, she felt her whole body shudder at the strength of their union. The heat and power of it fused them together into one entity.

They lay back in the grass and didn't move or speak for a long time. Then Annetta said in a whisper, 'I told you this was an erotic island.'

He raised himself up on his elbow and looked down at her in awe. 'I love you Annetta Peterson.' He kissed her but this time with great tenderness.

They spent five glorious days exploring the island and each other. It was interesting and exciting for James to see things through Annetta's eyes. He saw a beautiful coastline, whilst she saw secret harbours and pirates from another century. He saw Haute Corse as villages set in wild unspoilt countryside, she saw a patchwork of intrigue full of proud, deeply tribal people as strong as the granite of their island. Vendettas of honour. Independence gouging its way through the mountains like a river to the sea. He saw Pisan church towers rising out of the *maquis*, dedicated to St Theresa, she saw myths, legends, annual pagan festivals and harvest fertility dances.

They bought fresh fish from the boats at the port. Annetta cooked. He discovered the island's wine. They took long walks on empty beaches and swam in the still cold sea and lay in the warm, early summer sun. They feasted on each other and their new-found love. They took picnics into the hills and made love in the wild scent of the *maquis*. They stayed away from people, lost in each other. Their days all rolled into one. Then, sadly, it was over. They had to leave and both get back to reality and their individual commitments.

He asked her to marry him on the way to the airport. They were travelling back to London together before going their separate ways and the thought of not seeing each other for months weighed heavily on them. Annetta accepted his offer without hesitation. She had seen enough of life and had enough experience of men to know that what they had found in each other was a rare thing.

They sat quietly in their seats, each lost in thought, exhausted by their emotions. It was only after the meal had been cleared away by the stewardess, that either one of them had the energy to speak.

'Where will they send you when you get back to London?' James asked.

'I don't know. Northern Ireland or Lebanon, I think. Both places have flared up while we've been away. Nixon sent troops into Cambodia in April, so I may be sent back to Vietnam. It's important to be in the right place at the right time; that's how I keep my high profile. I was there when the Russian tanks rolled into Prague.'

'If the Russians drank wine instead of vodka, their politics would be different!' He grinned at her, lightening up a moment to relieve the tension.

'Profound psychology, Mr Minnelli – you should write a letter to Mr Brezhnev on your theory.'

'Your work is so different from mine,' he said more seriously. 'You are your own product. Flying all over the world hoping to catch the best market place, deciding which war zone has the most mileage in it, hedging your bets. My product is wine. Wine relies on stability, good soil, old vines, temperate seasons and dry cellars with a constant sixty-five-degree temperature. Time for the wine to age properly, then peace and comfort to enjoy its taste.' He put his hand over hers. 'That's why you must marry me as soon as possible. I'll be your stability, a perfect retreat away from the front line. I have my own wing at Eagles' Ridge, which you could decorate to your own taste. Or we could sell my apartment in San Francisco and buy a house, if you prefer. If we do decide to have children, I really don't want them to be born in a bunker.'

'You're not asking me to give up my job?' An edge of resentment crept into her voice.

'No, Annetta, you must always do what you want until you're ready to change things. Your world and life are so hectic that change is inevitable. I'm like my wine, I need stability to bring out the best in me but I'm never quite sure what each year will have in store. For me, this is the best so far because I met you and, like my wine, I'm here for you to enjoy. I hope I continue to make you light headed and happy, and that each year will have its own special taste.'

'Let's run away and get married. I don't want a lot of fuss. When the press find out I can just see the headlines. Messenger of Zeus marries Bacchus.' They both laughed.

James thought for a moment. 'OK. Let's go to Las Vegas. That's about as tacky as we can get, so let's give them something to write about. The next time you have a few days free, we'll fly down and join the queue of fugitives waiting to say, "I do." '

A month later they were married. The press had a field day and Annetta secretly liked the idea that she had given the gossip columnists a harmless gift. Lana was almost as disappointed as Annetta's mother that there was no big day, but they were delighted with their prospective in-laws and soon forgave the young their moment of folly.

Between Annetta's flat in London, James's apartment in San Francisco and anywhere else in the world that would work, they managed to be together for at least a week out of every month.

In the November after they were married, Annetta's grandmother died leaving something in her will for all her grandchildren. Some received money, others property. To Annetta she left her holiday cottage in West Cork. Annetta had spent all of her childhood summers there and was thrilled that her grandmother should choose her to inherit that particular treasure.

For the first time since James had known her she became involved in something outside her professional sphere. She started to make plans to update the interior. There was no central heating as the house had only been used by the family during the summer. There were open fires which all worked beautifully. She intended to keep them but add central heating. This would mean instant living if they decided to use the house at impromptu times during the winter months.

She reminisced with James about her childhood summers there, and one long May weekend she had spent alone with her grandmother stood out vividly. The woods at the back of the house and the fields in the front had been full of wild flowers and she had spent her time making daisy chains and posies. As she walked in the wood with her grandmother, she saw squirrels scurrying and birds flying from tree to tree. The gypsies and tramps were unseen but grandma had pointed out the traces they had left in the dead campfires and flattened grass in the glades.

She fell in love with the house that weekend for it seemed a magical place. In the evening they lit a fire in the drawing-room and she became familiar with every shadow the lighting in the room created. Her grandmother told old family stories and she learned about her grandfather coming from Denmark on his way to New York in an immigrant ship and deciding to stay because he met grandma. When she went to bed that evening her head was full of innocent childhood fantasies – Nordic heroes and beautiful princesses living in enchanted woods.

It took four months of careful planning to be able to meet in Dublin and spend some time in West Cork and during that time Annetta had organised a team of builders. Although most of the contact had to be long distance, she had managed to find the odd day here and there to pop in and see the results. Everything went ahead smoothly, without delays. By the time they arrived, the main work had been completed and the fun of turning the house into their new home could begin.

She had kept the hand-painted Scandinavian bed that had been her grandparents' wedding bed. It was beautiful to look at and she thought it romantic with all its wild flowers and love knots. However, James insisted upon a new mattress as sleeping in a feather bed didn't appeal to him. Apart from that, he left Annetta alone to play house. He drove her to antique fairs, art galleries and design shops. He paid attention and gave his opinion. In reality he was enjoying her pleasure so much that anything she wanted was all right by him.

When he first arrived he was delighted to find a small dry barn at the side of the house which would make a perfect *cave* for wine. He set about organising the work immediately and this project kept him busy in between shopping expeditions. He hoped the Corsican wine he had ordered – to remind them of that first week alone together – would travel well. The rest of his cellar would be his connoisseur choice.

By the end of the first week they were ready to invite friends for the weekend. For James, especially, it was good to rekindle friendships made at university which had been sadly neglected since his move back to California. He was sorry Anthony couldn't be there, but as usual he was in some other part of the globe, putting a business deal together.

Annetta's parents came to see them the second week and gave their seal of approval to all the changes that had been made.

'I think your grandmother would be very pleased with the results, my dear.' Her mother's soft voice sounded genuinely impressed. 'I love your idea of covering the sofas in the drawing-room in Donegal tweed and the red and cream silk cushions look very rich and warm against them.'

'Thank you, mother, I'm rather pleased with them myself but I can't take all the credit for the idea. I saw a picture of a room in a design magazine in England and for some reason I even remember the designer's name. It was Georgina Fox. I loved the idea she had of using tweed as a furnishing fabric. The room looked elegant but comfortable and I liked the combination.'

'Well, I think it's just nice to have the two of you living so close to us.' Her father spoke up in the matter-of-fact way he had of dealing with everything, including what he considered his daughter's maverick occupation. 'Perhaps now we will see more of you.'

After her parents left, they reluctantly closed up the house to leave themselves. They gave the key to Mrs O'Brian, who for many years had looked after the house for Annetta's grandmother. She seemed pleased when they told her that they would definitely be back for the summer.

Six weeks later James was waiting at the airport in San Francisco. Annetta had called him the night before from London and surprised him with an unexpected free week. They had decided to fly his father's plane down to Mexico. Annetta had her pilot's licence and insisted on flying whenever the opportunity presented itself. Firstly because she enjoyed flying and secondly to keep herself up to scratch; in her line of business it could save her life one day. The need to be able to pilot a plane to safety might arise at any time in a war zone.

James, himself a very able pilot, never had any problems sitting next to her in the cockpit; on those occasions he always referred to her as Amelia Earhart.

She walked through the barrier looking radiant, no sign of the ten-hour flight showing in her face. As they stepped out into the afternoon sunshine, James put his arm around her shoulders and guided her towards the car.

'I thought we would stay in town tonight and drive up to Eagles' Ridge tomorrow. I want to keep you to myself for the whole evening. I would like to take you out to dinner, fill you with champagne, good food and wine, then take you to bed and make passionate love to you.'

'Anything you say, Mr Minnelli, but our bed here can't do anything that grandma's hasn't done already. I'm pregnant.'

James was just about to put the key in the lock of the car as she made her statement; he dropped the whole bunch. Not even bothering to pick them up he stepped towards his wife. He pulled her gently to him and hugged her closely until he could feel every part of her body melting into his. 'Made in Ireland,' he whispered in her ear.

Being pregnant changed the course of Annetta's life. She gave up her job and started to organise their wing at Eagles' Ridge into a permanent home for her family when they were in California. Joe and Lana were delighted with her choice and insisted upon equipping the new nursery. Lana clucked around like an old mother hen and Joe was already the proud grandfather, long before the birth. There seemed no doubt in his mind that the child would be a boy.

Joseph Nicholas Minnelli was born on Christmas Day and from the moment he was named he was always known as Nikki.

Annetta was two months into her thirty-fourth year when Nikki was born. The birth had been difficult and the doctor advised her not to have any more children. Frankly, he said, next time neither one of them, mother or child, stood much chance of surviving. James obviously took the warning very seriously and they discussed it at length.

'I could always stay on the pill. It's almost one hundred per cent safe.'

'No that's not good enough for me. I would always worry in case you forgot to take it or something. I think I should have a vasectomy.'

'No, it's far too new an operation and anyway I'm older than you. You're still a young man and if I die and leave you a widower, you may want to marry again and have another family. Or, perhaps we could fall out of love with each other and then you would regret what you had done.'

'Don't talk like that, Annetta.' The mere thought was too much for him. 'You're not going to die and I will always love you.'

She squeezed his arm in reassurance. 'Well, it's nice to think we have so many choices.' She started to reel off facts. 'You probably don't know this but between the years of 1910 and 1925 three hundred thousand American women died in childbirth; that's more than all the men who died in American wars from the Revolution until World War I. Margaret Sanger, a trained nurse of Irish origin (which I find interesting because Southern Ireland is still in conflict over birth control), saw many women dying in childbirth. When she opened her first family-planning clinic in 1916, in one of New York's poorest neighbourhoods, it was closed down by the police, under the obscenity laws, and she was sent to jail. After her release, she refused to give up her fight and eventually found a way to give practical help to these women. In return for one of the devices, a man who delivered coal and had fourteen children helped her to smuggle the first diaphragms into the country. They also had the help of the captain of a cargo ship. The diaphragms were put into empty brandy bottles, crated and the crates marked with a cross. The captain dropped them over the side as he came into harbour. The crates were light, so they floated on the surface.

'That's an interesting story, especially as hypocrisy and illegal brandy bottles changed my life as well.' He loved her when she put on her 'broadcasting' voice.

'Oh, James, are you ever serious?' She poked him playfully in the ribs. 'Anyway, I've decided to be sterilised. It seems the most sensible answer to the problem. I'm the one whose life is at risk, so it is I who should take the responsibility.'

'All right, if that's what you want, but no more talk about death or divorce.' He kissed her as tenderly as always but he lingered a long while in her arms before he left her as if to reassure himself that everything would be all right.

Two weeks after Nikki's birth Annetta was back in the newly decorated wing of Eagles' Ridge, feeling stronger and enjoying all the attention that came with being mother to Joe and Lana's grandchild.

Joe insisted on giving a party to celebrate the birth of his grandson. Also, because Annetta had been obliged to spend Christmas and New Year in hospital, it would give them an opportunity to toast in 1973 belatedly at home.

So exactly one month after his birth, on the 25 January, a party was thrown for Joseph Nicholas Minnelli.

The house, adorned with blue-and-white flower arrangements, looked stunning. Each arrangement contained tuberose somewhere in its make-up and the air was heavy with the scent.

James and Annetta made their way into the drawing-room, where Joe and Lana stood chatting to their guests.

'Ah! here they are.' Joe opened his arms wide as if to embrace them across the room. 'Annetta you look beautiful, come over here next to me.'

She smiled at her father-in-law as she walked up to him to be kissed.

'We have an unexpected face in the group.' He glanced across and she followed his eyes. She had been so engrossed in Joe that she hadn't noticed anybody else.

'Anthony!'

Anthony Lawless smiled at her surprise. 'I couldn't miss this party, now could I?' His melodious voice had just the right tone in it to make it seem that Annetta was the most important woman in the world. He maintained the tone when he turned to James. 'Congratulations once again, my friend.' He lifted his glass.

'I so glad you could make it, Anthony. Lately, I only seem to see you in the States when you're here on business.'

At this point Annetta's eye caught Lana's and she knew it was time to circulate. She excused herself and left the old friends alone to chat.

'I must say that your father rallied some pretty interesting people together at such short notice.'

'They are all his friends, Anthony. You know how Joe is, impulsive; people are used to that with him.'

'I would guarantee that senator over there wouldn't be here tonight if he didn't think Joe was going to back him when he runs for Congress.' He winked at James.

'Well, I suppose dad does keep himself busy. He's the same as you, Anthony, he likes to be owed a few favours as he never knows when he may need them.'

'I have to hand it to him – when it comes to contacts, he's a past master. That's why I love his soirées.'

'And I thought you flew all the way out here this evening just to see us.'

'James, but of course I did, how could you think there would be any other reason.' His charismatic charm, perfectly administered to his old friend, was an art form in itself.

'How's business?' he said.

'Doing well, thanks. Californian wine is a bit like Joe, it has a good reputation these days. The world is beginning to take us seriously.'

'How do you see its future?'

'At the moment it is expanding so rapidly that it's hard to keep up with all the boutique vineyards that are opening up.'

'Boutique?'

'Yes, they're small, usually family-run, vineyards and they are popping up like mushrooms. To own a boutique vineyard is very fashionable, you know how California is.'

'Won't all this new competition affect your business.'

'I think it can only help. In the late sixties, Americans started to change their drinking habits, because of diet and health. They drink less hard liquor and more wine now, and the more of it they drink, the more discerning they become. Once they understand a subject, Americans start to demand quality, that's how we are. I would like to see our industry in America form some organisation for *appellation contrôlée*, similar to the French. I'm not like Joe. My only business is wine and I want to produce the best.'

'What does Joe think.'

'He leaves things more and more up to me. He loves business, any business, but for me wine is a passion. He sees that as an asset and supports all of my plans.'

'You're a lucky man, James.'

'I'm my father's son, Anthony.' They both laughed and turned back to the main group as people continued to arrive and they all needed to circulate.

Annetta had said her good nights just before the party broke up and was sitting up in bed when James came into the room.

'Not asleep yet?'

'No, I went into the nursery to look in on Nikki. Nurse was feeding him so I took over and we had a chat.'

'How is he.'

'Gorgeous, I kissed everyone of his tiny fingers before I left. It's hard to believe that they will be as big and strong as yours one day.'

James moulded himself into a Charles Atlas stance, then flicked his hair out of his eyes James Dean style and jumped into bed, snuggling up to her.

She giggled at his antics. 'I stayed awake because I wanted to analyse the party. Did you enjoy yourself?'

'Of course I did. When have you known me not to?'

'True.'

'Why? didn't you enjoy it.'

'Yes, I love to see Joe in action. There's nothing more interesting than to watch a professional networker. It makes war games seem even more stupid and crude.'

'Anthony is impressed with dad for that very same reason.'

'I overheard Anthony propositioning the senator's wife this evening, and with success I may add. He uses his willie like a magic wand; that's not your father's style.'

'Anthony's just a womaniser.'

'No, James, Anthony is a women abuser, there's a difference.'

'Don't you like him?'

'Yes, of course. I like the image he presents, but I know who he is. So I'm safe, I can afford to like him. If I were the senator's wife, I would probably end up hating him or myself, depending on my politics. Don't make the mistake of putting Anthony in the same league as your father. Your father has a conscience, Anthony hasn't.'

'Yes, mother.' He tickled her still flabby waist until she screamed for mercy.

'J–a–a–a–mes, pl–e–e–a–se stop.'

'Only if you tell me you love me.'

'Yes, anything.'

He stopped and drew her towards him. 'I can see you would be useless under torture.'

'Yes, I know, that's why I became a war correspondent and not a spy.' She turned herself around to be kissed.

During the next two years James worked on his dream of having the finest vineyard in America. He started to grow grapes farther up the rocky hillsides of their land. The thin topsoil put the vines under stress and the limited water supply produced a small quantity of concentrated juice which made better wine. This wine he gave a bin number. The claret he was looking to produce from these vines had to compare with the great châteaux of Bordeaux.

Prohibition had held back the Californian wine industry and for many years the only legal wine made was altar wine. With only a meagre living to be had from Californian wine, technology marked time. Intensive development had come with the fashion to drink more wine, and James was one of the many inspired growers who were taking full advantage of the new science and technology.

Along with his technical knowledge came a deep love for his vineyard. The wines of California owe their beginnings to the vineyards of the Franciscan mission stations. It was easy for him to understand the meditative qualities of tending and pruning the vines. He enjoyed the peace that came from walking around his estate and it was there that he did all of his deep thinking.

Annetta was enjoying her life in California and her long summers in Ireland. Being a mother gave her great pleasure. She was glad to have had the choice as to when she became a mother, leaving it until she had the time and the patience for the job.

When James went on business trips to Europe she often travelled with him, taking Nikki and his nanny with them if they were going to be away for more than a week. James always tried to arrange his travel plans in Europe either side of their summer holidays in Ireland, so as not to be separated from his family any more than was necessary.

Since Nikki's birth she had written a few articles for women's magazines, mainly about being a female war correspondent in very much a man's world. These articles had accelerated her interest in the women's movement. She felt there was a role for her to play in promoting the new female power that was emerging.

'If women were in charge of the world there would be no wars, just intense negotiations once a month.' This was one of the many jokes about women in control of the world; but would that be such a bad thing? As a mother she thought not . Yet men weren't all bad and women weren't angels. Life in the war zones of the world had taught her that. They both had a dark side to their souls that had to be looked at. One strength she felt women had was that on the whole they were better communicators than men. For that reason alone they should have a strong voice at a level that mattered.

James strove passionately to produce a wine that would cause Bacchus to swoon with delight. She saw her role as trying to help make the world a clean and peaceful place for people to enjoy that wine in.

She was a very fortunate woman, knowing who she was, enjoying the ease of being married to a man who wasn't threatened by her success. She knew that not all women had that privilege, even in her own culture. Men seemed much better at defining themselves and their achievements, always men first and whatever else next. Women mostly saw themselves as wives, mothers or daughters first and as women second. One of the first acts of imperialism is to de-humanise the native so that he sees his conquerors as superior. The patriarchal society has, consciously or not, dealt in the same way with women.

She needed to bring women together in any way she could. By talking to each other perhaps they would understand more about their strengths and weaknesses, thereby finding out who they were and regaining their identity. She knew her way around the media and she would use her knowledge to the best of her ability in the cause.

It was during the summer of 1976 she decided to go back to work full time. The weather was scorching and the fields in front of the house were parched. The summer in Ireland that year had been like California and James was able to use the barbecue day after day. Nikki, now three and a half, spent most of his time playing in a portable swimming pool James had bought for him.

'If the summers are going to continue to be like this, we should think about having a real swimming pool built.' James was in charge of the lunch and was barbecuing some halibut.

'I know, and a tennis court.' She smiled at him knowing his weakness.

'Perfect.'

'I would rather keep everything as it is. We do different things here than the things we do in California, simply because of the weather and the fact that we don't have a tennis court or a swimming pool. I like the contrast.'

'True. OK, you win, but if the summers stay like this we may have to renegotiate.'

'Don't worry, James, they won't. This is a one-off I can assure you. It has been wonderful though. It's hard to imagine wars and conflicts in a setting like this.' She walked over to her husband, her heart full of the love she felt for him. As she nestled herself against him, putting her arm around his waist, his dark brown, velvety eyes smiled down at her.

'James, I'm going to Ulster. It's time I got back to work. There's going to be a rally for peace on 8 August by the Women's Peace Movement. Children are being killed and there's no dialogue going on. Perhaps the women will be able to succeed where the politicians have failed.'

He pulled her into his arms and held her tight. 'I believe in you, Annetta; just be careful that's all, you're too precious to lose.'

'I will, James. I have an idea and I want to have a long chat with you about it. We'll talk after lunch, when Nikki and Nanny go for their walk.'

'Sounds like a plot. I can see it in your eyes; but first we must eat my splendid meal. Halibut marinated in lime juice and fresh ginger, *salade à la* James and wholemeal bread from Bewley's. I have selected, especially for madame, a superb Loire wine, a Sancerre rosé, to complement my oriental marinade.

The lunch was delicious, light and perfect for the hot weather. After Nikki had filled himself with ice cream, which was his treat for eating all his fish, he and Nanny went for their walk.

James and Annetta took the rest of the wine into the drawing-room and flopped on to the sofas.

'Come on, Net, thou trapper of my soul. Out with it.'

She chuckled at his nickname for her, which he always used whenever he felt that she was going to corner him into something he would have to give serious thought to, outside his own world of wine. The name was given without malice; he loved her and accepted the whole package.

'I have a plan, James. I want to form a company and I need financial backers.'

'What sort of company.'

'A company that won't make any profit.'

'Oh! That's going to be easy, there must be hundreds of people out their who don't want to make money.'

'James, please, I'm being serious.'

'Net, I know you are.' He poked his tongue out at her.

'I want to make documentaries and documentaries rarely make money, in fact they usually lose money. I have a specific plan in mind. I want to make documentaries about women for women so that they can develop a true sense as to who they really are. Women in art – artists, dancers, writers. Women in commerce, women in aviation.' She lifted one eyebrow when she said this and dared him to comment. 'Women in politics who aren't mimicking men, that's important.'

'How can I help, Net?' He was more serious now.

'Well, I think I can convince Anthony Lawless to back me. You have to work on Joe. Your job will be easy; mine will need a little more manipulation, but with Joe as bait I think I should be able to reel in my fish. Between them they must be able to form a syndicate of investors who need the tax write-off.'

'All right, I'll make a deal with you. If you promise me you won't get yourself killed, I'll promise you that dad will back you.'

'Mr Minnelli, let's shake on it.'

Anthony Lawless had not been as difficult as Annetta had expected him to be over the idea of her company. Surprisingly, he was very supportive as he saw lots of brownie points awaiting him for his association with it. Knowing Joe was involved was the bonus she had counted on when she had made an appointment to see him at his office in Dublin. He had apologised for not being able to see her until after five-thirty, as he was in meetings all day, but he would be delighted if she would join him for dinner afterwards.

His secretary showed her into his office and he stood up to welcome her, gesturing towards the chair in front of his desk.

'Annetta, take a seat. How are you, I must come and visit you both this summer.'

'The summer's almost over, Anthony.' She gave him a cool glance.

'Now, Annetta, don't scold me. When I'm here in Dublin I never seem to find the time to be social. It's much easier for me to find free time when I'm in the States.'

'Oh! and I thought it was because our Cork house wasn't grand enough for you. How unkind of me.'

'Annetta, I can see you're exhausted, this heat is enough to try the nerves of a saint.' He got up and went over to a mahogany door behind which was a well-stocked bar; he opened the refrigerator and took out a bottle of Dom Pérignon and two cold glasses.

'This will help to relax away the tension of the day.' He handed her a glass. 'Now down to business.'

It took just fifteen minutes to convince him to support her. He knew she was good at her job and the chances of her interviewing somebody who could be in a different arena in ten years' time, as women became more assertive and successful in politics, were very real. To be showing support, before the power was obvious, looked good. He always believed in buying futures.

Annetta had read him like a book and had given him all the arguments for her project with his self-glory in mind. The male ego never ceased to amaze her and Anthony's had reached its apogee.

They had an agreement in principle and were to meet with Joe at Eagles' Ridge the following month to form a company.

'Well, that's about it, Annetta. How about dinner?'

He had booked a table at the King Citric in Hose and they were greeted by the manager with great enthusiasm. He was pleased to see Mr Lawless arrive with such a well-known television personality as Miss Peterson.

Anthony was a charming host and centred his attention on her throughout the meal. He ordered excellent wine but without real knowledge; he just ordered the most expensive.

'How is James going to feel about you being away so much?'

'The same as me; we'll miss each other, but he respects my choice and supports what I'm doing.'

'I expect you will be spending more time in Ireland now.'

'Yes, I shall make it my base whenever I'm in Europe. I still have the flat in London, but I hope to work in California when I need use of a studio. London would be my second choice as I want to spend all my free time with James and Nikki. Now I'm freelance it will be far easier to manage my time. I see the Women's Peace Movement in Ireland evolving into something very important for women's movements everywhere. A lot of other issues will surface along the way.'

'I'll always be here if you need anything.' He sounded sincere.

'Thank you, Anthony.' She felt this was getting a bit to cosy.

'So you approve of married life, Annetta. I always thought you were a career women. I must say I was quite surprised when I heard that you had married one of my closest friends. I envy him – you're an amazing women. I should have married you myself.'

'I didn't think that you were the marrying type, Anthony. In fact, I didn't think you liked women,' she replied, not liking the tone in his voice.

'Oh, Annetta, what a thing to say; they are my pleasure.'

'So is whiskey to an alcoholic but he often hates the stuff.'

'Are you saying that you think I'm a misogynist?'

'I think it may be your one weakness. I used to think that you were without feeling, that would have made you really dangerous, but now I think that you were taught to hate. Deep hatred has to be taught by an expert. Your father must have detested your mother, or the other way around.' She want to see him lose his composure, if only for a split second.

He looked at her across the table, summoning the waiter with his hand at the same time.

'Annetta, you have such a vivid imagination. I'm going to order you a brandy to calm your lust for me. You obviously find me irresistible and are trying to come to terms with the feelings I have unleashed.' He laughed at his own joke and relaxed further into his seat. He really did find this woman, who was giving him such a hard time, unbearably attractive.

Annetta laughed too. If there ever had been a Garden of Eden and an innocent Eve, then Anthony Lawless could definately have auditioned for the serpent.

'How do you arrive at your psychological analysis of me? My parents were devoted to each other.'

'Because you want to enter as many vaginas as you can and poison them with your sperm.' She had read this theory somewhere and thought it applied to Anthony.

'Perhaps I just see myself as a king stag covering his hinds,' he quickly retorted, really enjoying himself now. 'A Celtic god enjoying his rights at Beltane.

'No, I fear your mythology is more ancient than that. Mercury the trickster would suite you much better.'

'Perhaps I just need to be taught to love, Annetta.' The tone of his voice became more seductive. 'In your arms I may find out how.'

'Don't even think about it, Anthony. For one thing James is supposedly one of your oldest friends, and secondly I am a married woman.'

'Neither one of those reasons has ever stood in my way before,' he said, as he waved his hand in the air in a sign of dismissal.

'Well, I'm sorry that you mix with such disloyal people,' she said disdainfully.

'One day, Annetta Peterson, you will be putty in my hands.' This thought gave him great pleasure.

'Not if I have anything to do with it, Mr Lawless.'

'Don't challenge me, Annetta.' He winked at her before he raised his eyes to the waiter for the bill.

It was the end of the summer of 1978. James was pleased with the way his work was going. He had started to get excellent results from his special reserve wine and was receiving a lot of recognition from the French. Annetta was becoming a well-known figure in the women's movement and she had even managed to make a small profit on some of her documentaries. They had stayed in Ireland over the Labour Day weekend because Nikki would be starting 'proper' school (as Nanny called it) in California that year. It was decided that Annetta should be there to take him on his first day, so they had arranged with the school for him to start late, because she was too busy to leave Europe before 12 September. The reason for this was that she had an interview arranged with Monique Pelletier, who was being appointed France's first minister for women.

It was the night before they were due to leave and go back to California. Annetta was relaxing in a bubble bath when James came in after reading Nikki a story.

'Smells good in here – would you like me to scrub your back?'

'Yes, please!' she passed him the loofah. 'I'm so tired tonight. I don't know why. I must be getting old.'

'You'll never be old to me.' He kissed her back. 'Would you like me to give you a neck massage.'

'Mm. You really are the perfect man to have around.'

'True.'

She felt his strong, sensitive hands begin to massage her shoulders then gradually move along to the back of her neck. Putting one hand on her forehead to support her head he spread the other either side of the base of her neck and slowly massaged away the pressures of the day. She was half asleep when he moved his hand to the front of her neck and she felt a sudden pain shoot through her.

'Ouch, James, what are you doing – that hurt.'

'It shouldn't have, let me have a look.' He gently felt the front of her neck. 'I think your glands are up, you seem to have a lump there.'

'That's probably why I'm so tired. I hope I'm not going down with tonsillitis.' She swallowed hard to see if her throat was at all sore.

'Well, let's see how you feel tomorrow; we won't travel if you don't feel up to the journey.' He dried his hands on the towel she had left on the end of the bath. 'Perhaps you should see a doctor anyway, it won't matter if we fly back later. Nikki is already late starting school.'

'Let's wait and see how I am.' She got up from the water and let him put the towel around her shoulders.

The next day they closed the house and went back to California. Annetta was feeling a lot better after a good night's sleep, although her glands still appeared to be swollen. She decided to see a doctor in San Francisco.

She had missed Joe and Lana this summer. They had both been very supportive of her work over the last two years and she had grown to love them as much as her own parents. She used Joe's plane as if it were her own, flying backwards and forwards to Los Angeles. Sometimes he accompanied her but he always let her fly the plane, which coming from an old Sicilian was quite a compliment.

Nikki started school and although his face puckered up as his mother waved goodbye to him, the teacher told her he didn't cry. He made friends quickly and by the end of the morning he was enjoying himself. He had grown into a very good-looking little boy, with his father's dark wavy hair and Lana's striking green eyes. He had a happy nature, and Joe, who adored him, called him Smiley. Annetta went to collect him from school and they called into the main house for tea so that Nikki could tell his grandparents about his first day.

'How did you like school then, Smiley?' Joe ruffled the boy's hair as he spoke.

'It's good fun, Joe, I have a new friend.' He smiled up at his grandfather.

'You do! what's his name.'

'Pete, and I told him all about you and I told him he could meet you. He doesn't have a grandpa nearby like me. His grandpa lives in Washington.'

'Well, I'd better come and meet you from school one day and take you boys out for a soda.'

'Thanks, Joe. I'll tell Pete tomorrow.' He knew Joe wouldn't let him down.

'Yes, but we have to arrange it with his mother. We can't go off by ourselves without letting the women know what we are doing, you know how they worry.' He raised his eyebrows.

'Yes I know, Joe,' he glanced across at his mother and grinned.

Annetta was finally alone with Lana in the sitting-room; Joe and Nikki had gone off to look for James. 'I'm going to see a doctor tomorrow in San Francisco.'

'Why, darling, are you ill or is it just a check up?' Lana studied her daughter-in-law's face.

'A check up, I suppose. I've been feeling very tired this past week and the glands in my neck seem a bit swollen. I think I may have an infection.' She tried to sound casual.

'Do you have a sore throat?'

'A bit.'

'Well, that's it. I'm sure that's what you have. Throat infections always make one tired; best to go and get it checked out if it's been going on for more than a week,' she smiled reassuringly. 'Don't worry, darling, antibiotics will sort it out very quickly.'

The receptionist showed her into the waiting-room; it was empty and unfriendly.

'Dr Wilson won't keep you waiting long, Mrs Minnelli, he's with another patient at the moment. Would you like something to drink – a tea or coffee perhaps?'

'No, thank you.' She sat down and filled in the form the receptionist had given her. Age, date of birth, address, profession, sex. Then
she picked up a magazine from the table in front of her and flicked
through the pages, not really looking at them. She hated anything
to do with sickness.

'Dr Wilson can see you now, Mrs Minnelli, would you like to
come this way.' The nurse picked up the form from the table and
opened the door of the surgery.

The doctor looked up from his desk as she walked into the room.
'Good-morning, Mrs Minnelli, do please take a seat.' She sat down
across the desk from him while he studied her form, which the
receptionist had handed him before she left.

'Now, tell me where it hurts.' He smiled across at her and she
relaxed.

'Well, I have swollen glands, a sore throat and I'm tired – but I'm
far too busy at the moment to be ill, so please may I have some
antibiotics, even though I hate taking them because they always give
me thrush.' She rushed all this information at him as if every second
was vital.

'Yes, doctor,' he laughed. 'Anything else?'

She laughed at herself. 'Oh I'm sorry but you know what I mean.'

'I think I had better take a look at those swollen glands of yours.
Would you mind going behind the screen and popping up on the
couch? Have you taken your temperature?'

'No.' It would have been the first thing she did if Nikki had a sore
throat.

'Well, I'll call the nurse in and we'll get her to take it.' He gave an
encouraging glance towards the screen.

As she got up on the couch she heard him call the nurse on his
intercom.

The nurse came behind the screen, shaking down a thermometer
which she stuck under Annetta's tongue; then she picked up her
hand to test her pulse. The doctor joined her just as she was taking
the thermometer out of Annetta's mouth.

'Thank you,' she smiled at the nurse in relief. 'I hate having my
temperature taken. I'm always afraid I'll sneeze and bite into the
glass tube.'

The doctor took over at this point, but he asked the nurse to stay as he wanted her to take Annetta's blood pressure after his examination.

He started by feeling her neck. 'What is this big work load you have at the moment.'

'My company has just made a documentary on women in politics and we are editing it next week.'

'Does that hurt?' He pressed a place behind her ear.

'Yes, a bit.'

'You say on your form you're a journalist. Do you travel a lot?' Then he said, 'Open wide,' in almost the same breath and she didn't know quite what to do next. She decided to open her mouth as a flashlight was now shining in her face.

'Say Aah.'

'Aah.'

'Good, where did you say you have been travelling?'

'I didn't.' She felt tetchy and wished she could get up and leave. Doctors and dentists always asked questions at the wrong times, making the whole ordeal even more frustrating than it already was. 'I have been working in Europe for most of the summer.'

'No tropical destinations in the last six months?'

'No.' Her imagination went to work and she began to fear a rare virus may be at the bottom of this.

He looked into her ears and then her eyes. 'Right, nurse, blood pressure please.' Then to Annetta, 'I'll see you after the nurse has finished, Mrs Minnelli.'

She tidied her clothes and went back to her seat in front of his desk; he was scribbling illegible things on her form. He looked up as she sat down.

'I would like you to have some blood tests, Mrs Minnelli. You don't have a throat infection but your lymph glands are swollen. We need to see what must be done as soon as possible; can't have you missing work now can we?'

'Is it serious, doctor?' she asked nervously.

'I don't know, Mrs Minnelli, that's why I would like you to have some tests.'

'When, doctor?' Tests, this was really becoming boring.

'This afternoon, if possible.'

'But I have to be back to collect my son from school; it's his first week and I promised him I would be there.' It was a genuine excuse.

'Is there nobody else you could trust with the job?' The doctor's face looked serious.

'Well, I could ask his grandfather – but then everyone at home would start to worry about me.' There was a slight panic in her voice.

'Mrs Minnelli, they are adults like yourself. Just tell them the truth, that you are having some tests on my advice and that you hope it will turn out to be nothing serious.'

'You're right, Dr Wilson. I'm such a baby when it comes to illness. I can go into a war zone with very little fear, yet the thought of illness turns my legs to jelly.'

'Yes, of course – Annetta Peterson. I thought your maiden name and face seemed familiar. I remember seeing you reporting on the Vietnam War and thinking what a strange job for a pretty young woman to be doing.'

'You sound like my father.' She felt comforted by the thought.

'Well, take my fatherly advice then and call home.' He passed her the paperwork for her tests.

She called Lana and told her she had been delayed and would explain when she got back. She couldn't face Joe and his Sicilian panic quite yet. She hoped that Nikki would understand as she rarely let him down and hated having to do so when school was such a new experience for him.

The afternoon was spent being pricked, pulled about and waiting, then waiting some more only to be pricked and pulled about again – the ordeal being enhanced by her fear of illness. By the time she finally landed Joe's plane on the airstrip at Eagles' Ridge she was ready for a drink.

As she climbed down from the cockpit she was glad to see James waiting for her in his jeep.

He got out and came towards her and she fell into his arms.

'Am I pleased to see you! It's been one of those days. . .' She hugged him tightly

He kissed the tip of her nose. 'I guessed it must be serious for you to let Nikki down.'

'Was he very upset?'

'No, Joe made sure of that. He called Pete's mother and arranged to take both of the boys for a soda, then he and Nikki drove Pete home.'

'I'm pleased one thing has turned out right today.' She sounded very down.

They walked slowly back to the jeep in silence. It was a clear night and the air was warm but she felt chilled with the foreboding wind of change.

James opened the door for her and she climbed wearily into the seat. He jumped in beside her and gripped the steering wheel but he made no attempt to start the engine.

'So what's up, Net?' If he was going to hear bad news he wanted it sooner rather then later.

'I've been to see a doctor today about the lump you found in my neck. I had some tests this afternoon but I won't know for a few days what the problem is. I'm sure it's nothing major.' She put her hand over her mouth and he could see her lip quivering behind it.

He hadn't given another thought to that evening in the bath. He had been so busy with the harvest since they got back. Annetta hadn't mentioned it again and she had seemed in perfect health. 'Annetta, we're a team, remember? Whatever is wrong we'll fight it together. OK?'

She felt stronger with James sitting next to her. The horrors of the day and the negative mood in which it had left her subsided; she was beginning to think everything would turn out to be just a simple problem. She look towards him and felt his arm go around her shoulder and ease her back into her seat.

'True, James.' She began to unwind a little.

She spent the next few days at Eagles' Ridge going around the estate with James and listening to his enthusiastic voice as he told her all about his plans and projects. She took Nikki to school and had tea with Lana most afternoons; they were joined by the men whenever they found the time.

She was at home when Dr Wilson called the house. 'Mrs Minnelli, please.'

'Speaking.' She recognised his voice.

'Mrs Minnelli, this is Dr Wilson. I have the results of your tests and would like to see you as soon as possible, please.'

'I can come and see you but I'd rather you told me now, doctor.'

'Mrs Minnelli, I'm afraid you have cancer.'

She felt the blood drain from her face and a shiver go down her spine.

'What does that mean, Dr Wilson.' Her heart was in her throat.

'It means that you are very ill, Mrs Minnelli, but there is treatment available to help you. I would like you to see a cancer specialist. I'm an ear, nose and throat specialist. The word cancer is the modern-day equivalent to the word plague in the Dark Ages. Many cancers are curable today and more people die of heart disease then they do of cancer. My colleague Dr Bennett is an excellent man and I would suggest you make an appointment to see him as soon as possible. I will ask my secretary to make an appointment for you, if you wish.'

'Thank you, doctor, I'll do it myself as I'm not quite sure of my schedule at the moment.' She needed time to digest all this.

'Well, I advise you to sort it out as soon as possible, Mrs Minnelli. Curing cancer depends a lot on early diagnosis and quick action.'

She wrote down the number he gave her and thanked him once again before putting the telephone receiver back on its rest. She stood looking at the number for several minutes, completely numb as to thought or feeling.

James found her in their bedroom, lying on the bed looking up at the ceiling. He didn't speak, he just got on to the bed and lay down beside her, Clasping her hand in his, he waited to be invited to share her distress.

When she finally said something, she seemed miles away. 'I have cancer.'

He drew her towards him and wrapped his love around her and held her for a long time before saying anything. He let his mind try and accept this bad but not completely unexpected news.

When he spoke it was in the voice he reserved for small children. 'I want you to try and fill your mind with every happy thought you can, I'll help you. We will start with the remember game. Remember the morning in the kitchen when Nikki took his first steps and we were both there to witness it. The surprise on his face when he lost concentration and ended up on his butt. Then he laughed, got up and tried again. By then you were kneeling down on the floor so that he could run into your arms and he did.

'Remember how happy we were running around getting our first home together in Cork. Those long walks on summer evenings; the woods and the sun filtering through the trees on to the floor of the glade, turning it into a magic carpet. We stood there, the sun warming our bodies which had been chilled by the shade of the wood. The sun's energy going through us and the energy created by our own passion made us make love right there on the grass, under the sun, like Adam and Eve.

'These are the feelings we are going to work on, happy thoughts and love. We are going to find the best doctors and between good medical care and our combined energy we are going to love you back to good health.

'You must not be afraid, Annetta – fear isn't a happy feeling. I am going to be with you every step of the way.'

The first hard step was telling Joe and Lana the following day. They had already arranged to have lunch together, so James decided that after lunch would be the best time. Annetta had made light of the visit to the doctor, as she hadn't wanted to alarm them if the tests were going to show nothing major. Her old fighting spirit had returned once she and James had talked about her illness and taken on the challenge. As they walked across to the main house, her heart was heavy with the pain this bad news would give her in-laws.

Lunch had been set out on the terrace in front of the drawing-room. The view over the estate and up to the mountains was breathtaking in the bright, autumn sunlight. The vines had taken on all the tones of a Titian pallet and spread like a carpet in front of them. The mountains in the distance provided a dramatic division between the russet of the land and the turquoise of the cloudless sky.

Lana's Japanese chef had prepared sushi, as it was James's favourite food. It had been artistically laid out on the table and was as colourful as its surroundings.

It had been decided between them that James would break the news. So after they had eaten and everybody had been served with coffee, he spoke.

'Annetta and I have some serious news to report.' He groaned inwardly, this was harder than he thought it would be. 'Annetta has been diagnosed as having cancer.' He paused for the news to register. 'We are going to need lots of help and support from you both to keep Nikki's life as normal as possible while Annetta undergoes whatever treatment is necessary.'

There was a long silence; even the birds seemed to be holding their breath. Lana found Annetta's hand across the table.

'Of course.' Her voice was steady, although she was stricken with concern and compassion for her daughter-in-law.

'Have you found out which is the best doctor to see?' Joe sounded businesslike but his old Sicilian eyes hid nothing. He loved this woman as much as his own daughters and now he had registered the shock he was responding to the news like any other challenge in life. He would inform himself thoroughly and then he was going to make sure she had the best treatment available.

'Dr Wilson recommended a Dr Bennett to me,' Annetta said confidently. 'I think we should start with him.' She looked at her father-in-law for approval. 'James and I are going to see him tomorrow.'

'Good idea, the sooner the better, and in the meantime I'll make some enquiries myself. Now, lots of fresh orange and lemon juice for you, my girl, that's a good Sicilian remedy for health, and I'll make sure the chef includes lots of garlic in your diet. We are going to get you well. Don't you worry yourself about Smiley either, Lana and I will be here for all three of you whenever you need us.

Joe did his homework and it was decided that Dr Bennett was the best in his field and that Dr Wilson had made an excellent choice. Annetta managed to fit in the editing of her documentary before the start of her chemotherapy. This she had been warned would be rather drastic and the first treatment had to be administered in hospital.

James was there to help her through those dreadful days, making it just bearable. When all her hair fell out she decided not to wear a wig but bought a lot of different coloured scarves which she tied gypsy-style around her beautifully shaped head. She wore big earrings and dressed herself in Ralph Lauren clothes. For evenings, she had black, white and beige silk turbans made, which looked very sophisticated when worn with her silk trouser-suits. She wore her happy thoughts in the shape of the diamond and pearl earrings James had given her when Nikki was born.

Anthony Lawless made a point of visiting them whenever he was on the West Coast. He showed genuine concern for her health and if she didn't know him better, she would have believed him to be a little in love with her.

'Annetta, you're are a marvel, you look wonderful.' They were at a dinner party given by a San Francisco society hostess who had donated a lot of money to the peace movement in Ireland.

'Thank you, Anthony, it must be all that garlic Joe makes me eat. I'm convinced his old Sicilian remedies have a lot to do with the way I'm responding to treatment.'

'His old Sicilian remedies have helped me in the past!' Something a little stronger than garlic had been prescribed on those occasions. 'As I've always said to you, if there is ever anything I can do for you, you know where I am.' His sincerity was genuine. 'I know how hard you are fighting and how supportive James has been and I'm proud of both of you.' His admiration sounded real too. 'I'm also pleased to see you're still as enthusiastic over your company.'

'That's another thing that's keeps me going, Anthony, my belief in a better world for all oppressed people.'

He raised his glass to her, studying her features. She was far too slim but it made her eyes seem even bigger and bluer than usual. The black turban she was wearing with such panache emphasised her high cheekbones perfectly. He knew it was one of her good days; her bravery throughout this whole ordeal had astounded him. His feelings for her had deepened into something close to love and that coming from someone as heartless as Anthony Lawless was something approaching a miracle.

Her treatment lasted six months in total. There were days when it was hard to be positive but between them they survived. Her cancer went into remission and she started to get well.

Her hair grew back, white at first but it gradually returned to its normal ash blonde. While it was very short and covering her head like a cap she brushed it around her face and took on the appearance of a devilish pixie, her eyes sparkling with the joy of her newly recovered health.

The bond that her illness had made between her and James had put their love on a different plane. During the past six months their highs and lows had been intense. Their joint energy had pushed them through the tough times and the elation of the good times they shared with relish. Their energy had become fused by suffering into an indestructible force.

'Let's go to Ireland for Easter.' James was sitting on the terrace watching her arrange some flowers for the dining-room table. 'You're looking so well and I'm sure it will please your parents to see for themselves that you're blooming.'

'Yes, that's a good idea. I'm ready to do some travelling and the thought of going home has been on my mind for a few weeks now.'

'Do you ever think of Eagles' Ridge as home, Annetta?' He had never thought about it until now.

'Yes, because it's your home and so therefore it's part of me too; but West Cork is different, that's a part of my childhood. Now you seem so much part of it, I can't ever imagine life there without you. I don't know how to explain it really, it's just about our love and making our mark on it and perhaps because Nikki was conceived there. It's well, sort of my nest.

September seemed a long time ago now, a lifetime almost, but she would always remember the day she found out she had cancer and how strong James had been for both of them. He had helped her take those first steps in coming to terms with her illness and taught her to look it straight in the eye.

James was a wise man as well as a loving husband. She knew she had been blessed with many precious things but James's love was the jewel in her crown.

They spent a wonderful week in Ireland and arrived back at Eagles' Ridge with a renewed sense of well-being. They managed to spend time with all of their family and friends, who had been so supportive over the long winter months. Affectionate, caring telephone calls had sustained her strength. There hadn't been a day that went by without somebody's eager encouragement.

Both of them were eager to get back to work. James had neglected his business over the winter months as he summoned all of his energy into assisting Annetta back to health. Now he was ready to give his full attention to his beloved vines. He was determined to help organise a system of *appellation contrôlée* for American wine. Technically California was leaping ahead; successful research was being carried out on virus infections and cloning of vines. For the *dégustation* of American wines to be respected on a world stage, a quality control had to be established. This was important, otherwise they would always be considered second class. James had an ambition for his wine to be on a par with the best, if not to be the best. He had studied the French system and would fight for similar controls to be adopted in America.

Annetta also went back to work with a vengeance; by the time the summer holidays arrived her work agenda was full right the way through the coming winter. She was to make a documentary on women and prostitution. To cover the section on how armies provided home comforts for their boys, she had trips planned to Bangkok and El Salvador.

She came back from the trip to Bangkok with so many issues to address it was difficult to know where to start. It gave her ideas and she realised she had enough material for the start of another documentary on women, which she intended to begin the following spring.

It was New Years Eve and they were at a party in San Francisco seeing in another decade, the 1980s. Annetta looked stunning, her hair had grown back thick and lustrous; it was now all one length and cut in a bob which she wore behind her ears. She was wearing her usual happy earrings, which she now wore as lucky talismans. Her shot-silk taffeta evening dress was off the shoulder and exposed her beautiful back and her iridescent, creamy skin. She wore no jewellery around her neck, which made it look longer and didn't detract from the delicate curve of her shoulders. But her real beauty came from within; she was elated with life; 1979 had been a successful year for her and her work. That year had ended with Mother Theresa of Calcutta receiving the Nobel Peace Prize for her work campaigning for the world's poor.

Anthony Lawless was at the party and he lost no time in seeking Annetta out. Still drawn to her by a magnetic force beyond his control, he wondered what his real attraction was to this woman. He regularly had far more beautiful women in his bed but he never felt for them the way he did for her. After a few weeks his passion for them always waned and he searched for new thrills. Women who, as he saw it, belonged to other men, held a fascination for him. Especially if the men found out but turned a blind eye, as often suited them because they needed Anthony's influence in some way. He enjoyed making those men squirm for a while. Afterwards he always had the problem of getting rid of their wives, who were usually, by then, completely in love with him. It wasn't like that with Annetta.

She was certainly a match for him intellectually and he felt the need to possess her body whenever she gave him a hard time. In fact, he laughed to himself, hard times from her always gave him a hard on!

'Annetta, you are literally glowing this evening; the light of your beauty drew me across the room to bask in its aura.' The resonance in his voice emphasised his statement.

'Anthony, the man of too many words, good-evening.' She gave him a stagy smile.

'How was Bangkok?'

'Interesting.'

'I hear you're going to San Salvador in the new year.'

'Yes, but I will be travelling all over El Salvador, interviewing women.'

'Be careful, it's a very dangerous place.'

'Of course I will, Anthony, I have a very experienced and professional team going with me. We are all used to the hazards of war zones.'

'Do you think this documentary will show women in a very good light?'

'Women need to understand all aspects of their personalities, Anthony, to recognise the good or reject what they don't like, but they need to know. Most women in war conditions who choose prostitution see it as the only way to survive. They often have starving or sick children, or some just feel the need of male protection. I interviewed a lot of Vietnam veterans. Some of the then young boys fighting in the war just wanted someone to love for the night; they were not professional soldiers, they were kids who should have been in college, kids who witnessed dreadful things. They were homesick and afraid; some of them created relationships with these women who became surrogate mothers, or girlfriends. I just wonder what will happen when the Americans leave the area.

'Prostitution in Bangkok grew out of the Vietnam War. The Americans pulled out of Vietnam in 1973 but there is still a war going on there and while there is a big American base in the Philippines, prostitution in Bangkok will be supported. In the Philippines the GIs will form relationships with local girls whom they will leave behind when they go home, probably having fathered a few children on them in the meantime. Then what will happen to these women?

'A lot of the women I interviewed in Bangkok had been there since the early seventies, many of them had been child prostitutes. Most can't go back to their villages and nearly all of them support aged family members on their earnings. It has become part of the economy of the country. Life has little value in poor, highly populated countries. A woman is just another womb that will eventually be filled with another hungry mouth. I suppose everything in life has its price and there are many different forms of prostitution, Anthony.'

'I know that, Annetta, I have quite a few examples on my pay roll.' He smiled at this thought.

Annetta, still serious, said, 'Anyway, a happy new year to you and thank you for all your support last year. I hope this year gives you everything that you wish for.'

'Well; my first wish would be you in my bed. Will you oblige me?' the tone in his voice was like a sexual caress.

'Anthony Lawless, you are an impossible man, you never give up.' She wished she was as annoyed as she tried to sound.

'That's why I'm a winner. One day, Annetta, you will be putty in my hands, as I've told you before.'

'Not if I have anything to do with it, Anthony, as I have already told you. Your success with women reminds me of one of the women I interviewed in New York who was a celebrated favourite of kings, politicians, arms dealers and drug barons. When I asked her why she, a beautiful, wealthy, well-educated woman, wanted to prostitute herself, she told me that sitting on the face of power turned her on.' Her cool eyes looked into his. 'Well, that's not me, Anthony.'

'Have I bedded her, do you think?' he said, his mind relishing the thought.

'No, Anthony, you're not quite powerful enough yet,' she said, still keeping her composure.

'Well, give me her number for reference, so I will know when I have arrived,' his eyes were full of satanic mirth.

That was it – she gave in and had to laugh. He really was the most impossible man.

James came over to them at that moment and she was pleased to change the subject.

'I hope you're looking after my wife, Anthony, and not boring her with all your old jokes.'

'James, whenever have I been boring?'

'Whenever you hold court, Anthony, which is becoming much too often.'

'James, you're the only man in the world I would let get away with a remark like that.'

'That's probably because I'm the only man in the world you have nothing on.' He grinned at his old friend, making it impossible for him to take offence. 'Dad wants to talk to you and I have come to reclaim my wife, so be off with you before I remember how much I enjoy your company and get embroiled in conversation with you.'

After a few more minutes of friendly banter Anthony took his leave and went off to find Joe.

'Do you want to go now, sweetheart? It's well past midnight and I always worry you will overtire yourself.'

'James, I'm perfectly well – in fact, I think I have more energy than before my illness – but I'm quite happy to leave now and spend some time alone with you.'

He took her hand. 'Come on then, let's say our goodbyes and be off. You are looking truly beautiful tonight, sweetheart. I've been staring at your bare back across the room all evening, thinking about running my hands over it when we get home.'

'Mr Minnelli, I can't wait.'

They were spending the night in San Francisco. They had not sold the apartment when they moved into Eagles' Ridge and found they still used it enough to justify keeping it.

They drove in silence, comfortable in the knowledge that their communication was at a level which didn't always demand conversation. Annetta hoped she and James would always be this close, a love as deep as theirs could only go one way if it went wrong and the thought of hating James as much as she loved him at this moment was a devastating one.

When she left for EL Salvador in March she could feel his distress. He didn't voice it; all he said was. 'Don't forget we have a deal, you're not to get yourself killed.'

'True,' she kissed him. 'Don't worry, I'll stick to my bargain.' They hugged and clung together for long time before saying goodbye.

During the following weeks, there were many moments when she reflected on those words. While interviewing prostitutes in San Salvador she was approached by a representative of the guerrilla army in the mountains. She couldn't resisted the opportunity to interview some of the camp followers. So, under the umbrella of reporting on the group's political aspirations, she and her crew were taken to one of the camps.

Leaving the plane by jeep, they headed through the coffee plantations until they reached the edge of the low volcanic mountains. At this point they were met by guerrilla fighters from the camp. They were obliged to travel on horseback, as the terrain allowed for no other means of transport. It was hot and humid as the volcanic rock gave off its nightly store of dew. As they travelled farther into the mountains, the sounds and smells of everything were exaggerated by their unfamiliarity with the dense vegetation. The beauty of the place, even under these tense conditions, couldn't be ignored; brightly coloured birds and enormous butterflies flew across their path and darted among the leaves. As they neared the camp they were blindfolded. Travelling blindfold on the back of a horse is a frightening experience, however sure-footed the horse or skilled the rider holding the lead rein. Annetta didn't know whether it was a man or a woman who led her into the camp. Women rode and fought alongside the men in this community. A number of its leaders were women who were well respected and obeyed. Once they were blindfolded they were told not to talk and the whole party entered the camp in silence. Only a few whistles and simulated bird-calls told her when they were almost there.

The camp was a whole community in hiding, bustling with life. Old women sat around the stove making tortillas, the staple diet of the camp. Dressed in their brightly coloured, hand-embroidered clothes, which depicted the birds and flowers of their native land, many of them wearing Panama hats, they worked deftly at their task. Annetta knew she had to get close to show the truth, but this was beyond her dreams, an unexpected privilege.

The only time they were in any serious danger was when the guerrillas decided that the crew was taking too much interest in filming their weapons. They accused the crew of being government spies. The filming had to stop and everybody involved was taken to the camp leader. It took some fast diplomatic talking on Annetta's part to defuse the situation; at one point, she even offered to destroy the film. After long negotiations she was allowed to continue, finding herself and her crew eventually back in San Salvador unscathed and the film intact. The reels were sent back to America by courier without delay.

It was 30 March, the day before they were scheduled to leave. They had decided to cover the funeral mass for Archbishop Romero who had been shot by gunmen the previous week while saying mass for his mother at the high altar. Her journalistic instincts told her she should be there to cover the funeral. A huge crowd had gathered outside the cathedral and access in and out was difficult. The mass was being conducted inside the cathedral when bombs exploded in the square and snipers with automatic rifles fired into the crowd. There was total panic and people started running in all directions, bumping into each other, screaming. People who fell were trampled.

Annetta remembered being pushed away from her crew and being jostled and buffeted by the stampede. Sub-machine guns were being produced by some of the left-wing mourners, who fired on the snipers. 'These must be government snipers, doing this to their own people, on behalf of a government supported by America.' These were her last thoughts before she was pushed from behind, fell and lost consciousness.

She woke up in hospital with a broken arm, several broken ribs and multiple cuts and bruises. She was lucky, at least twenty people had been killed, among them one of her own crew. The horror and stupidity of the situation was still vivid in her mind. America's fear of communism was allowing it to support Fascist thugs as the alternative.

James flew down to bring her home. He walked into the ward to find her interviewing a nurse about her daily life. He had to smile, she looked so pathetic with her arm in a sling and her poor face bruised and still swollen. But there she was, tape recorder in her good hand, the interpreter by her side and the nurse attending to the cut on her other hand that had been stitched and needed to be dressed before she left the hospital.

She saw him across the room and smiled a lopsided smile as he came over to her. He bent and kissed the side of her face that looked the least sore.

'Sometimes, Net, I wish you would take up knitting, at least then I would know where to find you.' All his pent-up fear and anger had subsided now he was with her.

'Oh, James, it's so good to see your face. I suppose mine looks a complete mess but I kept my promise, I didn't get myself killed.' She knew she had sailed too near to the wind this time.

'Almost though! I'm taking you home and I'm going to take charge of your life for the next few months, until I'm sure you have healed.' He assessed the damage to her face while he spoke. 'This is a dangerous place, Net, you should never have come.'

'The world's a dangerous place, James. Every time we make a scheduled flight we could be highjacked,' she said weakly, trying to justify her action

'True, but all I know at this moment is that I will feel much better when we are both back at Eagles' Ridge.'

She had all the time she needed while she was convalescing to formulate her ideas for her next documentary. In fact it was for this documentary that she had gone into the guerrilla camps. She knew she had to take the opportunity when it presented itself and the moment she had been approached by the messenger of the left-wing group, she hadn't hesitated. These people had been struggling for years and whole communities lived in the mountains. She wanted to speak to the women who had endured such long-term conflict and find out how they coped with daily life.

She would have her documentary, *Women and Prostitution*, ready to sell at the October market in Cannes and then she intended to start work on her next, and what she felt would be her most important, documentary, *Woman and War*. Under the present circumstances, she didn't feel it was right to mention it to James. He had been adamant that she should take fewer risks in her work, but that was because he was still a little shaken up over her brush with death, as he put it. Joe had also given her a lecture but she knew she would be able to talk them both around when the time came.

That year they left for Ireland earlier than they normally did for the summer so Annetta could make the most of her period of convalescence. By the end of June they were well ensconced in the West Cork house.

Mrs O'Brian had been there to greet them and as always was full of the local gossip.

'I hear you got yourself blown up, Mrs Minnelli.' Mrs O'Brian always folded her arms under her ample breasts when she stood talking.

'Well, not quite, Mrs O'Brian. I was knocked down,' Annetta replied sheepishly.

'I said to Mr O' Brian when I heard, she doesn't need to go to one of those South American countries for that, she can go to Belfast.' She took a good look at Annetta before she continued, 'Well, you don't look as if you came to much harm.' She did not wait for a reply. but went into the kitchen. Annetta followed her, wondering if she hadn't just been scolded.

'I've put the groceries away that you asked me to get, the bill's on the table.' She walked towards the back door. 'I'll be off now to get Mr O'Brian his tea. I'm glad to see you're still in one piece.' She left without giving Annetta the chance to say another word except for a weak goodbye and thank you through the closing door.

It's good to be back, she thought, as she looked around her home, mentally reclaiming it. I'm so glad we came early and that neither one of us has anything pressing to do as far as work is concerned.

That night in bed as she snuggled up to James, putting herself in just the right position to be really comfortable – her ribs and her arm were still sore even though they were now completely healed – she wondered why she was driven to do what she did. At times like these, when she was so contented, it didn't make sense, but she knew that by the end of the summer she would be impatient as usual to continue her work.

How did I ever manage before James? Life before him seems so empty now, yet at the time I was happy, my job excited me and I was never short of lovers. James filled a space in me I didn't know was there, and now we have Nikki growing up and giving us so much pleasure. I really am a very fortunate woman. She nestled her face into his shoulder; he stirred a little and automatically in his sleep fitted his body into perfect unison with hers. I love his clean smell, it must be all that tennis he plays. I just can't imagine sharing a bed with another man. She drifted off to sleep as comfortable and carefree as a child, her ordeal in El Salvador firmly consigned to the past.

James had arranged to take Nikki to the Olympic Games in Moscow the last week in July. They were meeting Joe in London and then all three of them would fly on to Moscow. Annetta had decided not to go with them; she thought it should stay a boys' trip and something Nikki would remember doing with his father and Joe.

Joe had organised all their visas before they left and the tickets and the hotels were booked. It had been quite difficult to arrange as America had boycotted the games but Joe could usually get things done if he chose to. He wanted to take his grandson to see Steve Ovett and Sebastian Coe run, so a few favours were called in and everything was arranged, including bodyguards.

She was looking forward to being alone in the house as she planned to work on the layout for her documentary. She thought she would start with Boudicca, Joan of Arc and Florence Nightingale – three different sides of women in war, the warrior, the martyr and the mother.

James and Nikki left in high spirits. Nikki, who at seven and a half was quite the little man about the house, was concerned about his mother being alone.

'You will be OK here by yourself without dad and me to look after you?' His face looked very serious.

She smiled at her son, who had become tall and skinny over the winter, with his adult front teeth now fully grown and looking too big for his mouth. 'I will be very careful, Nikki, and I promise to lock up when I go to bed.'

After they had gone the house seemed very quiet and empty. She wandered around for the first day doing nothing, getting used to the emptiness. She pottered in the garden, which, thanks to Mr O'Brian's love and attention two days a week, was looking a picture.

She cut some yellow rambling roses and a few sprays of white mallow and arranged them in the white glazed-terracotta vase her mother had given her when she came to stay the week before. The roses tumbled down over the sides of the vase and she put them on the Georgian mahogany table in the hall with a sense of artistic achievement.

The second day was better as she had got used to the quite and was beginning to enjoy the peace. She had spent all afternoon sitting in the garden working on her new project. The weather had been kind to her and at six o'clock when she went to take her shower it was still warm.

The water felt good on her body and she stayed under it for a long time, letting it relax her. After she had dried her hair and put on some body lotion she wished James would walk in and share her mood. She was missing him already; West Cork was about being together. She put on a pair of silk pyjama-style trousers and a silk caftan top embroidered with wild flowers. A pair of ballet pumps on her feet and a final quick brush through her thick hair and that was it, she was home alone and dressed for comfort. The silk felt sensual against her body and as she wore no underwear the softness of it caressed her as she walked.

She went down into the drawing-room and over to the drinks tray, poured herself a whiskey and took it out into the garden through the open French windows. She stood in the unusually warm evening air, listening to the birds and taking in the scents of the flowers, now thoroughly enjoying the quiet.

Her peace was shattered by the sound of a car drawing up outside the gate. She went around to the front garden to see who it could be. She didn't hide her surprise when she found a Rolls-Royce parked outside and a chauffeur opening the door for Anthony Lawless.

'Anthony, what are you doing here?' She had reached the gate at the same time he had and was opening it for him.

'I dropped in to see you and James. I had business in the area and I thought you would never forgive me if I didn't stop by to say hello and take a look at your charming little house,' he said, with warm-hearted sociability.

'James and Nikki are in Moscow with Joe. I'm here alone, Anthony, and by now the whole of Dublin will know you're here. Mrs O' Brian will be on the telephone this very moment and if it's engaged she will be using jungle drums to spread the word.'

'Should I leave?' he looked genuinely concerned.

'No, it's too late for that, but why didn't you telephone? It's very unlike you.' She didn't trust his motives at all.

'I wanted to surprise you both.'

'Well, you certainly did that. Come along in and have a drink.'

Anthony made a sign to his chauffeur and the car pulled away. They went into the house through the front door and she led him into the drawing-room.

'Take a seat, Anthony – what would you like to drink?' She was still flustered by the shock of his arrival.

'A whiskey, do you have a Jamesons there.' He was completely relaxed as he sat down, enjoying her obvious disquiet.

'Yes, that's what I'm drinking.'

'What a charming room,' he said as she handed him his drink. 'Who's the interior designer.'

'Me. Well, I must be perfectly honest and admit that I got the idea from seeing in an interior-design magazine the work of an English designer named Georgina Fox.'

'I know her work, I do business with her husband. She's very talented but it's a shame that she doesn't know a little more about real life. Her husband twists her around his little finger.'

'Perhaps she's in love with him.'

'In love? I don't know about that, but they are a good team. She's stupid and he's a manipulator. Good combination, don't you think?'

'Did she reject you, Anthony?' He was so vain, she thought. That could be the reason for him even having an opinion about this Georgina Fox woman, whom he seemed to think so little of.

'Not my type, darling, I'm waiting for you.' Her spirited reply inflamed his ardour.

She wished she had more clothes on; she felt vulnerable alone with Anthony in anything less than a suit of armour. She changed the subject slightly.

'Well, James and I are pleased with the house and for me it holds lots of childhood memories.'

'Here's to your childhood memories.' He lifted the glass and looked into her eyes in such a way that she hoped she wasn't going to blush.

'How about dinner? You're all alone here and it seems a shame not to take you away from your loneliness.'

'I'm not lonely, Anthony, in fact I have been enjoying the peace. I hope you don't mind if I refuse your invitation. I don't feel like dressing up and I have planned to eat something light. It's been hot today and I'm not really hungry.'

She noticed his glass was empty and got up to pour another drink. She turned round to see him looking at her with glazed eyes. She handed him his drink feeling the need to be out in the air. 'Let's go and sit outside. It's a beautiful evening and it's already quite warm enough to sit out.'

'Aren't you going to show me over the house, Annetta?' He stood so close to her that she could feel his warm breath in her ear.

'No, Anthony, I want to wait until James is here and we can show you together.' She walked into the garden and he was obliged to follow her.

'You're not afraid of me are you, Annetta? – or are you afraid you may respond to me?'

'Anthony, I would rather drop this conversation. James is your friend and my husband. It seems a little bit coincidental that you arrived to see us after he had left the country. I know you are in contact with Joe every few days and I'm sure he would have told you of their trip. Joe was very excited about it and I know Joe – when he's looking forward to something, he tells the world.'

'All right, Annetta, I did come to see you. I've told you before you could teach me to love. I want you, I want to turn the throbbing excitement I feel when I am with you into a joint experience.'

'But Anthony, I'm in love with my husband, doesn't that mean anything to you. I made a commitment to him and I have no reason to break it. That's what love is about, Anthony, it's not just about sex.' Her heart was pulsating in her ears like a drum, the energy was there between them, she had to admit it herself. Anthony had called up her dark side and she had let it surface. She stared him out.

He took a gulp of his drink. 'I'll not grovel, Annetta. May I use your telephone to call my chauffeur.'

'Yes, please do.' She drew a deep breath.

He went into the house to use the telephone and she allowed herself to relax a little. This wasn't the evening she had imagined.

He came back outside. 'He will be along in a few minutes; just enough time to finish our drinks.' He sat down next to her. 'You can't blame a man for trying, Annetta, and one day you may want something very, very badly – then who knows.' He lifted his glass to her again. 'To life.'

'To life, Anthony.'

When James came back he brought Joe with him. She was pleased to have her father-in-law visiting them at their house for the first time. He lay low, as he didn't want any of Lana's family to know he was in Ireland. The problems would arise over whom he should visit in his short stay and he intended to restrict his visiting to his immediate family only.

Annetta decided to tell James about Anthony's visit to the house sooner rather than later as by now the tongues of Dublin would be wagging. This was the only problem of a small, close community, and rising above the gossip wasn't always easy. So the evening after they had taken Joe to the airport seemed the right time to mention Anthony's call.

'Anthony came by for a drink while you were away. He said he was in the area on business. I was quite surprised to see his car outside.'

'Did he proposition you?' his voice sounded matter of fact.

She wondered what to say. This was new ground she was treading with her husband; she knew all about Italian honour and she hoped she was saying the right thing when she replied, 'Yes.'

'I think Lawless has an illness when it comes to women. He has to possess as many as possible.'

'You're not angry with him?' She inwardly breathed a sigh of relief.

'No, I feel sorry for him.' He was very calm.

'I was frightened to tell you, I thought all that Italian blood of yours would be stirred up into a passionate rage.' She was encouraged by his attitude.

'Anthony may be a fool where women are concerned but he isn't a rapist and I trust you, so why should I be angry?' he said, surprised by her question.

'And to think I've been fretting about telling you all the time Joe was here. In my past, jealous men have always been my biggest problem. I'm sorry I put you in that category.' She went over and sat on his lap, putting her arms around his neck. Her deliverance from the fear of a serious argument and the escape from having privately to assess her own feelings that afternoon alone with Anthony, made her feel quite light headed.

'Look, Net, don't think that I'm so easy-going when it comes to you. I'm sure that if I felt our relationship was threatened by another man, or that you were sleeping with someone else, I would be as jealous as the next guy. I didn't feel you had fallen for the Lawless charm, so I wasn't worried.' His face was solemn.

'I know what you mean, if I thought you were with another woman I would be jealous. Jealousy is only a manifestation of fear. Losing your love, or anything happening to Nikki, are about the only things that I would be afraid of at this point in my life.' She lay in his arms, thankful that she had been able to disregard a fleeting moment of temptation.

In October James accompanied Annetta to the MIP market in Cannes. They stayed at the Carlton Hotel. He had some business of his own to attend to while he was there. A vineyard had come up for sale in the Var and he was interested in buying it.

The wines of Provence most widely known were rosé, or 'blush' wines as they were called in America. He saw these wines becoming more fashionable and the thought of creating a top-quality product for the international market was on his mind.

He and Annetta had decided to turn the trip into a working holiday. He had made a plan and chosen the route and the hotels very carefully. It was the season for game and wild mushrooms and he intended to enjoy these autumn delights.

The vineyard was near Lorgues, in the area classified by its AOC as Côte de Provence. Some of the oldest vineyards in France were in this region and he intended to talk to the men who knew about their art and their vineyards. With their wine, which he saw as an expression of themselves, he was already acquainted.

The trip started well and then got better. Although the market was hectic it was good fun and Annetta's product sold easily. It seemed that the subject of prostitution pulled high ratings and that's what the market was really all about. Nobody gave a damn about women's issues.

By the time they had finished the whirl of social activity that her work in Cannes demanded, the contrast of driving into the peace of the Var was even more marked.

The leaves were just changing colour and the blue sky that presided over their journey heightened the beauty of the country-side. They had decided not to take the motorway and instead they drove to Grasse, the centre of the perfume industry. From there they took the back country to Draguignan, then pressed on down to the coast to spend a few nights in St Tropez. James had booked a suite at the Byblos and reserved a table at Lou Mouscadin's for dinner.

They sat in the cosy sitting-room of the Byblos in front of the fire; they had ordered pre-dinner drinks before going to the restaurant. The evening air had turned cool and the fire was a welcome sight.

'It's so beautiful here, James. I feel as if we are having a second honeymoon,' Annetta said, looking away from the flames.

'That's what I want it to feel like; this trip is a reaffirmation of my love for you.' He raised his glass to her.

'Have you seen any photographs of the vineyard?'

'No, I just had the specifications as to the type of vines, the yields and other technical information, like the acreage and the price, of course. All I know is there is an old *manoir* on the land but I don't know what state it's in.'

'I was just romancing about living here. At this moment I am completely under the spell of the place.' The adrenalin rush occasioned by working flat out for the last few days had subsided and left her in a mellow mood.

'I know. I feel the same. When we drove down through the countryside today, I felt I belonged here. I just imagined staying forever, it's so peaceful.'

'I'm really happy you came with me to Cannes and shared my crazy world for a few days – and now I'm here to share your world, which thankfully is much saner.'

'Well, let's see what tomorrow brings. If the *manoir* suites us, perhaps we'll make it our base and send Nikki to school in France.'

'I don't think Joe and Lana would like that idea very much.'

'No, neither do I, but things usually work out as they are meant to, if we let them. Perhaps this is the break on my own I've been looking for, something that doesn't need dad's backing. I love the old guy to death but everyone in the US sees me as Joe Minnelli's son, of which I'm very proud, but it would be nice for once to be just James Minnelli.'

'It's always hard to live in the shadow of a big personality like your father, but you do it with such style, James, that I think people see you very much as your own man.'

'Thank you.' He lent over and kissed her cheek then whispered in her ear, 'I love you.' He got to his feet. 'Come along, sweetheart, or we'll be late for the restaurant.'

The restaurant was excellent and the meal delicious; they left contented but not full, light headed but not drunk. They walked back to the hotel sauntering arm in arm like young lovers and their love-making that night took on all the sparkle of that first week together in Corsica. It left Annetta wondering, as she drifted off to sleep, how deep their love could go; at that moment it seemed fathomless.

They drove to Lorgues the following morning, after a leisurely breakfast of coffee and croissants. James had been sent a plan of how to get to the vineyard. The directions started in Lorgues so it made sense to go there and familiarise themselves with the village before going to the vineyard.

James had arranged a rendezvous with the agent for eleven o'clock at the *manoir*. The whole day had a feeling of adventure about it as they followed unfalteringly the path laid down for them by destiny.

Le Manoir de la Bouscarela reposed in the autumn sunshine like a mirage of their wildest dreams. Built in the seventeenth century, it was the colour of desert sand. The avenue of plane trees which led them to this seductive *bâtiment* was old and proud. The house stood on a high terrace with woodland behind it and the vines that flanked it on either side and in front were decked in their autumn red. Annetta held her breath, it was something out of a fairy tale.

The agent was waiting at the end of the drive to bring them back to reality. They got out of the car and walked over to where he waited talking to somebody who James imagined must be the manager. When he saw them approaching he broke off his conversation to greet them.

'Monsieur et Madame Minnelli, good-day. You had no problem understanding my directions?'

'No, they were very precise.' James answered him in English although he would have been just as comfortable in French.

'I would like to introduce Monsieur Gireaud. He is the manager here and lives on the estate.'

'Bonjour, Monsieur Gireaud.'

'Bonjour, Monsieur, Dame.'

They dropped into French and James asked questions about the estate.

Domaine de Bouscarela was owned by a family living in Paris. They rarely came to the estate and never stayed in the *manoir* when they did.

Le Manoir de la Bouscarela had been occupied by German troops during the war when it had been stripped of all of its works of art and furnishings. Nobody in the family had wanted to live in the house since, preferring life in the city. The only part of the house in permanent use was the kitchen, where Mme Gireaud prepared lunch every day for the estate workers.

The estate produced a small amount of wine for the family but the rest of the grapes went to the co-operative outside Lorgues.

'But the gardens are so beautifully maintained,' Annetta said as she looked at the fountain and the *cour d'entrée*.

'Yes, madame, they are the work of Pedro Gonzallez. His father was gardener here before him; he lives in one of the estate cottages and the gardens are his life. He remembers the old days before the war when the family was here every summer. He is very old now and nobody has the heart to tell him he should retire. He works in the garden from dawn till dusk and it will be a sad day for the house when he stops working.'

The agent changed the subject and the language. 'Shall we go into the house first or would you like to see the vineyard.'

'I think the house,' said James, looking at Annetta.

'Yes, the house.' She wondered what she would find behind this façade which showed such promise.

The agent opened the front door and stepped aside to let them into an L-shaped entrance hall. The floor was made up of black and white marble tiles, and from it a beautifully wide stone staircase with an ornate wrought-iron banister swept up to the first floor. To the right were two doors and to the left, one; directly opposite and under the high curve of the stairs was a fourth; all the doors were in carved light oak. The agent walked across the hall and opened the door under the stairs to reveal a cloakroom equipped for daily use.

The two doors to the right of the entrance led to what must once have been the drawing-room and the library.

The erstwhile drawing-room was full of boxes and broken furniture, disused bicycles and children's toys, but through all of the junk shone a room of beautiful proportions with a Louis-Treize fireplace and a high-beamed ceiling. The floor was old hexagonal terracotta tiles which reminded Annetta of the ginger biscuits her grandmother had baked in West Cork every summer. The room was sadly neglected but its spirit hadn't been broken and one could easily imagine its former glory.

The library was oak panelled with one wall of floor-to-ceiling book shelves. The same ginger biscuits were on the floor and the fireplace was of the same period as the drawing-room but the chimney breast in this room had a carved hunting scene depicted in the stone. Annetta fell in love with the library; she imagined the shelves filled with her favourite books and herself spending winter evenings reading in front of a blazing log fire.

The agent showed them back into the hall and through the door on the left of the entrance into what had been the dining-room. As they walked into the room they caught their breath.

'In wonderful condition, don't you think,' the agent enthused. The walls and ceiling were adorned with the most stunning frescos. 'They're attributed to Fragonard.'

Even with nothing in the room, it was alive and inviting. Annetta moved closer to James, and when the agent turned his attention to the terrace which led off the dining-room, she squeezed his hand to affirm her delight.

The kitchen was accessed from the dining-room and must have been original. It was in pristine condition and they felt as if they had gone back in time. It must have been Mme Gireaud's pride and joy. Although she was nowhere to be seen, the smells coming from the old iron range told them that lunch would be delicious. The kitchen door, which led to the gardens at the back of the house, was open. Annetta went outside to find a well-kept box-hedged *jardin potager* and herb garden. She wandered out and down the scented path to a stone building integrated into the surrounding wall. As she got closer she realised it was a chapel. The door was unlocked; she opened it quietly and it swung back on its hindges. As through a prism, coloured light filtered down through the stained-glass of the windows. The beams danced as the door momentarily cast its shadow. The simple altar was covered in a lovingly embroidered, white linen cloth and flanked on either side by huge brass candlesticks, glowing in the refracted light. A smell of garlic permeated the air. Three small pews to the left of the door were the only furniture in the room apart from the altar. She looked up, her gaze expecting a Fragonard canopy of spiritual enlightenment. The ceiling was stark but for the dappling of coloured light from the windows. It was on the wall at the back of the pews that the pungent garlic had been hung in plaited bunches. Annetta wondered if it was there to ward off evil spirits or whether, more simply, the chapel wall was just a convenient place to hang the garlic to dry. Perhaps she and James should have their marriage blessed here, if they bought the property. It was a far cry from the flashy surroundings of their Las Vegas wedding. It suddenly felt important that they should repeat their marriage vows in this place.

She went back in to join James and the agent who were still talking in the kitchen. They both looked up as she stepped back through the door.

'You found the chapel then?' the agent's enthusiastic eyes rested on her face.

'Yes,' she hesitated, still lost in her own thoughts. 'It's quite lovely in its simplicity.'

'Some say it dates back to the crusading Knights Templars.'

'I'm sure many a soldier has taken solace within its walls,' said Annetta, thinking of the young boys who had been part of the German war machine, whether they liked it or not.

The tour of the house continued. To the right of the kitchen door was another door which led into the laundry and boiler-room; this was the room that gave access to the cellars. The cellars were in good order and the bins were full of the family wine, which was shipped up to Paris when required.

Having been so pleased with the ground floor, they found the first floor disappointing. There was only one bathroom with a separate WC for all the rooms, of which there were so many it seemed like a rabbit warren. Apart from the master bedroom, the rooms had been partitioned into small units to house troops, and the scars of their occupation were everywhere. The views from the windows were breathtaking and in sharp contrast with the atmosphere created by this cramped accommodation; it took all of their imagination to envisage the original bedrooms.

The rest of the morning was taken up going over the estate. To the left of the house and down an avenue of plane trees stood the old coach-house; behind it, through a stone arch, was a terraced orchard and olive grove.

By twelve-thirty they had seen everything. James thanked the agent and said he would be in touch.

They left for Lorgues where they had booked lunch for 1 p.m. They talked about the vineyard all the way to the restaurant, enthusiastic, excited and a little in awe of the charm and beauty of Le Manoir de la Bouscarela.

'It would have to be carefully bought back to life,' Annetta said.

'Yes and it would need to be lived in again,' James answered pensively.

They were silent for a moment, each going through, in their minds, the meaning of such a dramatic change of culture and environment for themselves and their son.

'I'm going to make them an offer anyway. The vineyard is what I was originally interested in and now I've seen it I want it. The house was an unexpected treasure; the only thing we need to decide on is if we live here or not.'

'It's an exiting thought; perhaps in a few years' time, when Nikki is a bit older and he can speak a little French, we could give it a try. I can see myself retired and growing old here in the Var,' Annetta said dreamily.

'Perhaps Nikki could start private French lessons in the new year. He will be eight at Christmas and I know dad will be able to convince him that it's a good idea. All the Minnellis speak more than one language and French is the most important in the wine business.'

The rest of their trip continued as planned. They visited some of the many beautiful places in the area including Aix-en-Provence, Les Gouges du Verdon and the potteries in Salernes. The only thing which wasn't on the agenda were the almost daily visits made to Domaine de Bouscarela.

James had made an offer for the vineyard the day after their first visit and it had been accepted. He had arranged for the *compromis de vente* to be signed the day before they left for America.

Annetta couldn't keep away from the place now she knew James was buying it. While he talked business to Mr Gireaud, she would walk around the gardens and imagine living in the house. Every day she discovered something new, something to charm her. The house was like a magnet drawing on her imagination. She could see a Christmas tree in the hall, the dining-room soft and warm in the candlelight; a swimming pool near the coach-house, faceless grandchildren, nieces and nephews playing in the water; a tennis court for James by the side of the orchard; summer dinner parties given on the terrace outside the dining-room, the house ringing with laughter and happiness. She couldn't wait to start work on her daydream.

James came up with a good idea on one of their visits. 'Why don't we convert the coach-house. I'm sure we could get two bedrooms and bathrooms, a sitting-room and kitchen out of it. We can use it when we visit, then live in it when the time comes to move here and renovate the house. I'll ask the agent if he knows a good architect.'

Annetta was thrilled with the idea. 'Then we will be able to use it afterwards for guests who want to stay more than a weekend, parents for instance could stay for as long as they wanted. Then when we are old and Nikki takes over the estate we can move in there ourselves and potter around the gardens, remembering when we first made love in the open air.'

'Then I'll pull you into the shrubbery just to remind you I'm still not too old.' He let his hands drop from her waist and cup the exciting roundness of her buttocks.

When they left for America contracts had been exchanged and an architect had been employed to organise the planning permission and drawings for the coach-house. They had mapped out a long-term plan in their minds and envisaged moving to France in about two or three years' time. There was no need to share their plan with anybody yet, it would be their secret until the right time came to say anything. For now, that James had bought a vineyard and that they would be going there from time to time was all anyone needed to know.

The year ended on a note of excitement, with James flying to France the week before Christmas to complete on the purchase of Domaine de Bouscarela. Planning permission had been granted for the coach-house and before he left he gave the architect the go-ahead to start the work. He had some wine flown over to Eagles' Ridge and when he returned they gave a small party to celebrate his new venture. In retrospect, 1980 was the year his happiness reached a peak and no challenge in life seemed impossible. He always looked back on it with pleasure.

Annetta went back to work, reluctantly at first, as the holiday had transported her to another place and it took a while to get her feet back on the ground; but once she had centred herself, the work acquired its old importance.

By the beginning of January she had written her 'treatment', a brief overview of her new documentary, and was ready to present it to her company directors. This was more a formality than anything else as Joe and Anthony left everything on the creative side up to her and never had any comments to make. The only thing they were involved with was raising money for the projects.

The company had made an unexpected profit with *Women and Prostitution* but making money had never been the real motivation behind the company. Joe supported Annetta's work out of respect for her, also to please James and Lana. Lana had championed what Annetta was trying to achieve from the very beginning and had helped James when it came to convincing his father

Anthony Lawless had got involved for his own reasons but now his respect for Annetta outweighed his original motives.

She wasn't really looking forward to facing Anthony again. The last time she had seen him was alone in the house in West Cork the previous summer. Although he hadn't left on an awkward note, the memory of her discomfort and her vulnerability because of lack of clothing still bristled in her mind.

The meeting was planned for 22 January, two days after the inauguration of President Reagan. Joe, a Republican eagle, had been a big fund raiser for the Reagan campaign and was invited to the inauguration; so was Anthony Lawless, but Annetta wasn't quite sure why he qualified and she certainly didn't intend to ask him. They were flying back from Washington together and Anthony had been invited to Eagles' Ridge for a long weekend.

On the day of the meeting she was sitting in her office in front of her computer, putting the last-minute details to her presentation. Production had sent over the budget she had been waiting for and she was now prepared for her meeting at 5.30 p.m.

Satisfied that everything had been checked she got up from her chair and went over to the window. Her office was a small room next to the kitchen in their wing of Eagles' Ridge; it looked over towards the swimming pool and tennis court. Today the area was empty; everyone was working and Nikki was at school.

It was only the lull before the storm as the weekend would be hectic with dinner parties and a Sunday brunch was planned. At this moment she felt like going to bed and staying there until it was all over; she was exhausted and her whole body ached as if she was coming down with the flu.

She felt her neck but there was nothing. Her first thought was the return of her cancer but she could feel no lumps. She had been screened before they went to France last October and the tests were negative.

Perhaps if she went to bed for the rest of the afternoon she would feel better by the evening. She closed down her computer and wearily climbed the stairs.

Once in the bedroom she took off her top clothes and got into bed with her underwear on. Just half an hour's nap, she thought, and then I'll feel ready for Nikki's hyper energy when he comes back from school.

'Mom, mom.' The sound of Nikki calling through the house woke her up. She looked at her watch; it was 4.30 p.m. She jumped out of bed.

'I'm up here, Nikki,' she called back to him.

He came up to the bedroom and poked his face around the door; his sunny smile warmed her mood.

She had put on a silk kimono and was sitting at her dressing table. 'Hi, darling, how was school?'

He came across the room to give her a kiss. 'OK, I guess. Is Joe back from Washington yet?'

'Yes, he and Lana got home just after lunch but I haven't seen them. Mr Lawless is with Joe and I have a meeting with them at five-thirty, so we will go over together a bit earlier if you like. You can see Joe before our meeting, then while we are talking you can have tea with Lana.'

'How long will your meeting last?'

'Not long, Nikki, less than an hour.' She turned her attention to the mirror. 'I had better tidy myself up and so should you; go and wash your hands and face while I get myself ready. There are milk and cookies in the fridge if you want something to eat before we go.'

She looked back into the mirror; she felt dreadful but she seemed to look all right. The top drawer on the left of her dressing table had a bottle of aspirin in it. She opened the drawer and took two pills out of the bottle, put them in her mouth and swallowed them without any water. They tasted bitter but she couldn't be bothered to get up and do anything about it.

She took off her make-up, not being as thorough as she would have been at night, for she would be replacing it as soon as she had taken a quick shower to wake herself up.

By 5.15 she and Nikki were standing in the hallway of the main house. Joe came out of the drawing-room to greet them.

'Hello you two.' He kissed Annetta on the cheek then bent down to embrace his grandson. 'So how's it going, Smiley?'

'Great, Joe. Pete and I played baseball today and our team won. I scored the most runs.' His face beamed as he released this information which he had saved until they got to his grandfather.

'Well done, kiddo.' He gave his grandson a gentle punch on the shoulder. 'Now go and find Lana – she's waiting for you in the sitting-room. Then I'll join you after I've had a chat with your mother and you can tell me all about it.'

Annetta and Joe went into the drawing-room. Anthony stood up and took a step forward, 'Annetta.'

'Anthony, how are you?' she brushed his cheek with a kiss. 'How was Washington?'

'Splendid, but those things are such a lot of hard work. I'm looking forward to a relaxing weekend.'

She sat down and the men followed suit. She supposed a weekend with just one senator to dinner would be considered relaxing for somebody as ambitious as Anthony.

'Well, let's get our meeting over, then we can all relax for the weekend,' said Joe.

The mood in the room changed slightly as they got down to the business in hand. No problems arose, as Annetta had envisaged. A little concern was voiced by both the men as to who should interview the women in the areas of conflict mapped out in the overview.

Annetta waffled over the question, not saying directly that she thought it should be her. She knew the problems she had encountered in El Salvador last March were at the front of Joe's mind and that he would have discussed his fears with Anthony before she arrived. She had no intention of starting shooting on the part of the documentary she had mentioned until September. By then she felt that a lot more water would have gone under the bridge and it would be easier to convince her loved ones that she was the one for the job.

They wrapped up the meeting fairly quickly. Joe suggested that they all join Lana and Nikki in the sitting-room before they went to dress for dinner.

As Annetta got up she felt her legs giving way and her mind becoming totally disorientated.

'Annetta, Annetta.' She could hear her name being called in the distance. Somebody was gently slapping her face. She opened her eyes but everything was hazy and a nauseous pain shot across the back of them. She closed them for a moment before trying again.

As her focus returned she realised Anthony Lawless was sitting beside her, holding her hand. She instinctively pulled it away.

'Annetta, it's all right, you fainted. I carried you up here and Joe has gone to get Lana.'

She sat up, realising she was on Joe and Lana's bed. At that moment Lana appeared at the door.

'Oh, my poor darling, what happened?' She came over and put her arms around the still hazy Annetta.

'Where's Nikki.'

'It's all right, Nikki doesn't know what happened. Joe didn't want him worried.'

'Good,' said Annetta, feeling a little more life flowing back into her body. 'I think I have the flu. I felt dreadful after lunch so I went to bed and fell asleep until Nikki came home. Perhaps I should have stayed in bed.'

'I think I should call the doctor, Annetta, you don't look well,' Lana said, very concerned with her daughter-in-law's appearance.

'No, I'm sure it's nothing, Lana. I just need to sleep it off.'

'We'll stay here for a bit, and when you feel like it, I'll take you home and wait with you until James gets back.'

Annetta turned to Anthony. 'Thank you for scooping me up.'

'I felt like a Elizabethan cavalier, saving a damsel in distress,' he said, winking at her behind Lana's back.

God, the man was impossible. Fate had intervened so that he ended up having her completely at his mercy, even though it was for only a few minutes. She had literally been putty in his hands.

Just the thought of Anthony holding her in his arms had brought the blood back to her face. She swung her legs over the side of the bed and waited a minute, testing how she felt. She seemed a lot better, the pain in her head had gone and her legs belonged to her once more.

'I think I feel all right now,' she said to Lana. 'I would rather go home and get into my own bed. You and Joe are expecting guests this evening and I'm occupying your bedroom.' She got to her feet, and with Lana one side of her and Anthony the other, she walked across to her part of the house. Anthony waited downstairs while Lana made sure Annetta got into her own bed safely.

'There's no need to stay, Lana. James will be here shortly and the telephone is by my bed if I need to call you,' she said, trying not to sound as fatigued as she felt.

'All right, dear, perhaps you'll be able to sleep if I leave you. I'll call in about an hour and see what you and James want to do about dinner; he may decide to stay here with you; if so, I'll get the chef to have something sent over for you both.'

'Thank you, Lana, what would I do without you?' she managed a weary smile.

'What would we do without you? Now, you get yourself better by the morning or I will insist that James calls the doctor. I'll tell Nikki you popped home because you weren't feeling very well; he can stay with Joe and me for a bit longer.'

She lay in bed waiting for James to come home and as soon as she heard him downstairs she began to feel better. Just like his son earlier, he began to call through the house.

'Annetta, Annetta!'

'I'm up here in the bedroom.'

She heard him come up the stairs two at a time, as was his habit. He pushed open the door.

'What are you doing in bed, sweetheart?' He came over to her and kissed her. 'Are you ill or just waiting for me to join you?'

'I think I have the flu. I fainted in your parents' drawing-room. It was terribly theatrical.'

'Oh no, don't tell me Anthony picked you up in his arms and laid you on the sofa?'

'No, worse, he took me upstairs and laid me on your mother's bed,' she chuckled.

'How do you feel now?' He searched her face.

'Better, but I don't want to risk going to dinner tonight – falling at the feet of the senator would be too embarrassing. You go. Your mother said she would organise food for me here.'

'No, I don't feel like leaving you. I'll call mom now and tell her you need me here. We'll have dinner alone, here in the bedroom, and I'll open a bottle of Domaine de Bouscarela and we'll talk about France.

Neither of them was aware at that moment just how many similar evenings they would be sharing in the next eighteen months.

The following day Annetta felt a lot better. They joined in the weekend house party and her flu was put down to something she had eaten. However, by the end of February she was in no doubt that there was something very wrong with her health. She had noticed tiny lumps under her arms at the side of her breasts. She called Dr Bennett and made an appointment to see him.

She sat across the desk from him knowing the answer before he spoke.

'I'm afraid it's a recurrence of your cancer, Mrs Minnelli.'

This time she wasn't afraid. 'I thought so, Dr Bennett. Can you treat me?'

'Yes, of course; you responded very well last time, there is no reason why you shouldn't again.'

He looked down at her notes. 'I see you were a war correspondent. Were you ever in Vietnam?'

'Yes, I was very high profile at the time. I got all the best jobs.' She laughed at her contradictory statement.

'Were you ever exposed to Agent Orange?'

'Yes, I suppose I must have been. I reported on the environmental devastation it caused.'

'Well there have been a lot of Vietnam vets diagnosed with cancers similar to yours. There is definitely a link between this type of cancer and Agent Orange.'

'Yes, doctor, I know. I recently read an article about that. I did wonder when I read it if that was the cause of my cancer.'

They spent the rest of her visit philosophising about war and its innocent victims. Annetta left feeling more helpless than she had ever done before about the world's problems now she had joined the ranks of the victims.

Treatment for her returned cancer was to be started the following week. She went home to tell her family and organise her work schedule around her treatment. It seemed ironic to her that the Vietnam War had turned itself into a mini war within her body. She wondered if she should incorporate her personal war experiences into the script, but decided it would be too exhausting to play herself and fight her illness.

James took the news like the fighter he was.

'OK, Net, we did it once, we can do it again, and this time we have Le Manoir de la Bouscarela to look forward too. It's a dream we have to make come true.'

This time it seemed a long fight, but by September she had the all-clear. Her cancer had once more gone into remission. The only problem was her documentary was now six months behind schedule. Neither of her co-directors was worried, but she herself was anxious as she saw this as her most important project and she was determined to finish it.

James insisted they went to France after her all-clear in September. The coach-house was now ready to furnish and he wanted to take Annetta there and play house for a week or two.

'James, I am supposed to be shooting in the Lebanon, Northern Ireland and the West Bank this month. At least let one part of my disrupted project stay on schedule.'

'But why do you have to go, Annetta? Its dangerous out there and you have been ill. If anything happens to you, you won't have the resistance to fight.'

'James, I am at war with my own body. We may have called a ceasefire for the moment, but I have a feeling that the enemy will be back to fight another day.'

'Well, that's still no reason to go to Lebanon and get yourself killed.'

'Why should I be killed in Lebanon and not Northern Ireland?

Do you know, James, if you ask small children to draw a picture in a school there, in the worst areas, they won't draw houses and trees, sunshine and pets going for walks with mummy and daddy. They draw soldiers killing people and people killing soldiers. A picture is worth a thousand words, James.'

'But why does it have to be you that goes?' He was losing his patience with her stubborn attitude.

'Because I know what it is to fight the enemy within. Mine is my cancer, theirs is hatred. Hatred is just as destructive, it eats away at the spirit. The mothers of those children have to help them every day to see the sunshine. They have to fight their own confusion and pain, to love their children and give them hope. It's a lot of hard work for those mothers, James, just to try and keep everything as normal as possible. What would happen to the children if the mothers gave up hope? Those mothers need to know how much respect they deserve and that people do know how hard they fight for their children's future.'

'Annetta,' he drew her towards him, tears in his eyes, 'it's just that I love you so much and you being ill has made me realise that I could lose you. Somehow I don't feel the same old invincible James. I've always had everything I wanted in life, it has always gone my way. This is a new experience for me.'

She looked up at him and straight into his eyes, trying to replenish his emotional energy with love from her own.

'James, I promised you I wouldn't get killed. I keep my promises.'

'True.' But he said it without the normal ring that this code word was supposed to have between them. It was supposed to mean, 'Yes, I totally agree with you and I'm on your wavelength.' Somehow his 'true' came across with a 'I hope you're right' feel about it.

She didn't go on the shoot. She sent somebody else instead. Not because James wouldn't have let her go but because he would. She saw how tired he was and for the first time realised what a terrible strain her illness had been on him. He needed some tender love and care and he deserved it.

They went to France and stayed in St Tropez. They bought furniture for the coach-house and planned to come back in the spring and stay there. She told the crew not to send her the dailies, she would see it all when she got back. After accepting how selfish she had been over her work, she wanted to put all of her energy into her holiday with James.

It was James's honest statement that had made her realise how brave he was and how protected he had been. She had got used to the tragedies of life. She had seen so much suffering at close quarters that somehow the silver-spoon existence of James's world had always been a balance for her. But for James, it was all he knew. Nothing totally devastating had ever happened to him before. The thought of her being killed or dying had only been a thought, never a feeling. Things like that only happened to other people in James's world. James was the one who married the princess and bought her a fairy-tale castle and they lived happily ever after. For the first time in his life he wasn't writing his own script. He was losing direction and she had to be there for him one hundred per cent.

Nothing could stand in the way of the magic that La Bouscarela held for them and by the end of the holiday they were strolling in the gardens planning when they would renovate the house and deciding if they should build a tennis court now or later. Their dream was firmly on course by the time they boarded the plane for America.

It was the end of October. Annetta sat at her desk staring out of the window. She never regretted her decision to go with James to France but what she did regret was sending somebody else with the film crew to do her job. As soon as she saw the rushes, she knew the essence of what she had wanted exposed wasn't there. It wasn't anybody's fault, it had been just too difficult for someone else to express what she needed. The feeling was inside her and depended on her creativity to bring it out.

She didn't know quite what to do. The material wasn't bad it just had something missing. That 'something' she would have brought out in her interviews and it was crucial. She could do the whole thing again, but it would put them dreadfully over budget and she didn't have a good enough reason to do that. Also she knew Joe and Anthony would never agree if she approached them. They had joined ranks with James in the kid-glove treatment. A feeling of hopelessness came over her. Just this year, Anwar Sadat had been assassinated. President Reagan and the Pope had been shot. The Queen had been shot at with blank bullets and there had been riots all over the place. What was happening to the world?

Everything was ready to go by the beginning of January. All the editing had been done and her documentary was ready to assemble. She just couldn't bring herself to finish it.

She wrote notes to herself, and everybody else, as to what to cut, but didn't send them. Everybody she employed was freelance, so she had no permanent staff or studio to up-keep. She could put the documentary on hold for as long as she liked. As far as her business partners were concerned they saw her as a charity organisation and therefore any money lost, within reason, was written off as a tax loss and her budgets were always accepted, after discussion with the relevant accountant. Perhaps she should shelve it and go to them after April for more money to re-shoot the 'women in long-term conflict' part that she was so unhappy with. By then she would be physically strong again and they wouldn't refuse her.

She finally decided that this is what she would do and once she had made the decision she felt better. When the time was right, it would be ready and not before.

At the end of March, Annetta's cancer returned. The war within her body was on again. This time she didn't respond to the treatment and by July, after having followed up every second opinion, Annetta asked James if she could go back to Ireland.

'James, we both have to face the fact that, failing a miracle, I am going to die within a few months. I would like to go back to the country where I was born for that. I am not being negative, and I will fight for as long as I have to, but at this point I want to fight in West Cork.'

They were eating supper in their bedroom. Annetta was in bed and James sat at a table beside her.

'OK, sweetheart, if you feel up to it we can go next week. Anthony has already offered his plane if we need it.' His voice was flat and weary; he had been anticipating this conversation for the past month, but it still choked him when it came.

They flew to Dublin the following week. Annetta was having a slight remission and felt quite able to make the long-haul flight. Mrs O'Brian had everything ready when they arrived and her usual off-hand manner had been replaced by genuine warmth and concern. She offered to come in every day and 'do what was necessary', as she put it.

Annetta saw that her major challenge was to prepare her husband and son for her death. She had already faced its shadow herself and she wasn't afraid. But to leave James and Nikki emotionally unprepared, was something she could not do. Her body may be dying, but never had she been more in touch with her spirit.

The clarity with which she saw things at her weakest moments startled her and she tried to hang on to this in the exchange of energies as she temporarlily regained her physical strength. She spent many hours trying to explain this to James. She wanted to help him to understand that things didn't die, just changed. That their love would never die, just change. The energy of her love would always be there for him if he allowed himself to embrace it. The love would have changed into a spiritual love, but it was still the same love. He knew her as he knew himself and the more he understood himself, the more he would know her. He was a young man still, he must not live in the past, that wouldn't be any good for Nikki; he must stay strong and positive. If he looked forward, life would unfold as it was meant to. He had to believe that and keep his trust in life. She fought her illness because she fought for time. Time to prepare her family for what she had already accepted.

On 8 September 1982, Annetta Minnelli, née Peterson, died. She never completed her documentary.

The church was packed for the funeral service. James was still so stunned he went through the whole day in limbo as pain and desolation gripped his heart. Joe and Lana stayed strong in their own wretchedness, giving him all the support he needed to get through the ordeal. Annetta's parents were there for him too as he struggled to cope with the reality of the day.

Anthony Lawless did not go to the service. He couldn't face up to his true feelings for Annetta and seemed personally angry with her. How dare she die. It put him in a black mood. Then, for months afterwards, whenever he thought about her, which was more often that he liked to admit, the thought of his pursuit of her preyed on his mind; the fact that he would never have the chance to possess her left unfinished business in his soul.

He wrote James a letter of condolence and excused himself from attending the funeral because of ill health.

James didn't cry until he got back to Eagles' Ridge. He had wanted to before, but he could feel nothing, he was numb with grief. Once he did cry, his tears came from his very bones. Every night, for the next month, he went to bed and wept the soul-binding tears of a lost heart. Every day he learned what love was. The daily sound of the kind word. The smile, the knowing glance, the phone call, the soft touch, the smell of her scent still in the closet, the support of an idea, cherished dreams, valuing, empathy, openness. All of these things he had shared with Annetta. All of his life was expressed through his love for her. Now he had to deal with loss as she had told him he must. 'Don't put your feelings on hold, James, you must go through the whole transition of loss, for your sake and Nikki's. Remember the tears that flow are the ones that heal. I want you to heal, James, not live the rest of your life half a man. Use loss to expand your compassion and deepen your wisdom. Don't let the pain of it set into a hard heart.'

Joe and Lana were there for him and they were patient with his gnawing sorrow. Lana didn't allow him to become crushed by his grieving; she was there to listen when he needed to talk, to cry with him when he needed to cry and to try and fill the gap Annetta had left in his and Nikki's life.

Time was his greatest healer and gradually he began to function again. It took him a long while to want to do anything socially outside his immediate family but after the first six months he put his whole heart back into his work, making sure that all his free time was spent with Nikki. It was two full years after Annetta's death before he felt ready to face the world as a man alone.

He had gone straight into that world and met Tina. He had met her at a dinner party in London, given by mutual friends. She had shown a lot of sensitivity to his mood that evening. He had felt alone in the group and sorry he had accepted the invitation. It was still too soon after Annetta's death to leave his mourning at home and feel natural in a crowd. Tina seemed so small and vulnerable, and he felt a strong need to protect her. In her eyes he saw sorrow and loneliness and he wanted to hold her close and hug away the pain. His or hers, he wasn't sure. At that moment they were the same.

They left the party together and James followed Tina to her house in Grosvenor Square. They had spent the rest of the night drinking and talking. At five-thirty in the morning when James left, he didn't feel quite so alone and Tina Obstroullias was in love.

The following weekend was spent together on her yacht, where Tina learnt for the first time how tender and sensitive love-making could be. There was no theatre involved. This was a man who truly wanted to give pleasure for its own sake, not to display his macho ego.

That weekend she decided she would marry James. He would belong to her. This terrible need for ownership of things and people was an obsession Tina could indulge. Very few people said no to a woman as rich and powerful as Tina Obstroullias.

She showed genuine interest in his knowledge of and passion for wine. Even so, he did not tell her about La Bouscarela. He wasn't ready to share that. She played on his tender emotions, sharing some of her sad past. She told him about her own tragic love affair, with a man whose name she couldn't mention because she wanted to respect his marriage. How they had decided after great discussion and soul searching, on both their parts, that he should stay with his wife. This was the only answer to their dilemma, as his wife was mentally unstable. Then the terrible pain and anguish that followed and how it had taken her over two years to feel ready to trust life again.

'When I first met him, I didn't know he was married. He was introduced to me as a business adviser,' she said timidly, as if she were a victim of her money. 'I had a lot of property in America which I needed to take advice on.' She sighed. 'We became lovers, then I learnt he was married . . . ' she gulped back the pain of this knowledge . . . 'very unhappily to a woman who was mentally unstable.' Her face was filled with compassion for this poor deranged women. 'A temperamental artist living in a dream world. He felt he couldn't leave her as she couldn't have coped on her own. So, after a painful goodbye, we got on with our own lives.'

'Poor love, I know how hard it is to come to terms with loss and unfulfilled dreams; but we must, Tina, we owe it to life.' James felt his heart go out to this kind, sensitive woman.

She watched for his moods, gave him his space and tried to mimic what she thought he wanted in a woman, and gradually became part of his life. She tried to get on with Nikki when James finally introduced them, after two years. It didn't work. Nikki did not like her. She tried to be patient over his keeping Annetta's house in Ireland and going there every summer with Nikki. But after the third year she put her foot down.

'You keep that place as a shrine to your wife, James.' Her reproach had a venomous tone.

'That's not true, Tina. I keep it because Nikki loves to go there and one day it will be his.' He could feel his anger rising, as it so often did with Tina of late.

After that they continually argued about the house; she wanted him to sell it. They came to a compromise and he said that he would let it. He told Nikki he had done this because he wanted them both to stay with friends in Bordeaux so during the summer Nikki could work on his French. Nikki accepted the statement without question; as long as he was alone with his father for the summer holidays, he was happy to go to France and improve his French.

As their relationship deteriorated, James was pleased he had never told Tina about Le Manoir de la Bouscarela. One day when Nikki was older, and happily married, it would be his gift to his son, but only then would he share the secret he and Annetta had kept so well.

Life with Tina became more and more confused; after the sixth year he decided they were destroying each other and should go their separate ways. Raving with anguish, she threatened to commit suicide and frightened him so much that he hadn't the nerve to try again. Now she had given him the ultimatum – marry her or ... The question hung in the air. Would she kill herself? He wasn't sure; for the last two years she had hardly given him room to breathe, let alone think. It wasn't as if he expected to replace what he had had with Annetta, he knew that was impossible. But Tina's love gave nothing back. It was all controlling, all demanding. She grasped at his love like a drowning woman and made him feel guilty. Or was it that he felt guilty because he wasn't being honest?

He had insisted on having this time alone. Perhaps that's how he should stay. Alone was at least honest. He hoped he hadn't used Tina, because he certainly felt used. Perhaps they had used each other.

James looked across at Anthony, who was still engrossed in his paperwork. The steward went up to him.

'We'll be landing in ten minutes, Mr Lawless.'

Anthony nodded at the steward, 'Thank you.' He turned to James.

'Well James, did you enjoy your sleep?'

'Just been resting my eyes, Anthony; it's nice up here above the clouds.' Suddenly back in the present, his mind was clear and he knew what he must do.

Anthony Lawless smiled at his friend,

'Go for power, James, as I've already told you. It works.'

Destiny

Georgina and Jasmin arrived at Drummossie House in time for tea. As their car reached the top of the drive, they were greeted by three exited labradors and a springer spaniel. Jane and Camilla came out of the house to welcome them.

'Camilla has grown into a beauty,' thought Georgina as Camilla came up to kiss her godmother.

'Hello, Georgie.'

'Camilla, you're as tall as me. I have been away far too long; you were just a girl the last time I saw you and here you are a beautiful young woman.'

'Well, I'm eighteen today,' she said proudly.

'Yes, I know, darling, happy birthday. I've brought you something all the way from Provence.'

She turned her attention to Jane who had been talking to Jasmin.

'Thank you for coming all this way, Georgie. It's lovely to see you again. I know we keep in touch on the telephone, but it isn't the same, you look marvellous.' Jane greeted her French-style, with a kiss on either cheek.

'So do you, Jane. How is Marcus?'

'Oh, he's fine. You can guess where he is.'

'Fishing.' They both laughed.

Come on into the house and have some tea, then we can catch up on all the news. Leave the bags there and I'll get Billie to take them up for you.'

Billie MacClean was the general factotum at Drummossie. He cleaned Marcus's guns, plucked game, cleaned salmon, chopped wood, washed cars and did a million and one other jobs that made life run smoothly.

Marcus was a perfectionist and his home had to be in perfect order at all times. A speck of dust could send him into a wild fury.

They sat in the morning-room and by the time they had finished tea it was as if it were a matter of days rather than seven years since they had seen each other. Jasmin and Camilla excused themselves to go to Camilla's room and play music.

'Will Duncan be here this evening?' said Georgina when the girls had left the room.

'Yes, but later; he's driving over from Edinburgh after he finishes work.'

Duncan, Jane's son, was one year older than Georgina's son Giles.

'Does he like his job?'

'Yes he loves it. How is Giles?'

He's still sulking in his pet-food factory. I don't know how to help him. If he were happy, I wouldn't mind what he did.' Georgina sighed at the thought of her son.

'Some children take longer to grow up than others, Georgie. Giles is a charming sensitive boy; one day he will be a charming sensitive man. He just needs to find himself; don't let his physical age confuse you.'

'Your right, Jane. Oh, it's so good to be here.'

'Anyway, Georgie, what about your life. It's fun having a friend who is such a well-known artist. I'm really proud of you.'

'Thank you, Jane.' She smiled at her friend. 'There's nothing to tell really. I'm happy. I love my work and living in France.'

'What about men?'

'There's nobody at the moment. I'm involved with my work and Jasmin.'

'But Jasmin will be going to university this year. Once they do that they leave home, Georgie.'

'I know, Jane. I think about how different life will be without her around as much.' She reflected for a moment. 'I do meet men. In fact, I've just finished seeing someone who has been in my life for the past six months.'

'French or English.'

'French, a charming companion, but he was too young.'

'I wouldn't complain about that.' Jane grinned.

Georgina laughed. 'No, but he had never been married, never had any responsibility and needed too much attention.'

'Most men need too much attention, darling,' Jane replied, thinking about Marcus.

'You're right. I suppose he just wasn't the one for me.'

'What about that gorgeous man you rent your house from?'

'Samir is one of my closest friends – he's a wonderful human being.'

'Were you two ever lovers?' Jane had always been intrigued by Georgina's friendship with Samir Hariri.

'No, never. I often think about that. Perhaps it's because we started of as friends and over the years neither one of us wanted to take the risk of changing the status quo. We don't see each other very much but we keep in touch regularly over the telephone. He's an incredibly busy man and his work keeps him in America.'

'How about Paul, do you see very much of him?'

'A bit, he has been very supportive since our divorce and over the past few years he has taken to calling me when he has girlfriend trouble; he's become like another son.'

'Well, from what I hear his girlfriends are young enough to be your daughters.'

'I know Paul is impossible but he is good fun and there's no real harm in him; it's just that he's like Peter Pan, he never wants to grow up.'

'Well, I must say your attitude towards him is very generous.'

'Paul never meant to hurt me, Jane. I was just in his play; it's because I didn't like my part in the script that we parted company.'

'I don't know if I could be so forgiving to Marcus.'

'That's because you fell in love with Marcus. I fell in love with an illusion, the man I *thought* Paul was. When I found out the man I had fallen in love with didn't exist, all that was left was my friend Paul.'

'Oh, Georgie, we have so much to catch up on – but I have to go and see that everything is ready for tonight. Come and have a look at the marquee.'

They got up and went into the hall then across to the dining-room. The marquee had been erected on the lawn in front of the dining-room. It was entered by a covered vestibule leading from the French windows.

They went inside, it looked lovely. Jane had chosen soft heather colours for the flowers and there were bunches of heather on all the dining tables. The tables had been placed around the edge of the marquee and a wooden dance-floor had been put down in the middle with a disco next to it.

The women were standing discussing the plans for the weekend when Marcus Stevens walk in. They both looked across at him.

'Hello, Marcus.'

'Georgie.' He came over and kissed her cheek. 'Your looking fit, darling.'

'So are you.' She smiled as she pressed the fat on his stomach.

'Well, Jane likes me that way, don't you, darling.'

She looked at Georgina and pulled a face. 'I don't have a choice, Georgie.'

'Is everything ready for tonight?' He directed his question at Jane.

'Yes, I've double-checked everything.'

'Good, what time is Duncan arriving.'

'Late and there will be no time to go down to the river when he gets back.'

'OK, darling, point taken. I think I'll go and get myself a drink before I get changed. How about you girls?'

'No, thank you, Marcus,' said Georgina. 'I think I would like to go up and sort out my clothes for this evening.'

'I'll show you your room.' Jane put her arm on her friend's elbow and guided her out of the marquee. She looked back at her husband. 'I'll join you for a drink in a moment, Marcus; there are a few things I want to discuss with you about tomorrow.'

They went upstairs. 'I've put Jasmin in here with you; it's a full house this weekend. Anthony Lawless and his guest are staying at Tulcan Lodge – there was no room for them in the house.'

'Anthony Lawless? I haven't seen him in years. He seems to have made a name for himself.'

'Marcus is involved with him in some business deal they're putting together.'

'I don't know anybody who doesn't seem to be doing business with Anthony Lawless these days.'

'Does Paul see much of him?'

'Yes, I think they still have a few things they are involved in together. But Paul isn't so impressed with him as he used to be.

When we first married, that name drove me mad. Talk about hero worship,'

'Well, he's a man's man – and a ladies' man come to that.' She gave Georgina a mischievous grin. 'I've heard he doesn't wear underpants so that he can get his willie out quicker.'

'Oh, Jane, do you think that's true?' she laughed. 'That's what I told Jasmin yesterday in the car.'

'Yes, a friend of mine who has knowledge of the Lawless willie told me, so be warned, Georgie.'

'I don't think Anthony Lawless has ever really noticed me. Whenever I met him with Paul, I always felt as if I was in the way. Perhaps he knew how much I disliked him.'

'No, I don't think that would enter his head. He is in the world purely for his own self-gratification; he probably thought that you were shy from adoration; his own self-worship knows no bounds.'

'You don't like him either, Jane.' She searched her friend's face.

'It's not a question of not liking him, Georgie. With that magnificent speaking voice of his he only has to open his mouth and he has my full attention. He's big and bad and he fascinates me. It's just that I know danger when I see it and I'm far too astute a businesswoman ever to let him have anything on Marcus.'

Georgina was unpacking her suitcase and Jane was helping her hang up and put away her clothes while they talked.

'I don't know his guest; all I know about him is that he is an American from California. Perhaps you will know him, you lived there for a while.'

'I doubt it, Jane. California is a big place with thirty million people living in it. I never got to know many people who were important enough for Anthony Lawless to be interested in.'

'Anyway, Georgie, I would have taken more interest in him if he were single. I always hope to find a nice man to look after you one day.'

'But I have nice men to look after me. Paul helps me with all of my business affairs and Samir is only a phonecall away.'

'Oh, Georgie, you know what I mean, someone to keep you warm at night.'

'Don't worry about that, Jane; as I've already said, there have always been plenty of those. France is the land of love remember.'

'Sometimes, Georgina Fox, I envy you your life.'

'No you don't, Jane, you love being the *grande dame* and holding court.'

'Yes, I suppose you're right – talking of which I promised Marcus that I would have a drink with him. I want to go over a few things about tomorrow before I forget. See you in the drawing-room around seven-thirty.'

Georgina lay on the bed while her bath ran, thinking how good it was to see Jane again and to find the same person she had known as a child underneath the professional hostess mask she wore in company.

She had good feelings about her stay here and getting in touch with her past. She looked over at the dress, hanging on the wardrobe door, she had decided to wear for Camilla's party. She had bought it in St Tropez: it was long-sleeved and backless and the fabric was the most exquisite black lace; it was cut very short, as the fashion dictated, and she was glad her legs were still good enough to get away with it. She tried to exercise every day – a habit left over from California. During the summer she swam and during the winter she went to the gym. She would often go for long walks in the hills where she lived, taking in the colours and the smells of the sur-roundings which inspired her work.

Her hair was very blonde from the sun and the white streaks that age had put at her temples had been exaggerated by the hairdresser into highlights around her face. She was tanned and looked healthy; she knew time had been kind to her. The confidence she now possessed had been hard earned and it matched the good looks nature had given her.

Jasmin came into the room in a flurry of excitement. 'Guess who's coming to the party.'

Georgina had to smile to herself; her daughter was permanently on overdrive. 'No, who?'

'Tom Ashley.' He eyes were shining with excitement.

'Do I know him?' She looked blankly at Jasmin.

'Yes, mummy, of course you do, he's Sally Ashley's brother. They all came to stay one year when they were inter-railing, Don't you remember.'

'Jasmin our house was a campsite for most of the summer with all of your inter-railing friends. I think I remember Sally but I don't remember Tom.'

'Well, anyway, he's gorgeous and Camilla says he fancies me.'

'It sounds as if you are all going to have fun tonight.' She got up from the bed. 'I'm going to take my bath now but you can tell me all Camilla's news while I soak.'

Georgina was the last in the drawing-room; all of the other guests were engrossed in conversation when she arrived. She knew all of their faces as they were old friends. Camilla's godfather Nigel Scott was the first one she went up to, to shake hands. It seemed so alien, after living in France where friends kissed each other, but the warmth of the greeting was still there in the handshake.

'Georgina, it's been a long time but you just get better and better.'

'Thank you, Nigel, and you still as charming as ever.' He had been one of her favourite men friends when they were younger. 'It must be fifteen years since we last saw each other.'

'Yes, it must be about that.' Nigel wanted to linger on the subject but he knew she had to say her hellos.

How time flies, she thought, as she did the rounds of so many old friends.

'I thought it would be more civilised for the adults to stay in here until just before dinner. Camilla wants to welcome her friends herself. They are going straight into the marquee. We are all her guests tonight and she doesn't want me taking over.' Jane laughed as she said this, knowing how true it was.

Georgina was caught up in a hive of gossip. People were asking her about Mac and Lallie and Georgina had to report that Lallie became more eccentric every year but that Mac hadn't changed one bit. They all sympathised over the loss of Uncle Harry, who had been well liked and his cellars well remembered. Georgina was able to catch up on everybody else's news. There were plenty of marriages, births and deaths to be discussed after such a long time apart – and, of course, divorces.

The evening had gone well. Jasmin was in love – but that happened at least once a month. Georgina had danced the night away and Marcus had called all the women darling after midnight and all the men mate – because when he had had a certain amount to drink he could never remember anyone's name and Jane hadn't been at his side to prompt him.

Georgina finally went to bed at three o'clock; the party was still in full swing when she said good-night to Jane.

'Will you be coming out with the guns tomorrow?'

'No, I don't think so, Jane. I would love to sketch the house while everybody is away.'

'Whatever you feel like doing, Georgie, you're our guest. Lie in bed for as long as you like, then wander down to help yourself to breakfast. It will be in the dining-room until ten o'clock; after that you have to go to the kitchen and see Mrs Mackenzie.'

'Thank you, Jane.' She kissed her friend on the cheek and went upstairs.

Slowly taking off her make-up, she thought about the evening and how much she had enjoyed being surrounded with her past. She cleaned her teeth and got into bed, falling asleep almost immediately. The only time she stirred was when Jasmin came into the room at dawn.

She woke about nine-thirty and got up without disturbing Jasmin who would probably sleep until midday. Creeping into the bathroom, she took a quick shower, then put on her jeans and a cotton Blanc Bleu sweater, tied her hair back in a scarf, put on some big gold loop earrings, moisturised her face and applied a hint of colour to her full mouth. Once ready for her day she gently closed the bedroom door behind her as she left.

She arrived in the dining-room at five minutes to ten, just in time to grab some breakfast before it was cleared away. She was the only one there as the shoot had eaten earlier and left. She had let Jasmin sleep knowing she would be quite happy to get something from the kitchen later.

After her glass of orange juice, scrambled eggs, smoked salmon brown bread and butter, with two cups of coffee to follow, she felt ready to explore the gardens of Drummossie.

She knew from her infrequent telephone conversations with Jane that the gardens had become her personal responsibility and joy. She wanted to make some sketches and take some photographs as she planned to paint a watercolour for her as a thank-you present.

She didn't see Jasmin all day and could imagine the two girls locked in conversation, listening to their music in Camilla's bedroom, analysing the birthday party the way she and Jane had done when they were their age. For them every day was an adventure, every experience fresh and new. How she had enjoyed her daughter's growing-up, seeing her blossoming into womanhood with a confidence that she had never possessed at her age. These were the children of the new age, generation X. Her generation had been the children of the big change that had made it all possible, the baby boomers, out-numbering any other age group, important above all for their spending power. Her generation would not grow old gracefully as Mac's generation had done, there was too much money to be made out of them. They would be sold eternal youth because they could afford to pay for that dream. They would be the richest generation of retired people ever. That meant big business.

Over the next ten years some of those same baby boomers would be in positions of real power and she hoped their flower-power philosophy was still central to their thinking. As a student she remembered the make-love-not-war politics of the campus. She hoped they would all remember.

She was sitting on the front lawn, sketch pad in her hand, lost in that other place she always went to when she was engrossed in her work. She was sketching the house.

'Mrs Fox.'

She looked up to see Billie MacClean standing over her.

'Yes, Billie.'

'Mrs Stevens asked me to come and fetch you if you wanted to join the shoot for lunch down by the river.'

'No, thank you, Billie, I'm working on something I want to finish this afternoon. Will you please tell Mrs Stevens thank you for me?'

'Yes, Mrs Fox.' He gave an approving nod to what she was drawing as he left.

By teatime she was ready to stop and went into the house. Mrs Mackenzie had already put the tea tray in the morning-room as if she had expected her at that moment. Jasmin and Camilla came in and joined her for tea.

'Hello, girls, what have you been up to all day?' Their fresh complexions positively glowed, even after such a late night.

'Talking about last night,' said Camilla.

'Did you enjoy your birthday?'

'Yes, thank you, Georgie. Did you?'

'I had a lovely time, thank you, darling. In fact, it's been a long while since I stayed up so late – but it was nothing to you girls. I heard you tiptoeing in with the cockerel, Jasmin.'

'Jasmin's in love.' Camilla gave a dramatic flurry to the words.

'Oh, that must be with Tom Ashley, she told me last night that he was gorgeous.' Enjoying their frivolity, she sighed. 'How wonderful to be young and in and out of love the way you girls are.'

'Duncan is taking us to a party tonight and we are sleeping over,' Jasmin said snuggling into the sofa.

'Oh, I thought you would both be joining the shoot dinner.'

'Boring,' they both answered in unison.

'Come on, girls, we older people aren't that bad, are we?'

'Your not, mummy, neither is Jane. It's just when you all get together it's a bit much.'

'I know what you mean, that's how I feel about your age group.' She smiled at the two fresh young faces which looked back at her in total disbelief that their generation could ever be considered anything but good fun.

'Anyway I'm going upstairs for a nap before I get myself ready for my "boring" evening.'

It was six-thirty and she lay in her bath waiting for Jasmin to fly in and tell her the latest plans for the evening. She was sure they would have changed at least twice since teatime. The door burst open and Jasmin filled the room with commotion.

'Mummy, I can't stop and chat, I'm taking my things for tonight and I'm going to get ready in Camilla's room. Duncan's being a real pain. He came back in a bad mood from the shoot and he and Camilla have had a row and now he says he won't take us to the party. Camilla needs my support to talk him round. If not we will have to get a lift from Billie and go and see Sally.'

'Tom's sister?'

'Yes, but Tom will be at the party with Duncan.'

'Hasn't Sally been invited to the party?'

'Yes but she doesn't want to go because she just broke up with Gordon Grey and he will be at the party.'

'Why don't you ask Billie to drive you and Camilla to the party?'

'Oh, mummy, you don't understand,' she whined, frustrated.

'No, I don't.'

'It would be so embarrassing. It's like when you used to send me on a plane by myself when I was small and they used to pin a label on me like Paddington Bear.'

'Oh.' She tried to work out the connection but couldn't.

'Anyway, I've got to get back to Camilla, love you lots.' She rushed into the bathroom and kissed the top of her mother's head and then disappeared with a final ' 'Bye', round the door.

Georgina pushed herself farther down into the bath tub and, dismissing her daughter's confused conversation, began contemplating what to wear for Jane's special evening. She had better look her best, Jane would be counting on her to. There was even going to be an out-of-favour royal coming.

After she had dried and creamed her body she put on a towelling bathrobe and sat in front of the mirror. She took care over her make-up and her hair, which she brushed until it shone then twisted back into a knot at the nape of her neck. She was satisfied with the chic effect she had created and got up from the mirror to dress.

She put on a beautiful oyster satin embroidered *bustier*. Then her black silk Armani trouser-suit with satin lapels. The jacket was cut on the lines of a man's smoking-jacket, crossing over at the waist and secured by a satin toggle. As for her feet, she decided to go for comfort and put on her black velvet low-heeled shoes with the satin buckles.

She fiddled around in her jewellery case until she found the earrings she was looking for – a pair of Elizabeth Gauge gold discs which reminded her of roman coins. One final glance in the mirror and she was ready to support her hostess.

She arrived in the drawing-room just before seven-thirty to find the only other person in the room was Jane.

'Georgie, you look absolutely stunning, very chic. Yes, *très Française*, but then you're a quarter, aren't you?'

'Oh, you mean Grandma Williamson. Mac says I'm like her.'

'Wasn't there something strange about her? Didn't she see ghosts and things?' Jane asked.

'I don't know what you mean by things, but she did see a ghost once.'

'Have you ever seen a ghost, Georgie?'

'No, Jane, I see things.' She laughed and so did Jane.

If she only knew that I just told her the truth, thought Georgina.

Marcus came into the room with Nigel Scott. They were discussing the day's shooting and didn't notice Georgina and Jane until they were right next to them. They complimented both of the women on their appearance and Marcus asked Georgina where she had been all day.

'I wanted to sketch your house when there weren't five hundred people milling around it and today seemed the only day it would be possible. Tomorrow you have the big change-around and then another lot of guests for the weekend. I don't know how Jane organises everything so well.'

'Army family, darling, remember.'

The guests all began to arrive at once and in no time at all about sixty people had assembled in the drawing-room and the inner hall.

'Anthony Lawless will be late – he always is,' Marcus said to nobody in particular. 'I must say that mate of his shot well today – nice chap, too, for an American.'

Anthony Lawless arrived after eight-thirty; he was even later than the out-of-favour royal whom Jane considered fashionably late. Anthony's tardiness was just downright rude.

Jane was there to receive the apologies and forgive with her perfect balance of charm and grace, leaving Anthony in no doubt that she was the hostess. He, as an invited guest, had been politically incorrect not to have telephoned when he couldn't make a ten-minute journey by eight-fifteen at the latest.

She delivered this message with the softness of a dove and the power of an army boot on the shins.

She directed Anthony and James into the drawing-room. 'Just before we go into dinner I want to introduce you to an old school-friend of mine whom I think you already know, Anthony. She will be sitting on our table this evening.'

They reached Georgina, now deep in conversation with Nigel Scott's second wife, Becky, who was about fifteen years his junior.

'Ladies, I would like to introduce you to two gentlemen who will be on our table this evening, Anthony Lawless and James Minnelli.'

'Anthony! It's been a long time.'

'Good evening, Georgina.' He had forgotten how good looking she was. That full mouth and those high cheekbones and the way she wore her hair off of her face to keep her perfect features uncluttered. Well, not quite perfect – her mouth was too big.

'Lucky she had never had big tits,' he thought, 'otherwise I would have seduced her when she was far too young to know what was going on. Now she's really fuckable.'

'How's Paul?'

'Fine I think, Anthony, but you probably see him more than me these days.'

'Yes, I heard you two got divorced.' She had a confidence about her that wasn't even hinted at when she was young; his thoughts were racing. 'I also heard that you have made quite a name for yourself in the art world.'

'My work sells, Anthony.'

She turned her attention towards James. Anthony was pleased to see she was having the same effect on his friend. He knew James well enough to know that he was also liking the way Mrs Fox looked.

'And did you enjoy your day, Mr Minnelli.' She appraised his looks for the first time. His thick black wavy hair was silver at the temples and the rest had silver running through. He was tall – six foot she imagined – his shoulders were broad and he obviously played a lot of sport because he looked in excellent shape; she knew that if she prodded his stomach, the way she had prodded Marcus, she would find no fat. He was square jawed and had a strong face. His eyes were dark brown and mysterious; it was impossible for her to read them but they were definitely saying something to her.

'It was most enjoyable, Mrs Fox – but please call me James.'

His voice ran through her body and she was transported back in time to Californian beaches and stories of dolphins. It must have been the accent. A colony of butterflies had just taken up residence in her stomach and about four hundred of them were fluttering about at the same moment.

'And I'm Georgina.'

Where had she come from. He had never seen her before that moment and yet it was as if he knew her, had been waiting for her. Just looking at her beautiful face made him feel something he hadn't felt for the longest time. Happy.

They didn't have another chance to speak as Jane came over. 'We are all going into dinner now. Georgina you go with Marcus and everybody else will follow. Becky, you and I will go in with Anthony and James.'

Georgina found herself in between Marcus and the out-of-favour royal, who was on her left. Next to him sat Jane then Anthony, Becky then James who was sitting next to another house guest, her old friend Judy Walker, whom she still saw once a year when she went back to Tarn House for Christmas.

Judy still gave her New Year's Eve party and a bit of rivalry had started up since Jane and Marcus moved to Scotland and now gave their own New Year's Eve party. A number of their mutual friends had been put in the embarrassing position of having to make the choice as to which one they should attend.

Georgina was lucky; she had Mac and Lallie as her excuses for not travelling any farther north. It was good to see Judy there and to know that she and Jane were still friends. Silly situations like rival parties, in small communities like theirs, had been known to cause rifts that would go on for generations. Judy was sitting next to Marcus and she made up the eighth person.

Some of the tables from the previous night had been taken out. While Georgina was having her siesta, a lorry had arrived and taken them away and replaced them with a small stage on which now stood a piano. Jane had booked the Sonnie Brown Jazz Quartet to play for them after dinner. The dance-floor had been moved in front of the stage and the disco lights from the night before had been removed in favour of background lighting strategically placed behind the stage.

'Have you known Jane long?' the out-of-favour royal asked.

'Yes, we were at school together, but this is the first time we've managed to see each other in seven years.'

He asked about her work, he said he knew it and liked it. She asked about his horses and he told her. He held forth at some length and only needed her participation in the form of the odd 'Oh, really' or 'I didn't know that' or 'That's marvellous', which gave her an opportunity to observe the table.

Marcus, Judy and James all seem to be getting on well and Anthony had the full attention of Jane and Becky. She saw Becky falling under his spell and knew he had another victim.

By the time the main course arrived, the conversation around the table had become more open. 'What do you think of the wine, James.' Marcus was proud of his cellar.

James spoke with great authority on his subject without sounding pompous, as so many wine experts do.

The out-of-favour royal asked James about the Californian wine industry and Georgina suddenly realised that this was the man whose family produced her favourite Chardonnay. She thought about Uncle Harry and how he would have enjoyed talking to James.

After that Anthony took control of the conversation, his charm and wit dazzling everybody around the table. Even Georgina had to admit to herself that he certainly knew how to earn his supper.

The quartet took up their positions on the stage ready to play. The saxophonist delivered a few sensuous cords then the music began. Jane nodded to Marcus and they both got up. 'Come along, Georgina and Anthony, let's start the dancing.' She and Marcus went on to the dance-floor and everybody clapped.

Anthony did his hostess's bidding and asked Georgina to dance. The out-of-favour royal escorted Becky and James followed with Judy. The dance-floor began to fill up.

'Jane tells me you live in the South of France now.'

'Yes, I moved there ten years ago after Paul and I separated.'

'Have you married again.'

'No, Anthony, I'm very happy living alone.'

'Alone – but that's a tragedy your far too beautiful.' He squeezed her waist. 'You were made for love.'

'Not your sort of love, Anthony.' She gave him an indomitable look straight in the eye. 'I don't wish to become one of your cast of thousands.'

'Georgina, you exaggerate.' She reminded him of somebody.

'I don't think so, Anthony. Tonight I've watched you seduce Becky Scott; you're a modern-day Bluebeard.'

'I have made her feel like a queen this evening – how can that be wrong.'

'Because after you take her to bed, you will ignore her and she will feel like an ill-used doormat.'

'But, I wouldn't make you feel like that, Georgina. You could teach me how to love, perhaps that's what I'm searching for.'

'Over my dead body, Anthony, you're not capable of loving. To fall in love with you is to fall into the abyss. I've already fallen in once but I've climbed back out; the abyss has nothing to teach me, Anthony. It could teach you a thing or two but you will always be too afraid to learn from it.'

'What could I possibly be afraid of, Georgina.'

'Yourself, Anthony,' she smiled at him.

He laughed. 'Well, let me bed you tonight and discover myself in your sighs.'

'Anthony Lawless, you are impossible.'

As they got back to the table Marcus stood up. 'Come on, Georgie.' She was whisked on to the dance-floor again.

'Another wonderful party, Marcus; thank you for inviting me.'

'Any time, darling, you know you are always welcome.'

'It's been good fun seeing so many familiar faces.'

'Yes, it's a good crowd, and Anthony came up trumps with that friend of his. I like him.'

'I didn't realise that he was the Minnelli winery,' Georgina said, hoping to find out more about James.

'Yes, that's him. Anthony was telling me he is living with Betina Obstroullias. Has been for the past eight years. He thinks they will probably marry. Money goes to money, it's like a compass always finding north.'

At the mention of Tina's name Georgina felt a cold chill go down her back. She didn't think Marcus knew about Paul's affair with Tina. He spoke of her as if Georgina didn't know her, which in truth she didn't. Her dealings with Tina had been brief and Paul hadn't been faithful even to his mistress, which is what Georgina thought Tina must have seen herself as. It is very hard to know people who play games with themselves.

Her feeling of shock was more that somebody like James Minnelli, who had appeared so open and charming, could be involved with a psychotic, an emotional junkie; it didn't make sense.

Paul had told her more about his relationship with Tina, gradually, over the years. About their emotional game-playing and sexual fantasies; he hadn't elaborated but she got the idea from reading between the lines that it was a no-limits relationship. Once he had said to her that even playing with death hadn't been out of the question.

'Are you all right, Georgie.' Marcus's voice bought her back to the present.

'Yes, I'm fine. I was just taking a trip down memory lane.'

'We all go back a long way, don't we. It's our twenty-fifth wedding anniversary next year. Jane's already started talking about the party.'

She laughed with him. 'Jane loves a party.'

Towards the end of the evening, after dancing with the out-of-favour royal and several of her old friends, she was asked to dance by James.

'You're very popular, Georgina. It seems that every man here wants to dance with you. If you're not too tired perhaps you would put me at the top of your *carnet de bal*.'

'How could I refuse such a gallant request, James.'

Sonnie Brown had learnt to include a lot of popular music when he did 'parties', as he described all functions outside a jazz club – the latter where he played for love the former where he played for money. He had modelled his voice on George Benson's and had adapted a lot of pop classics to suit his style.

As they walked on to the dance-floor the saxophone went into a solo, then the band joined in and Sonnie delivered his adaptation of 'Will You Still Love Me Tomorrow'.

All evening she had been in the arms of different men. Some had held her too tightly, some too loosely, some, like Anthony, too suggestively. She was reminded of Goldilocks when she decided that this man held her just right.

He smiled down at her. 'Jane tells me you live in France, Georgina.'

'Yes I rent a charming old farmhouse from a friend of mind, up in the hills outside St Tropez. My family call it 'Sam's place'. Samir Hariri is the friend I rent it from and we call him Sam.'

'He's a writer, isn't he?'

'Among other things, yes.'

'Yes, I met him once a long time ago.' He remembered how much Annetta had admired the man. 'Have you lived in France long?'

'About ten years. It's home for me now. I don't think I would ever want to come back to England.'

'I've also been told that you're an artist but I have to be honest and say I don't know your work.'

'I'm not offended, James, not everybody is interested in art. I, on the other hand, do know of your wine. I lived in La Jolla for a short while before I moved to France. I was introduced to your Chardonnay by a friend and it became a favourite of mine. When you were talking about wine earlier this evening you reminded me of him. You have the same accent and you have found your bliss, which is how my mother describes being completely fulfilled with what one is doing.'

'Your mother sounds like a very wise woman.'

'Yes, she is.'

'Did you enjoy living in La Jolla?'

'Yes, I did, it was good for me.' She absorbed the truth in her own statement. 'My daughter went to school there for a while and we share some happy memories.'

'Do you have any other children?'

'I have two sons. What about you, James.'

'I have a son. He will be twenty on Christmas Day.'

'I expect you named him Nicholas.' Her smile was infectious.

'Yes,' he laughed. 'We are all so obvious, Georgina.'

'True but that's what makes life so wonderful.'

He held her a little tighter and she let her head rest on his chest. Her warmth and her scent flowed through his senses. He wanted this woman, wanted to make love to her. Not out of loneliness and pity nor out of wanton or physical lust. He wanted her for the way she made him feel, to discover her and share himself with her. To find his bliss with her, he liked that word and he knew he would like her mother.

The band played George Benson's 'In Your Eyes', and Sonnie didn't give his own rendition, he just mimicked George. There was no need to mess with perfection was how he saw it.

For the first time in ten years James began to think of the future and not dwell in the past.

'I sometimes have to go to the South of France on business, perhaps I could call you when I do and take you out to dinner.'

'Yes, James, I would like that very much.' She didn't give a second thought to Tina.

188

Politeness dictated that they went back to the group but he wanted to be alone with her. As they were going back to the table he decided to ask her if she would like to go for a walk in the gardens, but before he could mention it, Anthony was in front of them and Georgina was yet again whisked away.

The band began to play 'When a Man Loves a Woman' and Anthony held her so close that she could feel that infamous willie of his.

'I see you were getting on well with James,' he said, enjoying the nearness of their bodies.

'He speaks excellent French, Anthony,' she said, discreetly trying to push away.

'Good-looking bastard, too.'

'Yes, I had noticed.'

'So has Betina Obstroullias; he is about to marry her.'

'Is he really, Anthony?' She wasn't interested in what he had to say on the subject.

'Yes, he's known Tina a long time.' There was a pause in the conversation. 'He never really got over his wife's death. I don't think he ever will, he worshipped her.'

'How long ago was that.' Now she was interested.

'Almost ten years. Tragic business, cancer, she fought very hard but in the end she had to give up.'

'Oh, how terribly sad.' She hadn't known James was a widower; he could have been only around forty when his wife died.

'Yes, nobody will ever replace her. I think Tina understands that.'

Georgina thought how hard it would be to deal with the other woman when the other woman was dead. She didn't envy Tina the unfair competition.

She wondered why he didn't mention his wife in their conversation and remembered she didn't mention Paul. It hadn't been that sort of conversation.

As soon as the band stopped playing she eased herself out of Anthony's grip. There would be no second dance if she could help it.

'I need to sit down, Anthony. I've been dancing all night.'

'Of course, Georgina, I noticed your dance card seemed full.'

'I was at a teenage party here last night. I'm not accustomed to a social whirl. I live just outside a village of only twelve hundred people.'

'Yes, but you come to London quite a bit don't you,' he said as he escorted her off the dance-floor.

'About once a month – scarcely that, if I can help it.'

He gave her a sly grin. 'Georgina, I think your social life is a lot fuller then you would have us believe. You hardly look nun material to me.'

'I won't answer that, Anthony.'

A lot of people had started to leave. Jane and Marcus were busy accepting congratulations on the success of the evening and saying their goodbyes.

Georgina sat down; she really was tired. To her relief, Anthony had left her and she noticed he was talking to Becky. Poor Becky she thought.

'Georgina.' It was James.

'Why is Anthony the way he is?' She said this without thinking, as if to herself.

'Anthony likes to conquer, that's his pleasure. Everything else is incidental.'

She turned her head towards James, realising she had spoken out loud. Her face lost some of its anxiety. 'You know him well, James?'

'We've been friends for a long time.' He paused, studying her face before he went on. 'Georgina, I would like to see you again very soon. May I have your number in France?'

She reached for her evening bag. She had put some address cards in it before she came downstairs, knowing that she would be meeting a few old friends who didn't have her number. She handed him her card. 'I won't be back in France for another three weeks.'

'That's OK, Georgina, I can wait.'

She went to bed that night emotionally and physically exhausted but extremely happy. What a wonderful evening it had turned out to be. As she drifted off to sleep, her vision came to her as it so often did when she was very tired. The house was bathed in sunlight and she could smell the sent the jasmine was giving off in its warmth and for the first time ever the oak door was open.

The shoot dinner had been on the Wednesday. On the Thursday all of the house guests apart from Georgina and Jasmin left. On the

Friday more were arriving for the weekend.

'It's like musical chairs,' Georgina said to Jane as they sat in the garden after lunch on the Friday sharing a quiet moment together.

'I know – the others will be arriving around teatime; we had better make the most of the lull before the storm.' She lay back in her chair enjoying the soft breeze that was playing with her hair. 'Did you practise those dance steps I sent?'

'Yes, Jasmin and I set the cobblestones on fire, light-footing the Gay Gordons up and down the mews.'

'The mews!'

'Well, there was no room in the house, it's like a rabbit hutch.'

Jane was amused by the thought of her elegant friend and her daughter dancing out in the street like a couple of Whirling Dervishes.

'So you're all set for tomorrow night? Everyone is expected to join in the dancing, even the men. In fact after a few drinks most of them enjoy themselves. Some of them count out loud as they try to remember the steps. There's nothing like the bagpipes to stir up emotions in people, whether they are happy or sad. Every time I go to the Edinburgh Tattoo, and hear the lone piper play on the turret of the castle, it's all I can do to stop the tears ruining my mascara.'

'Yes, I know exactly what you mean. There's a beautiful eeriness about a lament floating through the sky and the silence that comes over the crowd. The energy of the moment catches the throat and suddenly a feeling of peace takes over. It's a wonderful experience.'

Jane looked at her friend. 'Perhaps you should move up here and paint. I could find you a nice single laird to marry.'

'Oh, Jane, you're impossible. I don't want to marry anyone. I have my life just as I want it. Thank you for your sweet concern but I've lived alone for so long I think it would be very difficult to adapt to another person in my life.'

'Yes, darling, that's how you feel at the moment. I know you look amazing but, let's face it, you're past forty now and Jasmin is off to university. Isn't it the right time to think of somebody to share your old age with?'

'There's no point in looking for somebody, Jane. If it's meant to be, it's meant to be. I would have to fall in love to want to change my life at this point and that's not easy when you've become as old and independent as me. I am happy, Jane. One day I hope to have some grandchildren to keep me busy but until then I have my work which I love. Not every woman has the opportunity to make a success of something they enjoy. I remember how it felt when I couldn't paint because I had blocked my energy.

'Feelings are like a water source in our body, Jane; if you turn the tap off on one, all the others shut off as well. I put my feelings on hold for so long, I forgot that I had any. I just stepped back from life and let everybody else direct me. The only thing that wouldn't accept the lie I was living was my art. I would never let that happen again,'

'You artists are so sensitive, it must be very exhausting for you sometimes.' She patted her friend on the hand. 'Come along we should be getting organised; the weekend begins in about half an hour and Marcus is on the river as usual. Come and help me sort out the tea.'

Jane was right – the Scottish country dancing was fun, even Jasmin and Camilla didn't complain about the boring adults. By the time they were ready to leave on Sunday morning, Georgina had promised her friend that she would not allow such a long gap before they got together again.

Jane had promised to try and come to France for a few days but Georgina didn't expect to see her there. It was far easier for Georgina to shut the door of her studio than it was for Jane to leave a large estate like Drummossie to run itself.

Back in London Drummossie took on shades of *Brigadoon* as she rushed around with Jasmin shopping and organising the things she needed for university.

Jasmin had been taking driving lessons on and off since her last birthday and her test was on 5 September. Paul and Sebastian were back from Atlanta, so it was arranged that they should all have dinner together to celebrate or commiserate over the outcome.

Paul had reserved a table at Bibendum. It was Georgina's current favourite and he wanted them to share a nice evening before she went back to France.

He missed her company and when they were all together as a family he wished he could be happy with just that. But he knew it was only his thought at that moment; he had learned to live with his restless spirit over the years and to respect the qualities he had found in Georgina, as a friend. He was proud of the pretty girl who had grown into such a beautiful woman and glad she was the mother of his children.

When he arrived at the mews to take Georgina and Jasmin to the restaurant there was no awkwardness in their greeting one another, just the closeness of old friends.

'Paul, come along in and have a drink. Jasmin is still upstairs.' They gave each other a friendly hug.

'Mm, you smell nice. How was Scotland?'

'Better than I could have imagined. How was Atlanta?'

'Rewarding.'

Jasmin ran down the stairs at this point. 'Daddy, daddy, I passed!' She flew into his arms.

'Well done, darling, I suppose now I will have to buy you that car I promised you.'

Georgina came out of the kitchen with a bottle and three glasses. 'It's a shame Sebastian couldn't have come here first,' she said as she passed the bottle to Paul. 'You open it, Paul. I always make a mess when I do it,'

Paul took the bottle and opened the champagne. The cork popped with just the right amount of force and the champagne tumbled unaided into the glass he had singled out.

'He tried to get away but he was still in a meeting when I left the office.' He passed the full glasses.

'Well, I'm glad,' commented Jasmin. 'He would only have had something sarcastic to say about my driving test.'

'Yes, but secretly he would have been proud of you.' Georgina raised her glass to her daughter. 'Well done, darling.'

When they arrived at the restaurant Sebastian was already waiting for them. He stood up as they came over to the table and walked around from his seat to greet them.

'Good-evening, mother, you look well.' He kissed her cheek. 'How was Scotland?'

'Most enjoyable, thank you, darling, and I hear Atlanta was rewarding.'

He looked across at his father and grinned. 'Yes, you could say that.' He turned to his sister and by the look on her face he could tell she had passed her test.

'Hi, Jazz. I got here early in case you were on the road the same time as me. My life insurance has run out and I don't want to take any risks.'

'Oh, Sebastian, you're such a pain. I told mummy you would have to say something stupid.'

'Well done, anyway. I can see by that daft grin on your face that you passed.'

They all sat down and got on with the business of choosing and ordering their meal. It was halfway through the main course before Paul brought up the subject of Giles's being absent from their family dinner.

'I wish Giles would make his peace with me, his stubbornness is wearing a bit thin.'

'He said he had to work overtime, Paul. I think he has to work very long hours.'

'Rubbish, Georgina! Anyway he won't be as eager to work so hard when he knows he is working for me.'

'What do you mean, Paul?'

'I have just bought the pet-food factory.'

'Oh no, Paul.' Her face looked shocked.

Sebastian and Jasmin burst out laughing and Georgina had to laugh in spite of her anguish.

'Now, Georgie, before you read me the riot act, it wasn't a premeditated decision. It's an excellent business deal. A foreclosure, the property was totally undervalued. The planning permission for the redevelopment of the site hasn't been passed yet, so it wasn't taken into consideration. But I know for a fact it will be passed as I have Anthony Lawless for a partner on this one.'

'That man's name comes up everywhere. He was at the shoot dinner. He doesn't change. Nigel Scott's young wife Becky is his latest victim.'

'Probably needs something from Nigel. He will get it through Becky, that's how he operates. It's always better to have a player like Anthony on your side than against you, that's for sure.'

'Talking about game playing, let's get back to Giles. He will see it like that, you buying the company he works for. I think you should tell him before he finds out from somebody else and feels a complete fool.'

'You're right, Georgie, though it would take a while for him to find out. I'll call him tomorrow, although I'm sure this will be the final nail in my coffin as far as Giles is concerned.'

'You never know, Paul.' Georgina thought hard as to what her son's reaction to this news might be. 'He has such an off-the-wall sense of humour that he may see it as the gods laughing at him, and when the gods laugh one had better laugh with them.'

Georgina arrived back in France to bright afternoon sunshine and the soft laid-back smile of Henri, who met her at the airport.

Although it was sad leaving the family in England she also had a warm feeling of belonging the moment she saw Henri waiting to take her luggage.

'Bonjour, Henri.'

'Bonjour, madame, vos vacances se sont bien passées?'

'Oui, merci.' They always spoke in French as Henri knew no English.

She had grown to rely on Henri and Rosie since she had moved to France. They looked after Sam's place and they looked after her. Rosie attended to the housework and always made sure she ate lunch when she was working and Henri looked after the garden and any other jobs around the house that he considered man's work.

They were not young and Georgina often thought how sad it would be for everyone when they retired and moved into the retreat they had organised for their old age, a place they would probably hate.

By the time the car turned off the motorway on the last stage of their journey from the airport she was up to date with all of the village news. August was always the best month to be away, as the road from the motorway to St Tropez was packed with tourists; sometimes it took two hours to make the normal twenty-minute journey to her house from it.

Henri pulled into the drive and Georgina took in the familiar surroundings with the sharp eyes of the traveller who want to make sure nothing has changed while she has been away.

She noticed the virginia creeper that grew on the east side of the house had already started to turn red and the cherry tree by the gate had some gold leaves among the green. Autumn was softly creeping up; by October one would be able to smell it as well as see it.

The car stopped in the carport and as she got out she saw Jasmin's little motorbike she used to get around on when she was home had been covered up, a reminder that her daughter was away for a long time – no longer the weekly boarder she had been in the Sophia Antipolis International School for the past five years.

She sighed at the thought of not seeing her until Christmas. They had shared so many adventures together and now Jasmin was leaving home.

No more crazy summer visitors; all of her inter-railing friends were either taking a year off to see the world or, like Jasmin, going to university first and seeing the world afterwards.

She wondered if Jasmin would ever live in France. She had hoped that she would choose to go to a French university but in the end she had chosen to go back to England.

Rosie was at the front door to welcome her back. She suited her name – her cheeks were like two small red apples glowing in her face and her smile was like the sunshine of Provence.

She had bought some fish for Georgina's supper and put it in the refrigerator; also fresh fruit, vegetables and bread were on the kitchen table along with a list of messages which had accumulated while she had been away.

She thanked Rosie, then patiently listened to the same news she had heard in the car from Henri.

Once alone, Georgina wandered over the house looking at all the familiar things that made it home. She picked up a photograph of Giles that was on the sofa-table in the drawing-room. 'I hope you and your father will make your peace soon,' she said aloud.

She went upstairs. Henri had left her suitcase in her room, but she decided she would unpack it later. She threw off her travel clothes and took a quick shower, then changed into a thin cotton caftan that her friend, Emma Davies, had bought her back from Morocco. Leaving everything in her room as it was, she went downstairs.

The sun was almost setting when she went out on to the terrace with a dish of olives and a glass of white wine. It was good to be back; tomorrow she would open the door of her studio and take in its feel and smell – but not before. She wanted to enjoy the house first while there was no work fever inside her. Once she opened the studio door, she could be in there for a few weeks, with only breaks to eat and sleep – and those so brief as only to allow for the minimum to survive. That's how work caught her sometimes when the creative ideas were flowing.

Autumn was her creative time and she didn't want to give her energy up to it just yet.

She cooked her supper and ate it without ceremony, then went up to her bedroom. She had decided to write her thank-you letter to Jane straightaway, as three weeks had gone by since the party. She had thanked her over the telephone but she still wanted to express herself in writing. It had been such a special stay. Being with her old friend had brought back so many memories.

Meeting James Minnelli had reminded her of the happiness she had felt when she first went to California and of the awakening of her independence. It had all ended in a nightmare but that had been the catalyst for her growth; she knew she would never again be afraid of life or death.

She pondered over her feelings when she met him. She wasn't sure if it was him or the fact that he reminded her of another place, another time, when she had loved another man. She certainly felt something extra in his arms – but love is lazy and he lived in California with odd trips to the South of France.

She wasn't a bright young thing who would give up everything for a man. She had her life and it was a full life. France was her home now and she was too old to want another major change.

There was also the big question-mark as to why he was living with Tina. Perhaps when his wife died he had put his feelings on hold and Tina had dragged him into her psychotic mess. It was quite possible that her money could be the attraction, after all she was one of the richest women in the world and that put her into a very exclusive category. Power was a drug that a lot of men couldn't resist.

The more she thought about James the more confused she became. The passion he showed when he had spoken about wine seemed to say his feeling were intact. He didn't seem like a powermonger, so where was the mystery? Marcus had liked him and Marcus was usually astute when it came to people's characters. She hoped he would call her soon as the more she thought about him the more fascinating he became.

She sat at her bureau for a long time thinking before she finally got around to writing to Jane. She wrote from the heart and when she reread the letter after it was finished she felt that it expressed her feelings exactly. She addressed the envelope, put the letter inside and left it on the top of the bureau to post the following day. She got up from her chair and closed the bureau, she was tired.

She undressed and got into her own bed for the first time in a month. It felt so right and she knew she would sleep well. She turned off the light and lay in the darkness listening to all the familiar noises that the house made.

She was just about to drop off when the telephone rang. It caught her at just the wrong moment; her heart was beating in her throat as she fumbled in the dark for the receiver.

'Hello.' Her voice sounded scratchy.

'Mother, are you all right.'

'Giles, I was just dropping off to sleep, the telephone startled me.'

'I'm sorry, mother, I didn't know that you were such an early bird.'

'No, I'm not normally, it's just been one of those days. Anyway, how are you?'

'I'm fine I just wanted to let you know I have given in my notice at work.'

'Oh!' Georgina's heart sank. Paul must have told Giles his news by now and he obviously had taken it badly.

'Mother, are you sure you are all right.'

'Yes, darling, I'm awake now.'

'Look, mother, dad called and told me what he had done. I had to laugh, it was too theatrical not to.'

'You're not angry, Giles?'

'Mother, of course I'm angry – but not with dad, not any more. I suppose I'm angry because unlike Sebastian I don't know what I want to do. I don't like the property business – which is OK, its good to know what you don't like – but I don't know what I do like and that's frustrating. I wondered if I couldn't come and stay with you for a few weeks and sort of think about it all.'

'Of course you can, darling, I will look forward to it.'

'Well I have to work my notice but I was thinking about the middle of October, what do you think?'

'I think that this is very good news I'm hearing, even if I am half asleep.'

'Mother,' there was a pause. 'I love you.'

'I love you too, Giles.'

The phone went dead.

She could sense his confusion in the darkness of the room. Her heart went out to her younger son. He had always looked up to Sebastian, always wanted to be like him when he was a little boy. Then when he grew up he wanted to find his own identity and he hadn't known where to look. Sebastian was very like Paul and that made it even harder for Giles. He was much more like his mother but he hadn't found an outlet for his creative sensitivity yet and it was strangling him.

A tear ran down her cheek as she remembered Giles the little four-year-old who had thrown his arms around her one day and told that her hair smelt like the fresh morning breeze. Jane was right, Giles would grow into a kind sensitive man in his own good time.

She was woken the following morning by a knock on her bedroom door.

'Madame, votre café.'

'Merci, Rosie.'

She got out of bed and opened the door. On the floor outside was a breakfast tray with coffee and croissants on it. She picked it up and put it on the table beside her bed and jumped back in.

Rosie left her breakfast outside the door every morning as she didn't like anyone in her way while she cleaned downstairs. Visitors soon got used to Rosie's little ways, as Georgina called them, and not many of them complained about breakfast in bed every morning.

As she drank her coffee she went through the messages she had brought up from the kitchen with her the previous evening. She eliminated a lot of business matters as she had already dealt with most of them while she was in England. She began to review all her social callers who had phoned inviting her to various functions and private dinner parties. Other messages were from friends calling to see when she would be back.

It was almost midday by the time she finally came down to the kitchen with her tray.

There was no sign of Rosie but the smell of baking and the spinach tart that had been left on the kitchen table for Georgina's lunch told her she had spent a busy morning.

Before lunch she went up to her studio. When she had first moved to Sam's place she had chosen a room that faced north-west. She loved the soft northern light and during the autumn the room was often clothed in a red glow from the magnificent sunsets that seemed to last for hours.

Everything was as she had left it. There was no furniture in the room apart from a couple of old kitchen chairs and her drafting table.

Henri had built some crude benches along one wall with shelves underneath and these served as storage. Her easel was over by the window where it waited, empty, for her return.

She had brought up with her the sketches and photographs from the gardens at Drummossie. She decided to make them her priority and start her watercolour for Jane that afternoon.

She rushed downstairs and quickly ate the delicious tart which was still warm, feeling a little guilty that she had managed to eat it in about a tenth of the time it had taken dear Rosie to make it.

Then, in her paint-splattered jeans and a big floppy T-shirt and with her hair tied back in a scarf, she went back to her studio to start work.

'Madame. It's seven-thirty.' Rosie called through the door. 'I've put something in the oven for your dinner.'

'Thank you, Rosie, I'm coming now,' she called back.

She had learned over the years to discipline herself to the knocks on the door. It was a rare occasion now when she didn't pull herself away from what she was doing.

Within half an hour she had washed her brushes, put lids on things that needed lids and generally tidied away. She did not intend to come back after supper. She went to her bedroom and threw off her dirty clothes, took a shower and changed into clean jeans and a sweatshirt. Then went downstairs to the kitchen.

Rosie had left a note on the table telling her that the food in the oven would be cooked by nine o'clock. On the kitchen table she had left a cup with some salad dressing in it and a bowl of salad ready to dress.

Georgina broke the end off of the fresh baguette that was also on the table and popped it into her mouth.

'What would I do without you, Rosie,' she said to herself as she looked around the kitchen. 'Starve most probably.'

She had just poured herself a glass of white wine when the telephone rang. People know my habits, what perfect timing, she thought as she went to pick it up.

'Georgina.'

A pleasant tingle passed through her body. 'James, how are you?'

'I'm fine. I'm here in France quite near to you in fact, just outside Lorgues.'

'That is near. How long are you here for?'

'Oh a few weeks. I arrived this afternoon.'

'You must be jet-lagged.'

'No, I'm OK. I had to stop over in London for two days before I came down here. I had some business I needed to finish there. Anyway how are you?'

'Glad to be home.'

'How busy are you tomorrow? I wondered if I could take you to lunch somewhere.'

'I would like that very much, James.'

'Do you have a fax?'

'Yes.'

'I'll give you my fax number here and perhaps you could fax me directions how to get to you.' He gave her his number. 'Do you like bouillabaisse?'

'I love it.'

'Good! I'll book a table at La Gruppi in Ste Maxime. What time suites you?'

'If you get here about twelve o'clock we are only fifteen minutes away at the most.'

'OK. I'll book the table for one o'clock then we won't have to rush.'

'Good, that means I have time to show you over the house before we go.'

'I would like that, Georgina; since I met you I've tried to imagine your life here in France. You must spend a lot of time alone when your working.'

'Yes, I need to, James.'

'I know. I've already thought about it.' He quickly changed the subject. 'Anyway, I'm looking forward to seeing you tomorrow.'

'I'll fax you the directions now and I look forward to seeing you too.'

They hung up. Georgina went upstairs to her bureau where she had a copy of the directions she sent visitors to find her house from the motorway. She faxed them to James. Then went down into the kitchen. She absent-mindedly dressed her salad, took the casserole out of the oven, laid the table and sat down to eat.

While she ate she chastised herself for feeling like a teenager. Her legs had gone quite weak when she heard his voice. She hoped that her feelings would settle down soon as this was most inconvenient.

She poured herself another glass of wine and tried to analyse why this man was affecting her so much.

'It's not just that I find him physically attractive. I had a dreadful need to go to bed with Oliver when I first met him but I wasn't really interested in what he thought about. That's probably why it only lasted six months. Sweet Oliver, he was such a young puppy of a man. Totally huggable but a brat of the first order. He could sulk for days at a time. He should have been an actor not a sculptor; he never gave me any space, yet he of all people should have understood an artist's needs.' Oliver was the last of the string of lovers she had had since she moved to France.

'With James I want to know all about him as much as anything else. In fact, if I'm perfectly honest, I'm fascinated by him. I feel as if I know him already and yet I don't know the first thing about him – other than that he is a widower who is living with a psychotic girlfriend who was once the mistress of my ex-husband. That in itself is bizarre. He has a deep slow laid-back Californian accent, which reminds me of the man I should have made love to but didn't because I thought I should respect my marriage vows, only to find out too late that it takes two to make a marriage. Having thought about it, I'm none the wiser. All I know is that I'm looking forward to seeing him tomorrow more than I've looked forward to anything in ages and, on that thought, I'm going to bed.' She got up from the table and went upstairs, a little less steady on her legs then usual, the extra glass of wine having had its effect.

By midday the following day Georgina was back to normal, although it had taken two aspirins with her morning coffee and the hot water from the shower spray on her head and neck for longer than usual. By the time she had got herself ready for her lunch date with James she looked her beautiful serene self.

He arrived at five minutes past twelve driving a yellow Ferrari Dino. Georgina knew nothing about cars but her designer's eye told her this was something special and not available for rent at Nice airport. A rather unusual car for somebody who only came to the South of France occasionally on business trips. She decided not to mention it.

'Hello, James.' She came out of the house to greet him. 'Did you have any problem finding the house?'

'No, your directions were excellent.' He came up to her and kissed her cheeks French style. 'What a beautiful old place.'

'Yes, it's really charming isn't it? Come along inside and I'll show you around. I've done very little to it since I moved here. It's still very much Sam's place.'

The floors on the ground floor of the house were made of olive-wood discs cemented into the ground like ceramic tiles; they must have been well over two hundred years old. Rosie and time had polished them until they shone.

All over the house were some of the most beautiful Oriental carpets that even Georgina in her days as an interior designer had ever seen. The furniture was mainly Provençal, of the same period as the house, with one or two Oriental things blended in. The antique Syrian tick-tack or hash-bash table in the drawing-room was one of her favourite pieces.

'Apart from these two lounge-lizard sofas, as Jasmin calls them, and the photos on the sofa-table, everything else downstairs is Sam's – and yet I never feel a guest in the house.'

'It's very you, Georgina.' James looked around the room and at the sofas placed either side of the fireplace; he liked the feeling of the house.

She showed him upstairs. Her bedroom was full of her own things, her brass bed, her bureau, her own painting of the beach outside their apartment in La Jolla, with Jasmin as a little girl walking towards the sea dragging her buggy board, and the crochet bedcover made by Grandma Williamson, which had finally come back to France.

They went out on to the terrace that led off the bedroom and looked at the view and the garden.

'It's very peaceful here,' James said as he took it all in.

'Yes, it is. Let me show you my studio before we go – not that there's very much to see at the moment. Almost all of my work is with the gallery in London.'

She opened the door of her studio and walked in. James followed. The first thing he noticed was the watercolour she had started the day before. It was on the easel and the light in the room was showing it to its best advantage.

'That's very good, Georgina, it looks like Jane's garden.'

'It is. I'm painting it for her as a thank-you gift.'

'That's a very generous gift, you must be good friends.'

'We are, Jane and I grew up together. I didn't have brothers or sisters but I had Jane.'

'Did you mind being an only child?'

'No, I don't think so. I had my Aunt Lallie as a companion when I was at home. She's like a child in many ways.'

'My son Nikki grew up an only child but there were lots of kids around for him to play with and my parents were always there for him. My dad spoilt him but he seems to have turned out OK.'

She wanted to ask him how Nikki got on with Tina but as James had never mentioned Tina to her she thought better of it.

'They usually do if we give them enough love.'

He gave her a comfortable smile. 'Yes, we all need that, don't we.'

'Yes we do.' She wanted to hug him.

'I think we should go to lunch now, don't you.'

'Yes, Mr Minnelli; lead the way.'

They drove into Ste Maxime and James parked the car at the port. He seemed to know somebody there to keep an eye on it while they had lunch.

They walked to the restaurant in the warm sunshine, looking at the boats and the view across the bay.

James seemed well known in the restaurant and they were fussed over from the minute they arrived.

He ordered a bottle of Pouilly Fuissé 1990. She didn't quite catch the name of the château, but when the waiter brought the bottle to the table, she could tell by it's shape and the L pressed into the glass at the neck of the bottle that it was one of her favourites.

'James has such an attractive accent when he speaks French. I suppose he must speak Italian as well, with a name like Minnelli,' she thought as she listened to him talking to the waiter and ordering the bouillabaisse.

That finished, he focused his full attention on Georgina. 'I'm glad you could make it today, Georgina. I hoped that you would be back by now and not in too much of a social whirl to see me.'

'The social whirl is over down here by the end of August.'

'I know; that's why I like to come here in September; the weather can be beautiful, like today, and the roads are empty.'

'Yes, but it can also rain for days on end.'

'Then you light a big fire and find someone to snuggle up with. Do you have someone to snuggle up with, Georgina?'

'Not at the moment, James, do you?'

'No. I recently ended a long affair which should never have started.'

'Was that hard?'

'Saying goodbye is always hard, especially when the other person doesn't want to.'

The conversation was interrupted by the bouillabaisse arriving.

'How often does Sam come to his house?'

'I think he's been twice since I've lived there. He rarely takes holidays. If he isn't lecturing, he's writing books. I speak to him almost every week and I always see him if it's possible when I go to America, but he's on the West Coast and I seem to be in New York or Chicago. That's where the American art world is.'

'How did you meet Sam?'

'On a plane flying back to Los Angeles from London ten years ago this month. Talking to Sam changed my life. I became aware of so many different things through him. He is a man with a great vision of a better world; he's one of the most positive people I know.'

'I remember Annetta talking about him; she was a journalist and she interviewed him on several occasions. They got to know each other quite well. She became a great admirer of his.'

'Annetta?'

'Annetta was my wife, Georgina. She died ten years ago.'

'I'm sorry, James.'

'Ten years is a long time, Georgina. I can talk about Annetta now and divorce my loss from the memory of her. She was a character and it gives me pleasure to talk about her.'

'Was she from California?' She did not really know what to say but she felt she should continue the conversation about Annetta.

'No, she was Irish, from Dublin.'

'How did you meet her?'

'My mother introduced us. I came home one day to find Annetta sitting in the drawing-room talking to my mother – she is also from Dublin and she and Annetta's mother are old friends.'

'So you're half Irish. Do you ever go to Ireland?'

'I was at university in Dublin and I try and keep in touch with my old friends but I don't go back as much as I would like. Annetta had a house in West Cork which she left to me. It was a bone of contention between my ex-girlfriend Tina and myself. She accused me of keeping the house as a shrine to my wife. She died there, you see.'

'And do you, James?'

'No, but there are happy memories for Nikki as well as for me in that house. Tina wanted me to sell it and I wouldn't. I told her I would let it but that wasn't enough for her and she was very upset about my decision.'

'Oh I see.' She could imagine Tina building the house up out of all proportion in her mind. She must have become obsessed by it over the years.

'Tina is a difficult woman to understand.' He sounded genuinely confused when he said this.

She wanted to say that she knew more about Tina then he would think but decided to drop the subject. It was all too complicated at this point.

The conversation turned back to the present and they talked about France and the South in particular, their likes and dislikes, their hopes for their children and their fears for the world they would be growing old in. They were the last to leave the restaurant but by the time they did they felt they knew each other very well and any awkwardness that had been between them was a thing of the past when they walked back to the car.

They drove back to Sam's place in silence, enjoying the pleasure of each other's company. The atmosphere was relaxed and as they reached the house James took Georgina's hand and squeezed it.

'I've enjoyed our day together, Georgina, and I don't want it to end just yet.'

'I know; come in and I'll make some coffee.'

She suggested that James sit on the terrace while she made the coffee. Finding some Armagnac in the drinks cupboard she warmed two brandy glasses over the steam of the kettle, then made the coffee and took everything out on a tray.

The sun was well to the west now and the shadows from the olive trees were long and dark across the garden.

They sipped their Armagnac, drank their coffee and digested the peace of the late afternoon. Georgina knew she would invite him to her bed, the question was when? The magnetism between them was drawing them closer and closer to that point. Their hunger for each other was building up slowly, there was time to consider its satisfaction. This was not the hunger of youthful lust that demanded quick relief. Growing between them was a desire for fusion, a mutual exchange of love through the ecstasy of sex.

When she finally stood up she took his hand. He rose with her and drew her into his arms. The warm desert breeze that had been gaining strength while they sat, caressed her face. The sensation of it ran down her spine, transporting her thoughts to the beach in La Jolla and the feel of the Santa Ana on her body.

The sun was low in the sky when she led him upstairs to her bedroom. As she opened the door the redness of its setting was filling the window, bathing the whole room in a soft warm golden light that played on the brass bed.

She relaxed into its glow, knowing it would create an illusion of youth on their bodies, enhancing the kindness time had already shown them.

They didn't speak, there was no need, the talking was all there in their eyes and in their kiss. The finding each other, the long discovery of each other's soul, was in that first naked kiss, the quality they each had to offer was in that kiss as their legs melted beneath them and they found themselves lying on her bed.

Each point of their love-making was savoured. There was no thought given to the end result, their enjoyment was centred on every stage. The undressing, the feel of their bodies entwined, the passing of lips over bodies and the natural resting places those lips found. The tenderness and yet the depth of their desire.

All of the elements were present to assist in their bonding – the air of their spirit, the fire of their passion, the earthiness of their bodies and the waters of their love – soldering their nexus by alchemy into gold.

Each movement, every touch reassured the other to let go and give themselves up totally to the experience. They rose above their past losses, naked and unscarred; they cleansed each other of any past pain.

They could enjoy every bittersweet experience that love and life brought them because they had both endured and now life was giving them their reward. The freedom to love again without fear.

They made love as the sun set, they made love as the moon rose in the sky and the stars one by one came out to join it. Then they slept in each other's arms as if they had shared the same bed for ever, such was the comfort of their slumber.

When Rosie knocked on the bedroom door the following morning and Georgina went to fetch the breakfast tray, she found an extra cup and a red rose on it. 'Quelle finesse, Rosie,' she murmured as she took the tray and put it on the table at the side of the bed.

She poured the coffee and looked over at James who was leaning on his elbow smiling at her.

'Milk or sugar?' She suddenly laughed at her question. 'Here I am asking you, the man that I made the most intimate love to last night, if you take milk or sugar? What do I really know about you, James Minnelli.'

'All you need to know about me is that I'm in love with you, Georgina Fox. I was from the moment I saw you in Scotland. I have fallen in love once before in my life so I know all the symptoms – and I had them all that evening. So please put one lump of sugar in my coffee and no milk then come back to bed because I want to have a serious talk with you.'

She did as he bade her, plumping up the pillows to make them more comfortable before she got back in beside him.

'Do you have anything planned for today?'

'No, James. I was going to work but I haven't really got back into the swing of it yet.'

'I would like to show you something,. About eleven years ago I bought a winery here, just outside Lorgues. It was a very small winery when I bought it, making just enough wine for the family who owned it. Since then we have planted many more hectares of grapes and I have built an up-to-date winery similar to the one we have in Napa. We produce over three hundred thousand bottles per year now and the wine is receiving accolades – which is quite an achievement for Côte de Provence with its stigma of generations of bad wine-making.'

'What's the name of your vineyard?'

'Domaine de Bouscarela.'

'I know the wine – the rosé is exceptional.'

'Yes, my first interest in buying a winery in Provence was to produce a good rosé. Anyway, when I bought the winery I planned eventually to spend a lot more time here but I've only ever spent the minimum that the business needs. I have a very good manager and everything has run smoothly over the years. Now I would like to spend more time here and I would like to share that time with you.'

'Living with an artist isn't easy, James. When I'm working I lose myself completely in another world and it can take a long time to come down to earth. It took me a year to complete the one-man show that brought me recognition; the only break I took in that year was during the summer when Jasmin was home from school. I became obsessed, all my energy was concentrated on what I was achieving. Those paintings are the only ones I can say I'm really proud of, they express my feelings exactly. Who knows when another spasm of work will take me?'

'Georgina, I was married to a war corespondent who went on to make documentaries on women's issues. I got used to losing track of her in very strange and dangerous places. At least I would know where to find you.'

'Annetta Peterson,' she suddenly thought. 'How stupid of me! She must have been James' wife. I admired her work so much and she inspired my one-man show. This whole thing is becoming more and more uncanny.'

'I would love to spend the day with you and visit your winery, James.' She curved herself around his body like a cat.

'One day soon I would like to see some of your paintings,' he said, running his hand down the sensuous line of her back.

'We need to go to London for that,' she purred.

'We will – but let's get going now, because if I spend one minute longer in this bed with you, we will be here all day; not that I am complaining, but you have one minute to make the choice.'

She jumped out of bed. 'Come along then. I have a toothbrush and a razor for you. I'll take my shower while you shave and then we won't get in each other's way.'

By ten-thirty they were in James's car and on the road to Lorgues. Georgina had left a note on the kitchen table for Rosie to let her know that there would be two for supper.

James took the back road which led straight to the winery. Although it was a modern building, a lot of sympathy had been shown in its architecture and to its surroundings. It was a stone-faced building with stone mullions over the windows and doors. Gardens had been planted around it and the flower beds were full of roses in their September bloom.

He parked the car, then came round to her side to open the door for her. 'We are harvesting at the moment so there is plenty for you to see.' He led her into the winery. It was an impressive sight with its huge stainless-steel wine vats reaching up to the ceiling.

James showed her over the winery and explained as they went all the processes that the grapes would go through. The importance of careful handling of the fruit, the different processes for white, red and rosé wine, the suitability of oak vats for traditional fermentation and a brief history of wine-making were all part of the instruction initiating her into his world.

'You're like an alchemist, James, creating magic for us all to enjoy.' She was being drawn to the pleasure his own art gave him.

'There is a touch of magic about it, Georgina. During an exceptional year when all the elements give their best to the grapes, something magical happens to the wine and its taste stays in the memory, like the great Bordeaux of 1961, for instance.

'Now let me introduce you to my manager.' He took her over to meet Mr Gireaud, who was busy talking to one of the workers.

After the introductions the men got into a conversation about the harvest and their hopes for the good weather to hold.

This gave Georgina time to take everything in. As she watched James and looked around to see what he had created out of passion for his art, she knew she was in love with this man who had come into her life bringing so many unanswered questions with him, and she knew it was meant to be. She remembered the tarot-card reading and felt she had a lot more to learn from it than just her ability to love again.

'There are always important decisions to be made at this time of the year. Rain now would be a disaster. Now, let's go. I have something else to show you.'

They got back into the car and he drove back the way they had come in. At the bottom of the road he turned left and then took the next road on the left which led them through the main gates and up the tree-lined avenue to the Manoir de la Bouscarela.

'Oh, James, it's beautiful.' She looked at the mansion set in it's impeccably maintained gardens and decided James must be a magician to have found such a beautiful house in an area not famed for its grand houses.

They parked outside the entrance. 'Georgina, before we go inside I want to tell you a story about this house.' He looked into her eyes and she felt his burning into her soul to be understood.

'Annetta and I bought this house the year before she died. We planned to live here one day but we never told anybody about it – all my father and mother knew was that I had bought a vineyard in the South of France. It was too early to tell dad that I planned to spend less time with him; we are a close family and our son Nikki was so much a part of my parents' daily life that at that time we both felt he was too young to move from the States to start school in France.

'I had to put the money into the winery before we could put the money into restoring the house. Also at that time Annetta was very involved with her work, so the house stayed a secret between us.

'When Annetta died I kept our secret, I don't know why. At first I couldn't come to terms with her death; then, when I had or I thought I had, I met Tina and something told me never to mention this place to her.

'After her reaction to Annetta's house in Ireland, I was glad I hadn't and I realised I just didn't want to share this with her or anyone else. I finally decided that when Nikki was married and happy with a wife and family I would give it to him.

'Then I met you, Georgina, and I knew that it is possible to love more than once. I hope you can understand that I want to share the dream of living here with you. I've thought about it since I met you in Scotland and I hoped I was doing the right thing as I was driving you here this morning. For me, it feels so right that you should be here with me. It's as if the house was waiting for you.

'Please understand, Georgina, I'm not trying to relive my past through you. This is an invitation you can refuse and I will give the house to Nikki later, as I had planned. I just had to tell you the truth now so that you can make your own choice.'

'I feel honoured that you want to share this beautiful secret with me, James.' She turned her face from the house so he could see the sincerity in her eyes.

He drew her into his arms and kissed her hard and long before they went inside.

As soon as Georgina stepped into the hall she felt a *déjà vu* sensation about the house. Even in its sadly neglected state she had a feeling of welcome from it. Nothing about it felt strange, and as James opened the door into what had once been the drawing-room, it was as if she had been there before when the house was alive. She felt she had once invited guests to sit by the fire and had offered them refreshment.

There was a feeling of coming home about everything, the feeling she usually associated with Tarn House.

'I feel as if I've been here before, James; it's the strangest thing.'

'I know. I felt like that the first time I came here and now it feels so right you being here, Georgina.' He held her hand and led her through the rest of the house.

When they reached the dining-room and she saw the quality and condition of the Fragonard frescos, for the first time in ten years she thought about creating her own home, one that wouldn't be taken away from her as if its only value was the money it was worth.

She even imagined a Christmas tree in the hall, a thought which shocked her in its disloyalty to Tarn House, where she had promised Jasmin they would always spend Christmas.

They walked out on to the terrace which led from the dining-room and looked out over the gardens and the vineyard.

'James, I love it,' she said, slightly breathless with the whole experience.

'And I love you, Georgina. Will you marry me and live here with me?'

'The last thing I ever thought I would want to do is get married again, but yes, James, I will marry you. I want to make a statement of my feelings for you.'

As she said it she realised how true it was. She had thought she knew herself until that moment. The independent woman who would never marry again, would always be in control of her destiny, had realised that nobody has control over their destiny – only destiny itself has that privilege.

Even if it would 'all end in tears', one of Aunt Lallie's favourite expressions, it was worth it for the way she felt now – whole and reborn with James's love.

They spent the rest of the day making plans and making love in the coach-house, where James had a base for himself when he spent any time on the estate. It was hard to get used to the speed of what was happening and to allow it to sink in. Georgina felt she should pinch herself to make sure it was real.

They drove back to Sam's place and Georgina lit a fire in the drawing-room. The smell of Provençal cooking was coming from the oven in the kitchen, where Rosie had left their supper prepared for them.

James had brought some of his special *réserve* wine for her small *cave* and was putting it away while she organised the fire. He had also packed a suitcase before they left La Bouscarela as they intended to drive down to Italy the following day and spend a few days in Portofino.

She set two places on the coffee table in front of the fire and put cushions on the floor for them to sit comfortably; she lit the candle in the middle of the table and as she did so her thoughts went out to Jasmin and the winter suppers they had shared in front of the fire and the cosy conversation of their friendship.

She wanted to tell her daughter about James, but she decided that it wasn't the right time as Jasmin was going through a huge transition period of her own in her first term at university.

Then Giles came into her mind. The telephone conversation they had shared just a few days ago in the dark of her bedroom. He was finally coming to terms with himself. Would he be able to cope with the news of his mother getting married again? Would he like James?

'Women must have choice without guilt,' she said to herself, feeling as guilty about her happiness at that moment as she had felt confident in her love for James an hour before. Her head started spinning with contradictions. 'Women need to break from their dependence on connections, they must see value in being firstly women, then mothers, wives, businesswomen, artists or whatever. I tell that to women through my art and when I am interviewed about my work. Yet here am I questioning it. Where is this guilt coming from? I am a woman who believes that anything coming from an act of love will work out. I came to France out of love for my art, and the children accepted and enjoyed the experience. I will marry James out of my love for him and yet here I am worrying that the children won't accept him. I have agreed to marry a man whom one part of me feels I have known forever and the other part of me has known for just a few days. I have never met his son or his family and he hasn't met my family but somehow that doesn't matter, although we both admit to coming from close families. Love really is blind.'

At that point James came into the drawing-room with a bottle of wine and two glasses.

'The food smells good.'

'It will taste even better. Rosie is one of the best cooks I know.'

'Do you like to cook, Georgina?'

'Sometimes. I used to do all of the cooking when the children were small but now I must admit I would rather leave it to somebody else.'

'I'm defiantly the man for you then because I love to cook. Especially here in France where all the ingredients are so inspiring.'

'James, there is so much about you I don't know, even though we haven't stopped talking since we met. I'm having a few problems adjusting to that; one part of me is feeling so comfortable it's as if you have always been in my life and the other is excited and fascinated by you.'

'That's how it is when you love somebody, there's always a small part that remains a mystery. That's the magic ingredient that takes it beyond friendship; that's why it's so rare, Georgina, and not something you turn your back on if it chooses you.' He kissed her playfully on the tip of her nose as he put the glasses on the table and began to pour the wine.

'Do you think Nikki will like me, James?'

'Of course he will, sweetheart. Nikki is almost twenty years old, he is in his second year at college. He isn't looking for somebody to replace his mother any more. He had a problem with Tina but he was younger then and also I think that his child's intuition told him Tina wasn't right for me or me for her. Now I'm sure he just wants to see me happy and I am happy, happier then I ever thought I could possibly be again.'

'It's strange how life works out. I know now that if I had met you before this point in time it would not have been right. My work or my children would have got in the way and perhaps the strain would have been too great. It's only now that I am truly free to love you completely. Before my one-man show, I was striving to reach that goal; all of my energy went into those paintings – it was as if a force outside of myself was assisting me in their expression. After I had finished the work I knew it was important and special. I felt different, as if my purpose for being here had been achieved and for that there would be a reward.

'Then I met you, James, and in some way I feel you are my reward for the pain and love I put into those paintings. I have never felt so emotionally drained from work in my life as when I added the final brushstroke to the last piece. Then the sense of peace that came afterwards healed me and prepared me for you.'

'What a beautiful thing to say, Georgina; the more I know you the more I love you. I want to see these paintings that paved the way for me.'

'You will, James, soon.' Unanswered questions were knitting themselves in the back of her mind but she pushed them away, thankful for her heart's content.

They drove down to Portofino the following day. James had booked a suite at the Splendido. It was the perfect time of year to be there, not crowded but enough people for it not to be dead.

They spent their days exploring the winding alleyways and eating in the colourful restaurants around the port. Georgina couldn't resist the Giorgio Armani shop on the quay; as she suspected, James spoke Italian like a native and she smiled to herself at the effect he had on the beautiful shop assistant, who was charmed by his accent and wanted to know which part of Italy he was from.

James's speaking Italian made everything just that bit better, not that it could get much better. There was a Jacuzzi in their bathroom and she decided that they had to have one in their bathroom at the La Bouscarela. She had been collecting ideas for the house since they arrived in Portofino; she had felt, even before they made the trip, that the house would lend itself to an Italian influence.

They made plans for a shopping expedition to Florence after Christmas and for Georgina to meet the architect, who had made such a good job of the coach-house conversion, when they got back to France.

They ended up staying a few days longer than they had originally planned as the good weather held and there seemed no need to rush. When they got back to France they were both ready to throw themselves into the renovation of La Bouscarela.

Georgina knew the time had come to tell her family about James. It had been at the back of her mind since they arrived back in France and now she needed to address it.

For some reason she felt the first person she must tell was Paul. She didn't want him to hear it from anyone else; that didn't seem fair somehow. She was a little nervous when she finally picked up the phone and she hoped he would be at home. Now that she had plucked up the courage she wanted to get it over with. She waited patiently while the phone rang.

'Paul Fox speaking.'

'Paul, it's Georgina.'

'Georgina, where are you? Are you in France?'

'Yes, Paul. Are you alone?'

'Yes, why?'

'Because I have some news and I want you to be the first to hear it.'

'Sounds intriguing.'

'Paul, I'm getting married.'

'You're what!'

'I've met somebody who makes me happy, Paul.' She added, almost humbly, 'I want to be with him.'

'How long have you known him?'

Oh dear, this was more difficult than she had thought it would be. 'Three weeks – a bit longer perhaps. I met him in Scotland.'

'You're going to marry somebody you've only known for three weeks? You must be out of you mind, Georgie.'

'Perhaps, Paul – but remember, when I first met you, we were inseparable after the first week and at that time I didn't know my own mind; at least now I'm out of the mind I know.'

'Georgie, you are impossible. You wait ten years then make a decision in ten minutes. Anyway, who is the lucky man.'

'James Minnelli, he's an American.'

'I know who James Minnelli is. He was living with Tina for years. You're not just getting your own back, are you, Georgie?'

'Does that sound like me, Paul?'

'No, but it does seem a bit coincidental. After all, Tina was the one who broke us up.'

'Paul, as I've told you before, Tina was only the catalyst for our marriage ending. I feel no anger for Tina, in fact I feel sorry for her if what you've told me over the years is true.'

'Unfortunately it is.' He was silent for a moment. 'Anyway, Georgie, I wish you luck and I have to admit to being a little jealous; and you can tell Minnelli that he had better make you happy, otherwise he will have me to answer to.'

'All right, Paul,' she laughed with relief, 'but please don't mention it to anyone until I've told the children. It must come from me.'

'Call them soon, Georgie, because these things have a habit of getting out.'

'Yes I will. I'm going now, Paul, but I want to thank you for being the best ex-husband a woman could have and to tell you that I love you.'

'I love you too, Georgie, and be happy – you deserve it.'

There were tears in her eyes as she put the phone down. Paul had been such an important part of her life, she hoped he and James would get on.

She called Sebastian first; as the eldest she felt he would have the least difficulty understanding her decision. He answered the phone straightaway so she didn't have to leave a message.

When she told him the news he was pleased for his mother but a little concerned for his father. She told him that she had already spoken to Paul and received his blessing.

Hearing that this obstacle had already been overcome he gave her his wholehearted support, and was sure that James must be a splendid person to warrant her love.

She left a message at the mews for Jasmin to call her back, then she telephoned Giles.

He asked her a thousand and one questions before he gave his approval, but qualified it by saying that he was glad he would be down in the next few weeks to meet this man who had swept his mother off of her normally well-planted feet.

When Jasmin called back and Georgina told her the news she was thrilled; she thought the whole thing 'too romantic for words'.

'When are you getting married, mummy?'

'Next May; the house will be ready then, so we can have a party there to celebrate.'

'Oh, I think it's too romantic for words living in a château in the South of France.'

'I think you will like the house, Jasmin; it *is* rather special and I am enjoying watching it come back to life.'

'What does Giles think about you getting married.'

'He wants to meet James before he can give his final blessing to us both.'

'Oh, Giles is such an old fart at times.'

Well, I think it's rather nice that he is so concerned.'

'Mummy, I think that this is something that was meant to happen – us going up to Scotland and you meeting somebody from the other side of the world who just happened to live a few miles away from you in France. I'm sure Giles will like him.'

'I'm sure he will too, Jasmin.'

'I can't wait to see you; it seems so long until Christmas.'

'I know, darling, I'll try and get over before then. I know this first term must be hard for you.'

After she put the phone down to Jasmin she picked it up again straightaway. 'Now, Mac,' she said out loud to herself.

She knew Mac and Lallie would be delighted and they were. Now she had told her family she felt she should call Sam and tell him about her plans.

She waited until later that evening because of the time difference. James was in Paris on business and it was the first night that she would be alone since they had met in France.

Before going to bed she called the university and left a message with Sam's secretary for him to call her – however late, it didn't matter.

She was sitting up in bed with her diary trying to work out when she could make a trip to England during November to see Jasmin and make arrangements with the art gallery who handled her work for an exhibition she had been asked to mount the following May. Next year was really going to be busy what with the house, the exhibition and the wedding.

Sam telephoned just as she was ready to switch off the light and was anxious to hear her news.

'Georgina, what's going on? Whenever I call lately, you're not there and Rosie tells me you have a special friend who is taking up all of your time.'

'Oh, Sam, Rosie is such a love. You are very lucky to have her and Henri looking after your house and I'm lucky to have Rosie spoil me and take care of me the way she does – it's as if she were my mother.'

'I know. Rosie needs to mother somebody, it's a shame that she never had children.' He paused. 'Now, Georgina, tell me your news.'

'Sam, I'm getting married next May. I've met a wonderful person and I didn't know I could be so happy.'

'Is he a Frenchman?'

'No he's an American, in fact I think you knew his wife quite well; he's a widower. His name is James Minnelli and he was married to Annetta Peterson.'

'Yes, I remember Annetta very well and her untimely death. It was caused by exposure to Agent Orange. She was a war correspondent and happened to be in Vietnam when the Americans were using the stuff to defoliate the forests. Now it seems a lot of Vietnam veterans have died from cancers related to exposure to that chemical.

'I know, Sam, James told me. His father has set up a trust-fund for important and relevant research. So she didn't die in vain; her father-in-law's is a voice people are used to listening to.'

'She was influential herself. I got to know her through her work with the women's movement – although while she worked as a war corespondent she did interview me several times over Middle Eastern issues. She was very active in the Women's Movement for Peace in Northern Ireland during the seventies and she made some excellent documentaries about women. I think they helped a lot of women to see where they had come from politically and socially and where they were going to.

'It was her documentary on women in war that was the inspiration for my one-man show 'Homework by Candlelight'.

'You didn't tell me this before, Georgina. I never knew she finished that documentary. Are you sure that it was hers?'

'Yes, Sam, I only saw it once when I was in Chicago on business but I will never forget it. I went back to the hotel for an early night. I remember flicking through the television channels and stumbling upon her documentary. It was already more than halfway through but the images of the women in long-term conflict stayed with me. I had total recall of those images when I started to paint.

'Well, I think it must have been somebody else's work, Georgina, because I'm sure that Annetta died before she finished her last documentary.'

'You could be right, Sam, perhaps I have got so used to coincidences that it seemed natural somehow that I would be influenced by Annetta's work.' She hesitated before she told him that James had been living with Paul's ex-mistress before he met her.

'I haven't told James about Paul and Tina – it all seems so incestuous and I don't want to give it more importance than it really has.'

'I can understand that, Georgina, and it really has nothing to do with you and James; some things are best left alone, my dear.'

'That's what I decided, Sam.'

'Now the big question – What are you going to do about renting my house? Will I gain another tenant or am I to lose the one I have?'

'I'm sorry to say that I will be leaving at the end of next May when our house is ready. I want to take this opportunity to tell you how much your house has meant to me and how I have enjoyed every minute of living here, Sam. You gave me a home when I needed one most. This house felt like home the moment I walked through the door and it has been a very important part of my children's growing up. I will be sad to leave it.'

'Times change, Georgina, and life goes forward. Perhaps I will be able to spend some time there myself once you leave.'

'Oh, Sam, that would be marvellous, we would be neighbours! Our new home is just outside Lorgues.'

'That was going to be my next question. I couldn't imagine you leaving France now.'

'I know, Sam, isn't it amazing how life works out sometimes.'

'Yes, Georgina, sometimes it is.'

After she had put the phone down she went over their conversation in her head. The information about Annetta stuck in her mind. Why had she been so sure it was Annetta's documentary and why hadn't she mentioned the connection to James. Oh well, it didn't matter now; she had been wrong and it was best that she had found out from Sam rather than having brought up the subject with James.

She was still feeling confused as she dropped off to sleep. Her vision came like a lullaby to soothe her and she noticed for the second time that the oak door of the house was open.

Giles arrived the third week in October. Georgina went to meet him at the airport. She had arranged with James that he would come over to Sam's place later to take them out to dinner, giving Georgina the afternoon alone with her son.

Georgina and James were virtually living together, dividing their time between the coach-house and Sam's place.

The work on the main house was going well and their living arrangements at this point suited them both. James had to do some business travelling but he was never away for more then two days at a time, they had become almost inseparable.

Georgina respected his sensitivity over giving her time alone with Giles. It had been James's idea that she go to the airport and bring him back to Sam's place.

He said that he had work to do at the vineyard so it all made sense but she knew he was purposely keeping out of the way.

Giles was already through customs and waiting on the pavement outside arrivals when she drove into the airport. She parked in front of where he was standing and he picked up his canvas holdall, threw it on the back seat and got in beside her.

'Hello, mother.' He reached across and kissed her cheek. 'The flight was five minutes early.'

'So I see.' She turned to face him. 'You're looking well, darling.'

'And so are you, mother – blooming in fact.'

'I'm very happy, Giles.' She put the car into gear and drove off. 'I hope you will like James; he's coming over later to take us out to dinner.'

'I'm looking forward to meeting him – he sounds very interesting; at least he isn't in the property business.' He sounded bitter when he mentioned property.

'Giles, do you hate it that much.'

'Well, that's all you and dad used to talk about when Sebastian and I were growing up. You could say we were weaned on it. I obviously didn't take to the diet.'

'Poor Giles, and I suppose Sebastian became addicted?' She glanced quickly across at her son and then back to the road, hoping she had made him smile. 'Have you had any more thoughts about what you are going to do, darling?'

'No, mother, but if I can, I think I may go back to university.'

'I'm glad, Giles, at least that will give you time to think about your future.'

'Yes, I've got to get it right eventually.'

'You will, Giles.' It felt good to have Giles sitting beside her looking happier than he had in ages and she could tell by his attitude that he would go out of his way to like James.

They spent the afternoon catching up on each other's news. Giles was pleased to hear James was a tennis player and hoped to be able to fit in a few games with him during his stay.

'There's a tennis court behind the coach-house at La Bouscarela. I think it was one of the first things James had built when he bought the house.'

'What's the house like, mother.'

'Beautiful Giles, you will love it. I can imagine my grandchildren growing up there.'

'Hold on, mother! – still Sebastian will soon be thinking of marriage, I suppose, or maybe Jasmin will be the first.'

'There's plenty of time for all of you. I don't want to be a grandmother just yet, I need to get used to being a stepmother first. James has a son named Nikki, he is almost twenty and a tennis player too.'

'Have you met him?'

'No, not yet, he's at Stanford University reading chemistry. James wants me to go over to California next month and meet him. I will also be meeting James's parents as we will be staying at Eagles' Ridge, their family home in the Napa Valley. I'm looking forward

to meeting his parents; evidently his father Joe is a real character –
his nickname is Lucky.'

'Lucky Joe Minnelli – he sounds like somebody in the Mafia.'

'Well, he does seem to have had a chequered past but like you he
eventually got it right.'

They had just lit a fire in the drawing-room when Georgina heard
James's car in the drive. She and Giles went out to meet him.

Giles put his hand on her shoulder and spoke quietly near her ear.
'You didn't tell me he had a Ferrari Dino, mother.'

'I didn't know that it was a Ferrari Dino; is that good?'

'Amazing, my favourite car; they are rare, mother – your boy-
friend has good taste.'

James came over to meet Giles. They shook hands with genuine
warmth and Georgina breathed a sigh of relief.

'Let's all go inside and open the bottle of champagne I put in the
fridge.'

The evening was a success, their conversation ranged over cars,
tennis and wine. Georgina was more an observer than a participant
in the conversation and by the end of the evening it was obvious to
her that Giles had found his guru.

Plans were being discussed for Giles to attend university in
Sacramento and study wine-making, then work for James in the
business.

In just one night Giles had finally grown up and found direction
and was going to California.

When they were finally alone, Georgina had the chance to thank
James for his help towards the transformation of her son.

'Giles found himself tonight, James, thank you.'

'He's a nice guy, Georgina, you must be proud of him.'

'I am, James, and I'm proud of you but I feel quite humble because
you have already given me so much and now you're helping Giles
to find his way. I would never have thought to introduce him to the
wine business. Uncle Harry was a connoisseur of wine and it was a
hobby that lasted all his life – even at the end when he was so ill. He
died of emphysema; it was a slow painful death and in the end he
went home for Mac and Lallie to nurse him. He died in Tarn House,
which was how it should have been; he was born there.

'Perhaps if he hadn't been so ill during Giles's teenage years he would have suggested to Giles that he did something in that field. Now I come to think of it Giles always asked Harry a lot of questions about wine – but *I* didn't think of it, you thought of it.

'I hope one day that I will be able to do something as special for you.'

'You already have, Georgina, you came into my life.'

Within three days James had arranged for Giles to start university halfway through a semester – or he had spoken to Joe which seemed to amount to the same thing. Joe was on the board of governors and Giles had the college credits required from his abortive attempt at university in England.

He was shipped off to England to organise his new life and arrangements were made for James's brother-in-law, who worked in the family business, to meet Giles in San Francisco and drive him to the university campus near Sacramento, where he would study oenology.

By the time she and James arrived at Eagles' Ridge at the end of November, Giles had settled into his new life and had found a second home with Joe and Lana. He looked tanned and happy when Georgina saw him again, walking off the tennis court with Nikki his new-found friend. They spent nearly all of their weekends together and most of their activities stemmed from having Eagles' Ridge as their base.

'Nikki knows all the best places to hang out,' Giles informed his mother when she asked him how he got on with Nikki.

'Well, he's a local. When he comes to London you will be able to show him the town.'

'He knows London as well as I do, mother. Nikki's a pretty international sort of a guy.'

Georgina and Nikki got on well. It helped that Giles had paved the way for their first meeting and had obviously given his mother some good press.

When they found themselves alone together he told her how pleased he was that his father was getting married again.

'I'm pleased to see my father so happy, Georgina; he has been a lonely man for a long time. I think you are very good for him.'

'I hope so, Nikki. He certainly makes me happy.'

'Joe likes you too, and that's a good thing; he may be in his eighties now but his opinion still has a lot of weight with dad. I know that it was important for dad that his parents liked you. My mother is a hard act to follow as far as they are concerned but I think you will do nicely, Georgina.'

'Well, thank you, gallant knight.' She couldn't resist giving him a hug and was happy to see that he wasn't self-conscious as he hugged her back. She had hoped that she and Nikki would be able to make friends, but the bond she felt with him was beyond her wildest dreams. She truly felt that she had gained a son.

Joe and Lana had welcomed her into their family with great warmth. Joe was still an impressive man and his soft brown eyes, though now a little watery, still had the same depth of mystery about them that was so alluring in James's. Behind the love and kindness he extended to his family one could still imagine the steel force he displayed to his opponents.

Georgina was glad that she was on the right side of the fence when it came to his opinion.

She guessed Lana was about the same age as her own mother but like herself had started her family young. She was still a beautiful woman and had never lost her Irish brogue, which Georgina found enchanting. She felt she had known Lana for a lot longer than the two weeks she spent with her on that first visit.

Georgina flew back to England alone, leaving behind all of her new-found loved ones and her son.

James had business to finish in the States and she had an exhibition to organise, apart from a house project to oversee. So they parted knowing that it would be after Christmas before they saw each other again.

James was staying at Eagles' Ridge for Christmas with Nikki, Giles, Joe and Lana. Georgina would go to Tarn House with Jasmin. Sebastian was spending Christmas with his new girlfriend Sophie and her parents. Paul was going to Australia on business and had decided to spend Christmas with friends who had just moved to Sydney.

Both James and Georgina had decided that their parents needed time to get used to everything that had happened so quickly and they both would feel guilty leaving their ageing parents over that first Christmas.

'Next year we'll be in our own home, James, then it will be up to everybody to come to us if they want to.'

'You're right, Georgina. Also, I don't want Joe to miss Nikki's birthday this year. I'm always thinking these days that this may be his last Christmas, but knowing Joe he will probably live to be a hundred.'

'Does that mean I will have another fifty years with you – they say that longevity runs in families.'

'I hope so, sweetheart.'

Christmas passed pleasantly for all of the spread-out family and James flew into Manchester to spend the New Year with Georgina.

She was there at the airport to meet him. As he engulfed her in his embrace the tension of waiting eased inside her.

'I've missed you, James; it seemed like such a long time.'

'I know, I feel the same. That's the last time I want to be apart from you for so long. I must be getting old. I used to value breaks, to reorder my thoughts.'

'Me, too. I fear we are going to turn into a proper old Darby and Joan.' She kissed him and then said, 'Mac and Lallie are dying to meet you so we had better get along home.'

It was fun to watch Jasmin and Lallie vying for James's attention; they were both besotted with him.

'He looks like a romantic Italian film star,' Lallie told her.

'I think you're the luckiest woman in the world,' said Jasmin. 'He's almost as good looking as daddy.'

Georgina smiled at her daughter's loyalty to her father and was pleased Jasmin's relationship with Paul had always been a good one; unlike so many girls, she wasn't looking for another father. She wondered how she would cope with Nikki, a green-eyed younger version of James.

The three of them were out together, taking Toby the labrador for a walk by the river. Toby had replaced Blue, who died the same year as Uncle Harry. Lallie had been heartbroken and Mac, who before Blue's death had said that he would be their last dog, had weakened when faced with Lallie's distress and brought Toby home for her.

'Do you think that you and Mac will join us if we have Christmas in France next year, Lallie?'

'I don't know, darling, we will have to see. It really depends on Sebastian – whether he brings home his bride or not.'

'You don't think Sebastian is going to marry Sophie, do you?' Georgina sounded surprised.

'Yes, I do, and they will come and live here; that's how it should be. It's time for the next generation to be born here.' She sounded so confidant that Georgina didn't dare comment.

Mac and James had stayed in the house. Mac was showing him Harry's cellar when they left. The cellars at Tarn House were not as full as they had been and Mac was delighted to take the advice of an expert over the restocking of them.

James was genuinely impressed with the cellar. He helpfully told Mac what he thought she should be drinking now and what she should keep. She made notes and he promised to advise her when ordering some more stock. After that they made their way up into the house, went to the morning-room and sat in front of the fire waiting for the others to come back for tea.

'James, I can't tell you how pleased I am that you are marrying my daughter. I never thought to see her so complete.'

'She has given me something I never expected after my wife died, a second chance to be genuinely happy.'

'How long ago is it since your wife died, James?'

'Ten years.'

'Perhaps it takes that long to heal; it's about ten years, maybe a little longer, since I feared for Georgina's sanity. She seemed so grief-stricken by life. But somehow she pulled round, she found herself through her painting – as a mother it was a tragic thing to watch happen and not be able to help. My sister never quite grew up as the result of a broken heart. I hoped that wouldn't happen to Georgina. Sometimes real life can be too much for sensitive people and Georgina has always been far too sensitive, like her grandmother. She even looks like my mother.'

She smiled at James; he reminded her of a man that she had once loved; she knew what it was like to lose a spouse early and was glad that, unlike her, he had found someone to fill the huge gap left by that loss.

They were interrupted by the laughter of the women returning from their walk, and by Toby, who bounded into the morning-room and had to be disciplined by Mac.

When it was time for James, Georgina and Jasmin to leave Tarn House, James felt very close to these extremely English, slightly eccentric old ladies who made up the rest of Georgina's family.

He also realised how brave it had been of her, in her time of great stress, to turn her back on such a comfortable nest and build her own world. He had his whole family around him when Annetta died and they were all there to help him. Georgina had only her art until Jasmin had come to live with her in France.

They arrived back in France to a building project that was miraculously going to plan. After a week, and leaving lists of instructions to the builder from Georgina, they left for Florence to look for fabrics and furniture.

They kept up this pace for the rest of the winter and the spring, travelling separately or together to achieve their goals. The demands of the house, the wedding and their individual business projects made the time fly by. Without a moment to rest it was suddenly the beginning of May, three weeks before the wedding and the day before her exhibition.

The house was ready to move into but they had decided to wait until after the wedding on 25 May at Caxton Hall. There would be a lunch on the day of the wedding at the Connaught Hotel for the few friends who had been invited for the civil service. Then two weeks later a party at Le Manoir de la Bouscarela which they saw as their real wedding day. The chapel would be festooned in white madonna lillies for the occassion, symbolic of the purity of love. There, with a nimbus of scent hovering in the air above their heads, they would truly pledge their troth. Two weeks would be the time needed for James and Georgina to iron out any last wrinkles in the house and be ready to receive their guests, who would be flying into Nice from all over the world. Giles and Nikki would be travelling home from university for their summer holidays, which they intended to spend together travelling around Europe.

On the evening before the official opening of the exhibition there was to be a cocktail party for the press and people from the art world. Robin Sutton, her agent and the owner of the gallery who carried her work, wanted her to be there.

This would be the first time James had entered her other world and she hoped that he wouldn't be too bored. Having a good eye and liking a painting wasn't quite the same as being surrounded by a crowd of arties analysing and discussing something to death.

She hoped he would like her powerful work which always provoked an opinion, whether positive or negative. The only work James had seen of hers was at Sam's place – the watercolour she finally finished and sent to Jane and the few paintings scattered around the house of California and Jasmin when she was a small child.

When she first moved to Sam's place she had painted an oil of sunflowers and poppies in a vase, with cornflowers and daisies by the side of it waiting to be included in the arrangement. She had hung this in the kitchen as her duty Provençal painting and her gift to the house.

James liked it and she had promised to paint a similar one for their kitchen at La Bouscarela.

All of these paintings, which she saw as pretty pictures, were a far cry from the more serious work in her one-man show. The Tate had bought one of those paintings but all the rest were on loan from their various owners.

'Homework by Candlelight' she had kept for herself but it hung in Robin's gallery on permanent exhibition. She had decided to give it to James as a wedding gift. Her spirit was in every brushstroke and it was too much a part of her to sell. She would give it to him with all the love that had created it.

She could imagine it in the hall at La Bouscarela; the contrast with the opulence of the hall would exaggerate the poignancy of the painting. The blind faith that the mother in the painting had in a better future for her child went beyond hope. Hope was like a wish, like taking a chance, in comparison with the uncompromising faith of that mother, under those adverse circumstances, in the existence of a future. No electricity, stuck in an air-raid shelter with only the light of a candle, but still the homework had to be completed. The school may not be there tomorrow, or it could be closed for months to come, but her child would be educated to the best of her ability to prepare him for that better future when it came.

There was nothing sad about the painting, it gave one a feeling of pride and self-respect. It had the qualities in it that make a human being human and not just a creature of instinct.

She was thinking about her gift to James and when she should tell him about it, as she got ready to go to the cocktail party.

They were staying in James's flat in Chelsea, as it was more convenient than living in two places. It also gave Jasmin the space to work and be with her friends, for the mews house was tiny and if two people shared it there had to be a great deal of respect for each other's space.

It was a mild evening and she had decided to wear a grey linen Armani trouser-suit and a cream silk blouse. As she dressed she could feel the nervous tension building up inside her.

'This is not about the exhibition,' she thought as she took deep breaths to calm her nerves, 'because this work has been seen and criticised already; no, this is about James's reaction. It seems more important than it should that he likes it.'

James was waiting for her to finish dressing; he was sitting in the living-room reading an article in a women's magazine Georgina had left on the coffee table. In contrast to her, he was completely relaxed, hoping she would be ready in time to open the bottle of champagne he had left in the fridge to celebrate the occasion before they left.

She came through from the bedroom a little calmer now; her face was alive with anticipation and he decided, not for the first time, what a beautiful face it was. He got up as she came towards him.

'Do we have time for a private toast, sweetheart.'

'Of course, James, that sounds like a wonderful idea. I must admit to being a bit nervous this evening.'

'Everyone will love the exhibition, Georgina.' He said as he went towards the kitchen.

'Not everyone, James. Whenever anyone makes a political statement, however slight, there is always someone to argue about it and disapprove.' She walked across to the window and looked out into the clear evening.

James came back with the champagne and two glasses on a tray which he put down on the coffee table. He expertly opened the bottle, poured the sparkling liquid into the glasses and took them over to where she stood.

He handed her a glass. 'To you, Georgina.'

'To us, James.' She raised her glass.

They took a taxi to the gallery. She had discovered his weakness for London taxis; he hardly ever drove while he was in the city and his car spent most of the time in the garage.

Robin was there to greet them and after the introductions Georgina knew she would have to leave James very much to his own devices, at least for the first half-hour, as she gave herself over to the job in hand and talked to the people Robin had arranged for her to meet.

It was almost an hour later before she could give her attention to James, and she found him lost in thought, looking up at 'Homework by Candlelight'.

'What do you think, James?'

He looked towards her voice but she didn't think that he saw her. His eyes were faraway and veiled and there was no way that she could read them.

'James, are you all right?' She reached out to touch his arm.

The physical contact seemed to bring him back to his senses. 'Yes, I'm fine, sweetheart. I'm sorry, I was miles away.'

'Well, what do you think?'

'I don't know what to say, Georgina. I think they are very good.' How could he explain that looking at those paintings was like going back in time for him; it was as if Annetta were standing beside him and he heard her saying, 'A picture's worth a thousand words, James.'

Tina had told him that she wouldn't compete with a ghost. How could he marry Georgina without explaining his confusion and how could he tell her without making it sound as if she were a substitute for Annetta.

'You must be bored by now – let's go. I've done my duty.' She smiled at the lost look on his face. This wasn't his world and she had left him alone for too long.

'Let's go and eat something – that's if your hungry, because I'm starving! All of that talking has given me an appetite. Let's go to Le Suquet. I want to be back in France and that's the next best thing.'

'OK, Georgina, lead the way and we'll say our goodbyes as we leave.'

They sat opposite each other in the restaurant, the enormous *fruits de mer* in between them now nothing but shells and the bottle of Chablis in the ice bucket next to them almost empty.

James felt more relaxed and hoped that he was acting normally.

'I'm glad that's over,' Georgina said tiredly. 'I hate that side of the business, but I suppose that every business has a downside. What do you dislike about yours, James?'

'The fact it sometimes takes me away from you,' he said honestly.

'You always come up with the right answers, Mr Minnelli.'

'True.' The moment he said it in the old way, made the old sign, he could have bitten his tongue, but Georgina just smiled at him completely unaware that the word had struck a chord.

'James, I want to give you 'Homework by Candlelight' as a wedding gift. It's the most important thing I own and I want you to have it as a testimony of my love for you.'

Tears sprang into his eyes; he didn't know how he stopped them spilling over. 'I feel honoured and I thank you.' He found her hand across the table and put his over it. 'Now, let's go home. I need to talk to you.'

They went back to the flat in silence. She could feel the tension and couldn't think what had happened between them; she wanted to be back in France, living in their dream, not here in this taxi with no idea of what to say. The panic was building up inside her by the minute. She tried to focus on the moment when things had changed between them but she couldn't; perhaps nothing had changed and it was just her imagination working overtime. It was probably the wrong time to give him his wedding gift; it would have been better to have had it sent to France and given it to him on the day of the party. Well, *tant pis*, it was to late for regrets; she had misjudged the moment and there was no going back.

She stood on the pavement waiting for James to pay the taxi driver; the evening was still mild but she felt suddenly cold.

He put his arms around her as they went into the building and she was grateful for the physical contact, even if the rest of him was in another place. She knew that she had to wait for him to speak first, anything else would have been an intrusion.

He turned the key in the lock and opened the door, letting her pass through; she went into the living-room and threw herself down on the sofa, allowing the exhaustion to take over for the first time.

James had gone into the kitchen and came out after a few minutes with two glasses of brandy.

'Georgina will you come to Ireland with me tomorrow?' He passed her a glass as he spoke.

'Yes, James, if it's important – and by the look on your face it is.' She held the glass tightly for fear her hand would shake.

'I want to take you to Annetta's house; there's something I want to ask you and I feel you have to decide for yourself whether I'm keeping the house as a shrine or not. I don't want it to loom up in our future and spoil our life together. I would rather resolve everything now.'

'I understand, James; if you have any doubts about me, it is better to leave while our lives are still easily separated.' She could feel the lump in her throat choking her as she spoke.

'Georgina, I don't have any doubts about my love for you. I want to tell you something, and I say this without any disloyalty to Annetta, because she was always one to accept the truth. Annetta would never have been truly happy living in France. Well, for the first year perhaps. Then she would have needed to go off and fight some cause somewhere and I would have been chasing halfway around the world looking for her or rescuing her or whatever was demanded of me. That's all right when you're young, Georgina, but once middle age takes a hold of the bones, the need for a more tranquil life sets in.

'I don't think Annetta would ever have settled for that, she was a restless spirit. Old age would not have sat well on her shoulders.' He sat down beside her and put his arms around her and drew her towards him, his closeness comforting her chilled body.

'I don't want to live a lie, James. I've given up too much for that.'

'I know, Georgina, that's why we must go to Ireland tomorrow; it's important because what I want to ask you is very delicate and your answer has to be an honest one, not one to please me.'

'I hope Annetta won't come between us, James. I don't want to feel I'm competing with her memory for your love. I don't want you to be afraid to mention her for fear of upsetting me, either, that would be too horrible.

They sat in silence for a long time, taking solace from their physical closeness but each locked in their own thoughts as to what tomorrow would reveal about their feelings and their future together.

For the first time since they had met in France they spent a restless and troubled night. There was too much at stake the following day to allow for peace of mind.

They flew into Cork airport in the sunshine. James hired a car at the airport and they set off for West Cork.

He had called Mrs O' Brian, who still held the key for the house and acted as housekeeper; somebody else cleaned these days but Mrs O'Brian hired and fired.

Georgina took in the countryside. Ireland was a beautiful country and as green as people said. The whole place was soft like the lilt in Lana's voice. She liked the way it felt and she was beginning to feel better about the day.

James pointed out different landmarks along the route and told her some stories of his university days with Anthony Lawless; she noticed he was also more relaxed now they were on their way, and he was clearly happy to be back in this enchanting country.

Some of the stories made her laugh, and she was glad that they had Anthony in common so that she didn't feel such an outsider.

'It's good to hear that Anthony has been dreadful all his life and didn't grow that way later. I like to think he has a birth defect; it would be sad to discover that life had made him the way he is.'

'Oh come on, Georgina, he isn't that bad is he?'

'He's worse.' She laughed again at the story James had just told her about Anthony and the vice-chancellor's wife – a typical Lawless story. Was nothing sacred with that man?

They turned a corner and came upon a hamlet 'Here we are. I've asked Mrs O'Brian to open up the house. I thought she should air it and put some flowers around, to make it feel a little lived in. I never did let it, you know, Georgina. I just stayed away when I knew it was upsetting Tina. Mrs O' Brian keeps everything in order, though. I let friends use it for weekends during the summer; it's good to think it's being enjoyed.'

He drove through the open gates at the side of the house and parked the car. He got out and came around to open her door and she was grateful for his arm when he offered it to her, as she needed the support.

They walked around to the front of the house and she stared at it for a long time before she dared to speak.

It stood in the sunshine, its white walls reflecting light, it's slate roof glistening, and the jasmine and yellow roses around the door in full bud, ready to burst in the next few weeks. The oak front door was half open and its brass knocker had just been cleaned and glowed with pleasure.

She could feel the happiness welling up inside her as she tried to find her tongue. She looked at James and the smile on her face reflected the joy in her voice when she finally said, 'I'm so glad we came, James – so, so glad.'

He smiled down at her, caught up by the feelings she was exuding. 'So am I, sweetheart.'

At that moment Mrs O'Brian came out of the house. 'I've been waiting a good five minutes for you to come inside, Mr Minnelli. I haven't got all day, you know. I have to get back and give Mr O'Brian his lunch.'

'I apologise, Mrs O'Brian. I didn't mean to hold you up. Please let me introduce you to Mrs Fox.'

Mrs O'Brian softened at the sound of James's calm deep voice and with a big smile shook Georgina's hand. 'Pleased to meet you, Mrs Fox. I didn't mean to go on so but you know what these men are like if they're not fed on time.'

'Yes, I understand.' She smiled back at the wrinkly old lady with the twinkle in her eyes and decided her bark was definitely much worse then her bite.

Mrs O'Brian bustled back to her own home and left them to go into the house alone.

As they walked through the front door Georgina quite expected it all to disappear, like the first time she had thought she could enter the house in her vision; but no, this house was planted solidly on the ground on which her feet were firmly placed.

He showed her through the hall and into the drawing-room. Mrs O'Brian had put some freesias in a vase on the coffee table and their scent filled the room.

She took it all in – the Donegal tweed on the sofa, the red and cream silk cushions. They were still as good as new. It took her back more then twenty years, seeing this room. Uncle Harry had got her one of her first design commissions, an apartment in Kensington. She had used Donegal tweed and grey flannel in the reception-room. The apartment had been featured in *Home Design* magazine, naming her as an up-and-coming young designer.

She looked around the room with pleasure, the room proved to her that good designs stood the test of time. She had always liked to get away from conventional fabrics in her designs and now that for the first time in ten years she was back at work – on La Bouscarela – she had adopted her old ways, using navy and white bed-ticking for the curtains in the kitchen and covering the cushions in the library in Cerruti cashmere suiting material, which looked rich and warm against the light terracotta linen which she had used to cover the sofas. There was not a room in the house that looked as if a lady decorator had popped by to pretty it up. She was in a class of her own when it came to style and would have gone on to become a truly great designer if that had been the path fate had mapped out for her. Success had come in another way and she had no regrets.

'Would you like a drink, Georgina.' James was a little bit lost now they were in the house. It was as if Georgina knew something he didn't and the secret was giving her a lot of pleasure. 'There's only whiskey, I'm afraid.'

'That will be fine, James, but lots of water, please.' She had sat down on the sofa, feeling very much at home.

'What was the date of Annetta's death, James?'

He looked at her bewildered by the question. For some reason it seemed at that moment, and with the relaxed attitude that Georgina appeared to have about the whole experience, a strange thing to ask.

'It was 9 September 1982.'

'That was the worst day of my life too, James, a day I will always remember. The day my emotions reach crisis point. The day I wanted to die and didn't. Annetta had wanted to live but couldn't, how strange.'

That was the day she had taken Jasmin to boarding school, the final nail in her emotional coffin. She remembered hyperventilating in the car on the way back to Tarn House, with the emotion of all the dreadful things that had happened during the prior three months, starting with Frog's death.

It was as if her feelings had been gathering in her throat and blocking the flow of air. When her car hit the tractor, she had given herself up willingly to death, only to wake up in hospital cheated by it.

'Georgina, I want to tell you about something that happened before Annetta died. It's to do with a documentary she was making that she never completed. I have that documentary. I bought it from the company she formed with Anthony Lawless and my father. I bought it when they closed the company. In fact, the documentary was completed, it's just that she was never happy with it – or should I say the final footage of it.

'It's a documentary about women and war; she wasn't satisfied with the part about women in long-term conflict, she felt the interviewer hadn't brought out what she was looking for from the questions. She had wanted to go herself to interview the women but because of me she didn't. I had stopped trusting life at that point and I felt something would happen to her in Lebanon. I don't know what – taken as a hostage or perhaps shot. I was very emotional at the time, she had fought so hard with her cancer. I knew she wasn't strong physically and I was selfishly trying to control her activities. She never blamed me but I know that it was because of me she didn't finish what she saw as her most important project.

'When I saw your paintings, I knew what she meant, what she was talking about. I could see all the depth of feeling she was trying to capture, and would have captured, if she had gone herself to interview those women. There, in your paintings, was what was missing, what the documentary needed to be complete. There, before my eyes, painted by you.

'I want to ask you if I may use your work to bring out the essence of those interviews, Georgina. I owe it to Annetta to finish her project and I have to ask you, regardless of what you think and how it will affect us.'

She looked at him for a long time before she answered him, arranging her thoughts so as to be able to explain what had happened to her, how she knew now that part of Annetta was in her and always would be because they had bonded somehow. Her out-of-body experience a few days after Annetta's death had something to do with that bonding. How could she explain the experience and communicate her now total belief in the collective subconscious?

'James, I think I told you that when I did those paintings, I was like a woman possessed with an energy outside of myself; it was as if I were a vehicle for that energy. I was drained by the experience but it was also exhilarating, every fibre of my being was alive in the creation of those paintings. I felt every emotion portrayed by the characters and I loved every breath I breathed during those hours and days that made up the experience. I was glad that I wasn't afraid to feel and I saw that the sweetness of my joy was all the sweeter for being carved out of my sorrow.

'Perhaps that energy came from Annetta's restless spirit, as you called it. Perhaps her energy needed to complete her work, before her spirit could relax in another world.

'All I know, James, is that our love has Annetta's approval, and so I thank you for bringing me here to feel that and understand a little more about myself and our love through this experience. I will be more than happy to help you, in any way I can, to finish her documentary.'

She didn't tell him that she had already seen it on a television screen in a hotel room in Chicago. Some things should stay between her and Annetta.

'I love you, Georgina,' was all he could reply as he allowed the tears to trickle down his cheeks.

She kissed their saltiness. 'Good! Now take me to lunch somewhere, I'm starving. I think Nikki and Giles should spend some time here this summer on their trip around Europe. I think it would be good for both of them; this is a very special house James and I'm glad you kept it.'

It was late in the evening when they boarded the plane back to London. Everything she had seen that day had made her determined to come back. Ireland was a beautiful country, full of warm hospitable people, and she wanted to come back and explore more of it.

They settled themselves in their seats in a much better frame of mind than they had been in when they arrived earlier in the day. She was pleased to discover that James was as emotionally brave as she had become. She knew that their relationship would always be an honest one and thought how lucky she was.

James looked at the newspaper he had picked up automatically as he had boarded the plane. His sudden chuckle drew her attention.

'What's so funny?' she asked, wanting to laugh at the contagious sound he was making.

He handed her the newspaper and she read the headline: ANTHONY LAWLESS TO MARRY BETINA OBSTROULLIAS.